SILVER LININGS AND ANGEL WINGS

Kaden Shay

Supposed Crimes LLC • Matthews, North Carolina

Published in the United States.

ISBN: 978-1-938108-13-6

www.supposedcrimes.com

This book is typeset in Goudy Old Style, licensed by Ascender Corporation.

This book is dedicated to the ladies of the Mesa Women's Novel
Writers group. Jacky, Peggy, Adriana, and Gillian. Without their
input, Silver wouldn't have the glowing personality she ended up
with. Thanks ladies, for everything.

Chapter One

Breaking the Rules

I eased my grip on the limp form in my arms, supporting the weight as my hand raised to check for a pulse. It was there, weak and on the verge of failing but would recover eventually. I dropped the body to the plush crimson carpet with a soft thud. Without a second glance at it, I reached up to wipe the blood from my lips with the back of my wrist. The check for signs of life was the only concession I would make for the human who had served as my meal.

I stepped over the still form and crossed my bedroom, opened the door and gave a sharp whistle down the hallway. A head popped around the corner and with a quick flick of my wrist the rest of the young man attached to the head appeared. He closed the space to my doorway, his eyes on his feet, he had been in the manor long enough to know better than meeting my eyes.

"Yes, Mistress?"

"Remove that from my room and make sure the carpet is cleaned."

He nodded and if he felt any kind of solidarity or sympathy for the form lying in the room, he knew enough to not show it. I tugged my coat off the stand beside my door and stepped into the hall, leaving the boy to clean up after me. Things ran more smoothly when I went out and left him to clean up without my attentions on him. I made him nervous, as I should, and he worried about failing or falling short with me.

"Oh and Ivan?"

The sandy-haired head peeked around the frame of my bedroom door, eyes on the wall just to my left.

"Yes?"

"Make sure some care is received, I'd like to see that one back at some point."

Another quick, respectful nod of acknowledgement and he vanished back into my room to complete his tasks. I knew I would be seeing my most recent meal again in a few weeks. The human body was quite fragile and recovery time would be needed after a day spent with me. A wicked smile stole over my features as I took the stairs to the ground level of the manor and crossed to the front door. The poor thing had known exactly what was waiting in my chambers but was unable to refuse.

A tall, well-muscled man in a smart-looking suit pulled open the front door as I approached, his eyes on my boots as he held the portal open. I stepped through without more than a passing glance in his direction and stood on the front porch. I moved to the edge, standing on the uppermost of the ten marble steps and turned my face to the painted sky.

Sunset had tinted the horizon in a brilliant flare of color, pink, purple, blue, orange and red all vying for supremacy in the fading light. I took a deep breath and let my eyes slid closed, my senses heightened after my recent feeding. My mind drifted back to the afternoon and I chuckled to myself, the sound low and very pleased. The subject of my latest feed had been a lovely thing, a bit shorter than myself with a cascade of lovely golden hair and pale green eyes.

I ran my fingers through my own dark hair, always unable to decide if it was deep brown or black. The recently-cut strands fell from my fingers to flutter against the shoulders of my coat. I decided I liked it short. I licked my lips as a replay of the day flashed through my mind. The girl had known the moment she was brought to my rooms what was in store for her. The terror in her eyes had been almost as satisfying as the fear I could smell rolling off of her. I had always enjoyed the taste of blood flavored with a twinge of fear, gave it a kick.

"Silver."

I took a slow breath, exhaled it sharply and then opened my eyes with an exaggerated roll. I pointedly ignored the tall woman who had stepped up beside me. I started down the stairs but my progress was halted by a hand wrapping around my elbow and dragging me back up. I growled under my breath and turned to face the blockade trying to keep me from leaving. I didn't think I would ever get over how much I looked like the woman standing there staring at me.

"Mother."

"Another one? Why can't you reign yourself in and follow the rules like everyone else?"

I grumbled at the comment, having heard it more than a hundred times and not wanting to listen to the lecture sure to follow. I rolled my eyes again where she could see it this time and then turned and started down the steps once more. My progress was halted by a massive, mountain of a man blocking my path and I huffed as my shoulders sagged. I stuffed my hands into the pockets of my jeans and took a single step back to look up at the hulk of a man.

"Silver, your mother was speaking to you. Stop being rude and answer her."

I growled at the man and his bright blue eyes narrowed at me as he returned the sound. While my growl could be fierce and inspire fear in many beings, his was downright terrifying. I flinched, shook my head at the fact he had won so easily and then turned and faced my mother again. The massive man stepped up behind me, placing a hand on the back of my neck and forced me back up the stairs.

"Apologize to your mother child."

"Sorry."

Apparently he didn't like the sarcastic tone in my voice because a second later his large hand connected with the back of my head. I jerked with the force of the blow and even though it didn't actually hurt I reached up to touch the spot and turned a glare on him. Anyone else who had dared to look at Ianos in such a way would have found themselves short on life very quickly. As it was, I was treated to a second blow, this one only a bit lighter, aimed at my right temple and leaving white sparks in my vision.

"Properly, Silver." The deep, rumbling bass of his voice commanded respect.

"Okay, okay. I'm sorry mother, I got carried away with the girl."

"Thank you."

"You're welcome, dad."

He responded to my snide remark by shoving me hard enough that I landed on my ass in the dirt at the bottom of the stairs. I pushed myself back to my feet, brushed myself off and glared at him as I climbed the stairs again to stand beside my mother. I crossed my arms over my chest and growled at the man again, provoking him. As I suspected, it worked and he moved toward me which was what

I assumed he would do. I sidestepped his movement and stuck a foot out to trip him.

He landed on his face, sprawled at the bottom of the steps and I turned toward him with a smirk on my face. By the time he rolled over he was laughing and I dropped my arms to my sides while he righted himself. He took the steps in two strides and picked me up, tossing me over his shoulder as I kicked and pretended to protest.

"Would you two put your bonding on hold long enough to allow a proper scolding?"

"Oops, now we're both in trouble. Sorry love."

He dropped me to my feet and brushed himself off as he crossed the few feet to my mother and dropped a kiss on her cheek. He moved to whisper something in her ear, melting the scowl from her face and replacing it with a small smile. She shook her head as he squeezed her shoulder, shot me a stern look over his shoulder and then disappeared into the manor.

"Silver, I don't what to do with you."

"Why do anything with me?"

"Do you think that just because you are my daughter you are free to break all of our rules?" Her voice had risen as she spoke and knew my constant disregard for our rules, her rules, were wearing on her.

"No. I don't break them all."

"Only the ones you feel are too strict for your liking."

"I just don't understand why I can't feed freely as long as I leave them alive. The girl isn't dead so what's the problem?"

"The problem is that now she'll be taking up a bed in the hospital for the next few weeks and there is nothing wrong with her other than my daughter being irresponsible."

"Irresponsible? Mother, really. They're food, nothing else. Your ruling if you remember."

"I remember well child. I also remember laying rules about their treatment. What you did is bordering on torture. You know our calming doesn't work when they are so close to death. She spent the last several minutes of your feed in pain. Knowing you she spent the entire feed in fear. It's not how we do things."

I rolled my eyes at her again and waved at hand at her as I turned to try and leave again. I had heard the whole argument before and I didn't want to hear it again. Humans were only good for two things, food or pets. The latter was only allowed if a human happened to have some special skill we found intriguing or entertaining. The former, well, they were dinner, bred to feed our population and nothing more. Though my mother had always been obsessed with their humane treatment.

"Silver please. Try to understand why the rules exist."

"I understand why they existed when they were written mother. Now they don't have a place anymore. I know that when you wrote them, most of our kind was vulnerable in daylight and treating them well kept them from rising against us. That isn't the case anymore. You haven't been prisoner to the daylight for well over five hundred years. Others have followed and even I've been walking in the sun for two hundred years. It's time we stopped worrying about them killing us and start making them fear us again."

She sighed and something I didn't recognize flicker behind her eyes. It made me raise a brow and tilt my head to one side. She reached up to rub her temples with her index fingers. I wondered for a moment of I really did inspire a headache in the elder Vampire or if it was only for show. I sighed and shook my head, deciding she was done with me and turned to walk away when she spoke again.

"My child. I didn't write those laws out of fear. I wrote them out of compassion."

"Compassion? For what? Cattle?"

She moved so fast I didn't have time to react before the back of her hand connected with my left cheek. The blow rocked me back onto my heels, throwing my balance off so I stumbled backwards down the steps. My hand went to my cheek and I looked up at her. In my entire eight hundred and sixty years I couldn't remember my mother ever striking me. I stared into eyes the color of molten silver, a trait I had inherited from her, for several seconds. I tightened my jaw against a pain that wasn't in my cheek.

"Watch your mouth. Being my daughter will only spare you from my wrath for so long, Silver. I can't allow you to continue as you have been. You need to follow my rules... Or leave."

The last word was like a solid kick in the stomach and I staggered at the force of it. The thought of leaving the only home I hand known for almost nine centuries threatened to actually make me cry. I pulled myself together and swallowed hard as I studied the ground at my feet. I forced my gaze up to the manor, taking in the gleaming marble façade tinted pink in the last minutes of the dying sunset.

"Okay. I'll... Try."

"That's all I ask, for now. You have to understand that without them, we cease to exist."

I nodded and turned on my heel, leaving my mother and the manor behind me as I beat a quick path to the end of the driveway. Once I made it out of the gate I turned right and started toward the forest flanking our estate. We had lived on this expanse of land my entire life and I knew the woods I headed toward like my own backyard. I stepped into the trees and stripped off my coat, leaving it hanging on a low branch as I weaved through the foliage. My shirt followed, then my bra, my boots, my jeans and finally my underwear.

I broke into the clearing I'd played in during my childhood breathing in ragged gasps around the tears I had been fighting back. I stood under the light of the rising moon completely naked and let the cool autumn breeze wash over me. I knew exactly what I needed to regain my composure but I had to take a moment to breathe before attempting it. Once I had regained my normal breathing pattern, I reached deep within myself. It only took me a span of two deep breaths to find the part of my lineage I hid away, locked in a prison made of magic, runes and my own weakening willpower.

I had two sides of myself and one of them had always been ignored, left in the background, forgotten. Every so often I would reach inward and touch that piece of my soul I spent so many centuries pretending didn't exist. I wondered at times what would happen if I let her completely out, let her have the freedom she had been denied for so long. I pondered this for several minutes as the moon finished rising overhead. I had given in to the pull before but always with protections in place, always under my terms, tonight I felt the need to let her run free.

I looked down at the bracelet on my right wrist, the solid silver gleaming in the moonlight. The skin around it permanently reddened due to my allergic reaction to the silver. The intricate runes etched into its surface glowing a faint blue in the pressing darkness. I took a deep breath and gripped the bracelet, gritting my teeth against the bite of the silver on my opposite palm. I ripped it free of my wrist and allowed the half of myself I inherited from my father to rush to the surface. Sudden pain ripped through me, dropping me to my knees as I cried out, the sound turning to a howl as I blacked out.

Chapter Two

Consequences

THE FIRST thing my mind registered was the cool breeze drifting across me. Next was the chirping of birds around me and, once the breeze died down for a moment, the warmth of the sun on my back. Without opening my eyes I knew I was outside and nude. I sincerely hoped I wasn't where anyone could see me. I took a deep breath and smelled the familiar scents of the forest underneath me, a good sign.

I forced one eye open a sliver and groaned as the sun blinded me. I closed the eye tight again and attempted to move. I was sore, my muscles aching in protest to the shifting around I was subjecting them to. I rolled onto my side, reached up to rub my eyes in hopes of easing the sandpaper that had overtaken them and tried opening them again. I succeeded this time but regretted it instantly when the world spun around me before I could gain my bearings. After three tries I had them open without the world swimming or my head pounding. Progress.

I sat up and shook the leaves and dirt from my hair then looked down at myself. I covered my mouth with my hands. I was smeared with crimson streaks everywhere I could see. Some were only smudges but several appeared to be handprints. I took a deep breath and swallowed hard against the sight. I wished I hadn't when I tasted the iron tinged coppery flavor of blood in my mouth. Whatever I had done overnight couldn't have been good to have this much of the crimson fluid all over me.

I shuddered hard at the sight and fought to keep the contents of my stomach where they belonged, trying not to think about what I might have done. I pushed up to my feet, unsteady and staggering for half a dozen steps before I regained my sense of balance. I looked around and tried to figure out where I had ended up, got my bearings and started off in what I thought was the right direction. I stumbled into the clearing I had started in the night before and had a flicker of memory. I had been so hurt and angry at my mother I had taken my bracelet off. I shook my head at myself and the sheer stupidity of the action as I set to looking for it.

I found it near the southern end of the clearing and slid it back into place with a grimace. The familiar burn of pain from the silver held an edge for fifteen seconds or so as the magic reasserted itself. As it faded away I sighed in relief and turned toward home, hoping my clothes had survived the night. As I retraced my steps from hours earlier I wondered exactly what I had done and how much trouble I would be in. I knew I could dig into my memory and try to find out what I'd done but I was terrified to attempt it.

I was thankful to come across my underwear and jeans after walking a handful of yards through the trees. I pulled both on, found my boots and tugged them into place before I tied them and moved on to find the rest. By the time I stepped out of the woods near the manor I was fully clothed with most of the blood covered. I was also exhausted and knew I must have been active until right before dawn to be so drained. That meant I'd had more than ten hours to wreak some serious havoc and I shook my head at the thought.

I worked my way across the open field toward the front gate of the estate but stopped just short of entering. The grounds were alive with activity and my stomach twisted into a tight knot when I scanned the individuals and counted at least two dozen of my father's guards. Anything that could bring out more than twenty Lycan enforcers wasn't something good. I had the sinking feeling the 'anything' was me and whatever I had gotten up to the night before. The sudden urge to turn tail and run gripped me but I bit the feeling back and pulled in a steadying breath.

Whatever I had done, I would have to deal with the consequences of it. I set my jaw, steeled my nerves and stepped through the gates. I crossed the yard with purpose, my chin up showing a confidence I didn't feel. I took the front steps two at a time, reached for the knob on the front door and was grabbed before I could get a grip on it. The strong grip on my wrist tightened and I was spun around, about to lash out when I saw my father looking down at me. My temper flared for a split second before I saw the look in his eyes and it made me deflate instantly.

My father was already an imposing man at six feet nine inches tall with jet black hair that fell right past his shoulders and glacial blue eyes. When he was angry the animal within surfaced, turning those blue eyes a vivid yellow that could pierce right through to your soul. I shivered as he leveled those eyes on me and I knew I was in trouble. Whatever had happened must have been worse than I imagined for him to look at me the way he was.

I had seen my older brothers on the receiving end of a look like this one but never me. I had always been his princess, even when I had screwed up, even when he was reprimanding me. His youngest (not by much, but still youngest) and his only daughter he had kept a more lenient approach with me. Now I knew how the boys must feel when they pissed him off. I started to say something but couldn't find the words and had to swallow and try again.

"Daddy..."

He growled at my whispered word as the door behind me opened and I felt my mother's energy on the porch with us. He dropped my arm and yanked the coat from my shoulders so he could get a look at my arms. The bloody streaks marring my pale flesh made his brow furrow as his nostrils flared in anger. I swallowed hard and tried to speak again, cut off once more when he grabbed my right arm above the elbow hard enough I cried out. He pulled my arm up and turned his eyes down at the bracelet on my wrist.

"What the hell have you done, Silver?" The tone my mother used clenched my heart and made my eyes mist over as my father set his jaw and shook his head.

"She took the bracelet off, Ayana."

My eyes went wide as my mother gasped behind me and I stared at the bright yellow eyes boring into me. I couldn't understand how he could possibly know I had taken it off. I tried to remember if it had some kind of alarm on it if I removed it but if it had they would have found me the night before. I would have been in a cage before I had the chance to do any damage to anyone or anything.

"How did you know?"

His hand moved down toward my wrist and he raised it so I could get a good look at the bracelet. The runes which had always glowed a steady pale blue had changed. The angry red flares of light flickering from the etchings made me take a sharp breath. The usually red skin at the edges of the silver had turned a dark shade of charcoal. My heart rate picked up and I had the span of four heartbeats to absorb what I must have done. My father yanked hard on my arm, dragging me into the house and up the stairs to my room.

He tossed me into the space and I stumbled, putting my arms out to catch myself before I ended up face down on the carpet. I turned over and looked up at him, my mother standing behind him, smaller but possibly even more terrifying. She shook her head as my father took a step back out of the doorway.

"I'm sorry Silver, but you finally crossed the line."

I tried to process why she was saying she was sorry as she raised a hand. By the time I saw the charcoal pencil in gripped between her fingers it was too late. She drew the final rune on my door frame and when I moved to leave I was pulled up short, hitting the barrier she had put in place. I put one hand on the invisible wall my own mother had erected to keep me in and looked up to meet her eyes as a tear slipped down my cheek.

"Why?"

"I know you don't remember what you did last night. That's the only reason you're still alive." The pain in her voice twisted through my stomach like a knife.

"You ended up in Xander's territory. You slaughtered almost a hundred of his humans." The disappointment in my father's voice was worse than his earlier anger.

"Maybe it wasn't..."

"It was. You have a very unique wolf that no one outside this family has ever seen. Until last night. He described you perfectly then you show up this morning covered in blood. He wanted your head but your mother managed to convince him that you wouldn't have known what you were doing. The wolf was in charge."

I leaned my forehead on the unseen wall holding me captive and released a shaky breath against it. There wasn't really any doubt that I had done what he said, even as unthinkable as it was. My mind reeled as I tried to come up with anything I could say to get myself out of the trouble I had landed in. Even knowing I hadn't meant for any of it to unfold didn't help. When nothing came to mind I looked up and let my gaze flicker from my mother to my father and held his gaze.

"Dad, you know I didn't mean for this to happen. It's why I had the bracelet on in the first place. I never wanted to cause this kind of destruction again." I shivered hard against the visions of centuries long past. "So much death."

My gaze fell away from his as my eyes misted over with tears I absolutely refused to shed. I had messed up, caused more damage than I could excuse but I wasn't about to cry over the punishment I deserved, no matter how much I hated it.

"I know you didn't. You've worked so hard to keep this from happening, that's why it's so hard to understand."

"I know, I wish I could explain but I don't understand it either. I was angry and I just... Acted. Wasn't thinking it through." I forced my eyes back up to his and took a slow breath before asking, "How long am I caged?"

"Until Xander no longer wants to kill you. He agreed to let you live as long as you weren't allowed to wander around free to do it again."

I nodded at my mother's words and turned to press my back against the wall next to my door. I slid down to the floor and pulled my knees up to my chest. I was trapped, the room I used to call home now my cage. I suddenly knew how the animals some of the families kept for entertainment felt and I didn't like it. I crossed my arms on top of my knees and leaned my head on them. I didn't have the energy to argue so I didn't try.

"If you can show us you won't attempt escaping our punishment we'll give you more space. You may be allowed the entire house eventually. Until then, you have this room, your study and the bathroom. Your mother was kind enough to allow you access to the balcony but don't try anything, it's warded as well. As are the windows."

I nodded as I fought back more tears. I hated crying and I had already done it more in the last day than I liked or wanted to admit. I heard my parents retreat, leaving me to my own thoughts but I didn't move for a long time. I finally talked myself into standing up and moving to my bed, finding it was dark outside. I collapsed onto the mattress, pulled a pillow under my head and curled up on my side. I spent the next couple hours staring at the wall and wondering what I could do to get my freedom back.

I needed sleep but the persistent burn of the bracelet against the skin of my wrist and the knowledge I was trapped indefinitely made relaxing difficult. My mind was a tumbling wreck of 'what if's and 'should have's that kept repeating over and over again. I did know that if I was ever allowed to leave the house again, I would make sure the damn bracelet never left my wrist. Though now, who knew if it was even still working properly. I closed my eyes and willed my thoughts to still.

CHAPTER THREE

HOUSE ARREST

AFTER SIX weeks in my warded prison I had exhibited good enough behavior to warrant an extension in my range. I had access to the entire second and third floors which allowed me the library as well as the kitchen on the first floor. The thought of the library might have excited me, had I not read and reread every book in the room several times. Thankfully my in home gym had also been included so I could waste hours working out, which I did. After a few days even that became more like a chore and had proven boring.

I needed a new distraction and fast before I went absolutely bat-shit crazy in the huge house all alone. My mother showed up the day after my seventh week began and offered me a solution. It wasn't one I was particularly fond of but it was better than any of the ideas I had for keeping myself entertained. She suggested a 'pet', a human with a specific skill or talent who could keep me company. I had a feeling it was her way of forcing me to bond with a human, making me see things from her point of view.

As much as the thought chapped my sense of pride and independence I didn't have a choice if I wanted to maintain my sanity. After a week of arguing with myself about it I finally caught her in the kitchen one night. She had settled at the counter with a cookbook and was flipping through desserts when I walked in. I plucked the book from her hands, gave it a quick glance then rolled my eyes and tossed it aside. I would never understand why she bothered with such human habits as cooking.

"Is there something I can help you with or were you only

interested in interrupting my relaxation time?"

"I give. You're right."

"I'm right about ever so many things, child. You could be a little more specific for me."

"About me taking a human pet. It might be good for me and at the very least it would give me someone to talk to while I'm stuck in this house all day."

"Oh good. I'm glad I managed to get through that thick skull you inherited from your father."

I rolled my eyes but couldn't help the grin that turned up my lips at the comment. I was so much like my father I was sometimes amazed she hadn't murdered us both in our sleep centuries ago. I sat myself on the stool across from her and leaned forward, arms crossed on the top of the island. I drew in a slow breath then exhaled on a sigh as I forced my gaze up to meet hers.

"Look, I'm not saying I'm thrilled with the idea. I actually still think it's a waste of time but I'm going crazy and I've started talking to myself."

"Well we can't have that. Any particular type of pet you'd like?"

I thought about it for a minute, trying to decide what I might want in a companion. That was exactly what this human would be, more than a pet, someone to keep me company. After a pause I furrowed my brow and tried to mentally compile a list. I needed someone who wouldn't annoy me in the first two days but wouldn't be impossible for my mother to actually find.

"Okay so, let's see... Female."

"Obviously." I smirked at the older woman, knowing she wouldn't have brought me a male even if I hadn't asked for a woman specifically. She'd known my personal persuasions from the time I was fourteen years old.

"I'd prefer if she wasn't taller than me."

"Five foot five or under. I remember your preference in regards to height."

"No one with a boring talent like painting. I want someone interactive. A musician or a singer."

"I think that can be arranged. Any preference on looks? Age?"

"Not really just, easy on the eyes. I don't want to spend all day every day for the foreseeable future with someone who makes me cringe when I look at her."

My mother rolled her eyes but managed a small smile at my comments and then sighed and nodded. She would do her best to find someone who matched everything I was looking for. I actually had every confidence she would find someone I could tolerate for a few days at least. It was about the best I could really hope for given the circumstances. I had never kept human pets simply because humans bored the hell out of me. I doubted anyone my mother could find would change that.

"Now the rules."

"Oh great. Okay, hit me with them."

"No eating your pet. You will not be allowed to feed from her."

I waited, expecting more than the single requirement she had thrown my way. When nothing further followed I raised an eyebrow at her expectantly. She sat there, stoic and staring at me until I realized she had actually finished speaking. I couldn't remember a time in my life when my mother didn't have at least half a dozen rules for things so I was shocked.

"Really? That's it?"

"That's it. She stays alive and relatively unharmed and you get to keep her. You bleed her and you not only lose your pet but your range will be restricted back to the second floor only. Permanently."

"That's... A terrifying thought. Okay, I got it. I think I can manage to leave her be. I've been well fed since there's plenty sent up and I'm not exactly using a ton of energy."

She nodded and then slipped from the stool and walked away from the island. She didn't voice it but somehow I knew I would have a new companion by the next morning. I wondered what my mother would consider good looking in a human female. It made me wish I had elaborated a little on the physical attributes. What my mother found attractive might be so far off my mark I couldn't be in the same room with my new pet. Oh well, I would just have to wait and see what she brought for me.

I sat there and thought it all over for a few minutes longer before I pushed away from the island. I needed to do something, move and sweat a little so I took the stairs two at a time up to my gym. I stared into the room, trying to decide what I wanted to do first and settled on beating the hell out of a punching bag. I tipped the wraps for my hands off the small shelf they were on and started getting ready to wail on the thing. I didn't necessarily need the wraps with my super-fast healing, but they made the process less of a pain in the ass.

CHAPTER FOUR

A NEW COMPANION

I WOKE up pleasantly sore the next morning, remembering falling into bed sometime around midnight. I had taken all my frustration out on the poor punching bag. The process had strained my muscles to the point that even my super healing was still attempting to repair everything. It wasn't often I got to wake up sore after a workout so I spent a few minutes savoring the feeling. I stretched, grinning as the burn worked its way through my arms and legs then rolled over. The clock on my bedside table read seven which prompted me to turn and face the window.

The early morning sun peeked through the small gap in my curtains. I yawned as I rolled out of bed and crossed the room. I threw the heavy window covering back and stared out at the sprawling expanse of our back yard. The woods at the back of the property called to me and the wolf whined below the surface. I knew my mistake had caged not only me but her as well and she was suffering even worse for the imprisonment. She needed to run, to be free, even if I was still the one in charge. Wolves weren't meant for cages.

I sighed heavily, turned away from the window and crossed to my bathroom, stripping off clothes as I walked. I was bare by the time I flipped the bathroom light on and stepped over to turn on my shower. I still smelled like I'd sweated it out at the gym for seven hours, which I had, and I desperately needed to get clean. I turned the water all the way up as hot as it would go and climbed in once the room filled with steam. I winced as the heated water contacted my skin, sucking in a sharp breath through clenched teeth. It hurt, but I liked it so I stood there and let the steaming water cascade over my body for a few long minutes.

I finished my shower as the water began to chill and turned it off, stepping out into the cold room. The tile was like ice against my heat reddened feet and I shivered as I pulled a towel around myself. The sudden shift from hot to cold woke me up and got my blood pumping. I felt alive for the first time in weeks and only wished it would last. I pushed the thoughts aside as I walked back into my bedroom, leaving the now soaked towel in the middle of the room.

I pushed my closet door open, grabbed one of the several pairs of black jeans and a random tank top then kicked it closed. I pulled the jeans on, the tank tossed over my shoulder as I moved to my dresser and yanked on the first bra I pulled out. The tank went on then I shoved my feet into a pair of socks and found a pair of chucks that matched the blue of the top I'd grabbed. Dressed and mostly dry I ran my fingers through my recently trimmed hair, glad I had decided to keep it shorter. It would dry more quickly and wasn't soaking the back of my tank.

I descended the stairs quickly but pulled up short when I heard my parents talking in the kitchen. I stepped up to the doorway and took a breath to clear my throat. My mother raised a hand before I had the chance and motioned me into the room without looking away from my father. I smiled at her ability to tell I was there without sight or sound and stepped into the room. In the several seconds it took for either one of them to acknowledge me I realized they weren't alone. It seemed my mother had made good on her word and found me a pet.

"Silver, come meet your new companion."

I took two more steps into the room as my father decided my mother's words were his cue to leave. He exited the space as my gaze worked over the girl standing with her hip leaned against the counter. She looked to be about five foot five with golden blonde hair about four inches longer than mine. She had a great figure, the right curves in the right places. I raised an eyebrow at that, a smirk tweaking my lips as I reminded myself to praise my mother on her taste later.

She had worked herself into a pair of tight jeans and a plain light gray tee shirt, both of which hugged her curves perfectly. She was toned and obviously fit, not rail thin, and I thanked the Gods for it as I raked my eyes back up her body. Her full lips were twitched up at the left corner in a smirk of her own. She apparently knew she was being given a once over and didn't mind in the least. My eyes finished their circuit by landing squarely on hers and I was stopped dead for a moment.

Her eyes were a bright, sparkling blue that glittered in the early morning light coming through the kitchen window. They were stunning and beyond that, she met my gaze and held it, something no human had ever done. All those on our lands knew who I was and wouldn't dare look me in the eyes, terrified of what might happen. I could easily roll the mind of a human in a matter of seconds and have them agreeing to pretty much anything I wanted.

It was a rare one indeed who would dare to meet my eyes and the fact she had elevated my pulse a bit. I pushed the thoughts already assaulting my mind out of the way and tried to focus. The process was made infinitely harder when I caught the familiar scent of arousal. Apparently she had been appraising me as well and it appeared she liked what she had seen. I winked at her and it threw her enough that she glanced down at her shoes, offering me a reprieve from my swirling thoughts. I swore I saw her cheeks tinting pink but my mother spoke and drew my attention away.

"Silver are you listening?"

"No mother, sorry, I wasn't."

"I was saying, this is Angel Kent."

Angel seemed like a perfect name for the girl standing in my kitchen. I looked her over again while she had her eyes turned down, not having removed her gaze from her shoes. I wondered what kind of talents she had but wasn't left in the dark long.

"Angel plays the guitar. She also has a lovely voice I'm told."

"Great."

I couldn't really think of anything else to say since I was completely new to this companion human thing. I glanced at my mother when she cleared her throat and raised one eyebrow at her. She nodded toward Angel and then crossed to the door.

"I'll leave the two of you to get acquainted."

She swept from the room in a graceful swirl of lace and I chuckled at the sheer theatrics of it. As much as my mother liked making an entrance, she really loved making an exit. I stared at the empty doorway for a few beats then turned my attention back to the girl. I realized my mother hadn't told me how old she was and I wondered if she had been cruel enough to hand me a human pet under twenty-five. She knew I didn't have many lines to draw. I preferred humans I had contact with be adult enough to know what they were getting into at least.

"So, how old are you anyway?"

"Eighteen."

"Perfect."

Her head snapped up and her brow furrowed sharply at the sarcastic huff the single word carried. I waved her off, not wanting to explain how my mother had found a way to sabotage my fun. She had found exactly what I wanted and tossed that perfection at my feet, knowing I would be hard pressed to touch the girl thanks to her age. I sighed and shook my head, the woman was devious and it might just drive me insane this time.

"Come on, I'll show you your room."

I turned and left the room without making sure she would follow but somehow knowing she would. I led the way up the stairs and down the hall to the room beside my own. I opened the door and stepped inside, finding her things already piled at the foot of the bed. I crossed to the window and threw back the curtains, dust flying from them and making me sneeze. The room hadn't been used in several years, a fact which was glaringly obvious. I narrowed my eyes at the layer of dust coating everything and moved back to the door.

"Ivan!"

The sandy haired boy who acted as, well, basically my personal cleaning boy, popped out of my room, his eyes on my shoes as usual.

"Yes Mistress?"

"We have a... Someone will be using this room for the foreseeable future. Clean it up."

He nodded and started for the room Angel would be housed in and she raised a hand to stop him before he could go inside.

"Oh no, it's fine, I can do that."

"Don't be stupid. It's his job. Go on Ivan, and unpack for her while you're at it. Then get back to my room and finish up. I expect both rooms to be spotless by dinner."

"Of course."

"Oh, and Ivan."

"Miss?"

"When you're done with the rooms, go clean up the gym. I put several holes in the wall that need patched and painted. I expect it presentable for my spar with Casper tomorrow."

"Of course, Miss."

He gave a quick bow of his head and ducked into the room without another word. Angel stared after him for a full ten seconds, her brows furrowed down before she turned to me. I saw something like anger flash behind those dazzling blue eyes but it was gone as fast as it appeared. I tilted my head slightly to one side, questioning the look she was giving me.

"Why did you do that?"

"Do what?"

"I could have cleaned and unpacked. And from what I gather, you can't leave this house so what could you possibly have to do that would keep you from cleaning up after yourself?"

"Why should I clean up after myself? That's why he's here."

"So even when you could do it yourself, he has to do it for you?"

"Uh, yeah. What else would he do?"

"I don't know... See his friends, his family, take a walk?"

"He has no friends, his family is dead and even if those things weren't true he's not allowed further than the porch without an escort."

"And who set that boundary for him?"

"I did."

"Why?"

"It doesn't matter why. I don't need to have a reason. He's human, he does as he's told."

"Or what?"

"Or he gets replaced."

"You mean you kill him and bring in someone who won't defy you?"

"And what if that is what I mean?"

"I'd heard you could be harsh but I thought everyone was just telling stories. Turns out you really are a monster."

I glared at her as I took two steps, closing the gap we'd had between us and getting in her face. She was a full three inches shorter than I was but you'd never know it the way she squared her shoulders and met my glare with her own. I growled at her, the sound resonating from deep in my chest but she barely even twitched at the sound. Instead of backing down like I had expected, she set her jaw and fisted her hands at her sides. I didn't like the humans I had to keep company with to be so dominant and confrontational.

She needed to be knocked down a few pegs and I'd never been one to go easy on my humans. I leaned away just far enough to get my arm up between us. The blow I landed on her right cheek rocked her hard and made her stagger back several feet. She gasped in pain, reached up to cover to spot the back of my hand had connected with and turned that glare on me again. The beginnings of tears shimmered in her sapphire eyes but I wouldn't be swayed by crying.

"You will respect me or at the very least keep your damn mouth shut. Understand?"

"And if I don't? What then? You'll just kill me too?"

I narrowed my eyes, my lips twitching into an evil grin as I stepped back into her personal space and leaned in. Our noses were almost touching but again, she showed no signs of backing down. Apparently this one learned the hard way. I was fine with the hard way, it was more fun for me anyway. I huffed at her, dropping my voice to an almost demonic sounding growl as I spoke into her face.

"Oh girl. There are worse things than death you know. Cross me and I'll hand you over to my guards. They like human girls and they are anything but gentle. They'd have all sorts of fun with you. Think you can take on three Lycan males at once? I don't know that your poor little mortal body would handle the pain well. You'd be begging me to kill you by the time they were finished."

Her eyes went wide at that and I had the feeling I'd gotten through when she took a full step back and ducked her chin to her chest. I let out a satisfied grumble despite feeling a little disgusting for the threat. Not to mention I knew my guards would do no such thing and would be mortified I'd even threatened they might enjoy such activities. Lycans could be real brutes but the males learned respect for women, Lycan, Vampire or otherwise, early in life. It had always irritated my father that I hadn't managed to inherit this trait.

My point made, I turned and headed back down the hall toward the stairs. I ran up them and slipped into the library as my keen hearing picked up the sounds of soft sobbing from below. I couldn't help the smile that stole across my features at the sound, glad she was finally beginning to understand. Life ran so much more smoothly when everyone near me understood their place and she needed to learn hers. Despite the thought, seconds later a deep ache hit me directly in the area of my heart and I couldn't make heads or tails of it so I shook it off and went about my day.

CHAPTER FIVE

TURMOIL

AS I expected, Angel spent the next two weeks avoiding me whenever possible. I had forced her to sit and play something for me on a handful of nights but I could tell she wasn't happy about it. As her third week in the manor began I wondered if her behavior was out of fear or defiance. I made my way into the kitchen one morning to find her sitting at the small table settled at the end of the larger island. I poured myself a cup of coffee and turned to lean against the counter.

"Morning, Angel."

Her shoulders rose then fell again as she took a deep breath then she pushed away from the table and turned to leave the room. Curiosity piqued and anger beginning to flare I set down my mug and followed her. She started up the stairs but I cut her off, my inhuman speed coming in handy. She paused for a beat and then moved to go around me. My hand shot out, catching her around the left wrist and halting her progress.

"Let me go, Silver."

"Excuse me?"

I didn't appreciate the demanding tone in her voice. Not to mention all the humans in the house called me Mistress or simply Miss, never my name. The disrespect she had shown me over the last fourteen days had stoked my already volatile temper to a fever pitch. I was one comment away from rather literally throwing her out of the house. Her heavy sigh caught my attention in time for her to begin speaking.

"Please. Just let me go to my room and stay out of your way.

You've made it clear I'm unwelcome in your company if I intend to think for myself. I'm just trying to avoid pissing you off until you get bored with me and send me back to my family."

Her voice had cracked a couple times during her short speech and it brought my temper up short. She didn't sound as defiant but the fear she'd shown two weeks earlier was gone as well. She sounded almost, defeated. For the first time since the day she had come into the manor I really looked at her. Her eyes were on the stairs over my shoulder, her arm slack in my grip, the confident straightness gone from her posture.

I couldn't help myself as I released her wrist, reached over and hooked my finger under her chin. I lifted her face until I could see her eyes and found the sapphire orbs dull, lacking the shine and sparkle I'd seen those first few days. She was broken and I was the one who had done the breaking. The thought sent an unfamiliar and unwelcome pain through my heart. A sudden wash of sympathy hit me and I pulled my hand back at the emotion, recoiling as if she'd struck me.

I didn't know if she was unaware of my reactions to her or ignoring them, either way I was infinitely glad she stayed silent. I took three deep breaths, trying hard to steady myself and return my heart rate to normal after the spike it had just taken. Almost a full minute passed before I managed to form words and fight them out of my mouth.

"Go back to your room. I... If you... I'll be in the gym."

It was the best I could manage given the turmoil crashing around in my body. I turned and fled up the stairs, heading for my gym. I needed to release some frustration and punching things was the second best option I knew of. The first was unavailable to me in my present situation since the only female nearby was Angel, who apparently hated me now. I stepped into the large room, went right for my hand wraps and crossed the room to the punching bag.

After almost three hours taking out my aggression on the bag, I had put a hole in one and broken the chain on a second. A well placed kick to the third and last ripped the bracket right out of the ceiling, tossing the bag across the room. I backpedaled to the wall, leaned hard against it and then slid down slowly. My knees came up, my forearms resting on them with my hands dangling as my head dropped, my eyes on the floor between my feet, a regular sitting position for me. My breathing was ragged and labored as I tried to make sense of the things flying around in my head.

I'd never experienced any of it before and the sensations, while not completely unpleasant, were very new and a bit frightening. As my heart rate steadied and my breathing leveled out I worked the wraps off my hands and dropped them to the floor. I pushed myself to my feet and left the room, wandering down the hallway in a kind of daze. I wasn't sure where exactly I wanted to be right then, only that I needed to be moving. Sitting still was playing with my head and making me think things I didn't want to even consider.

I ended up outside Angel's room, her door pulled closed but not latched. I could hear the tones of her guitar from inside, the tune she plucked out slow, almost sad. I used the toe of my shoe to ease the door open ever so slightly, the motion slow so no sound gave me away. She was seated on the end of the bed, barefoot, her legs crossed and her guitar settled on her lap. She was playing with her eyes closed, accompanying the strumming with a wordless melody, her voice sounding haunted. I pulled my gaze to her face and saw the shimmering trails of shed tears on her cheeks.

My heart seized for a moment and something inside me broke at the sight. I'd never cared if I hurt the humans I kept and I had expected this one to be the same. I still wasn't sure how she was different but Gods help me, somehow she was. I discovered I hated seeing her looking so hurt, hated hearing the pain in her song. I also discovered I had absolutely no clue what to do about it. I backed away from her door slowly, leaving it pushed open so I wouldn't alert her to my presence.

Once I was back in my room I flung myself on my bed, arms spread and eyes on the ceiling. I watched the fan blades spin slowly, willing my mind to clear of the weird shit it had been spewing at me. The task was made more difficult by the mournful music making its way to me from the room next door. A tight knot formed in my stomach causing me to roll onto my side and curl into myself. I finally drifted off, the sound of Angel's voice still washing over me.

Chapter Six

On Lycans, Nudity and Other Family Quirks

I WOKE with a start as a very cold, very wet nose was pushed against the spot on my lower back my tank top had left bare when it rode up. I yelped and turned over as I lashed out, catching the side of a massive muzzle with the back of my hand. The owner of said muzzle whined at me and I rolled my eyes as I planted both hands in his ribcage and shoved, pushing him off my bed with a thud. He popped up a second later, his chin rested on my bed, tongue lolling out and looking pleased with himself.

"Screw you Casper."

The huge white canine barked at me then leaned over and licked my face, leaving a trail of sticky wolf drool on my left cheek. I glared at him, using my tank top to wipe my face off and then reached over and smacked him in the middle of his forehead. He went cross-eyed for a second and then his tail thumped on the wood floor several times. As hard as I tried I really couldn't be angry with him, he was my twin brother after all. He was older by a whopping six minutes and forty-three seconds, and he never let me forget it, even after almost nine hundred years.

"You're an ass, go shift so I can attempt to hate you properly. You're too damn cute this way."

He barked at me happily and then pranced away to shift back to his human form. I shook my head at him as he left, somehow still finding his prancing funny after so many centuries. He returned a few minutes later, human and unfortunately not clothed. He walked over and threw himself onto my bed, right on top of me and I heaved out an overly-dramatic 'oof' before I shoved at him.

"Get your fat ass off me before I suffocate!"

He laughed and wiggled around, not even pretending to roll off of me as my anger actually did start to flare some. I growled at him, a warning that if he didn't move on his own, I would move him. He ignored it, patted my forehead and shifted to flop onto his back, still pinning me to the bed. I loosed a deeper, louder growl as I got my hands between us, planted them in his back and shoved. He flipped off of me, missing the bed and hitting the solid wood floor hard.

"Ow! What the hell?"

"I warned you, Cas!"

"Damn, Si. That actually hurt."

He stood up beside my bed, rubbing his right shoulder which I assumed he had landed on. His brows knit together as he looked down at me, obviously shocked at my behavior. We had always been the rough and tumble type of siblings, getting into scrapes and accidentally hurting each other. We had always apologized though and the fact I hadn't this time had apparently thrown him off.

"Hey, you okay, sis?"

I shrugged and the look he gave me said he wasn't about to give up so easily which elicited a huff from me. He turned and sat on the edge of the bed, patting the spot beside him until I moved to occupy it. He wrapped his arm around my shoulders and I leaned my head on his chest with a sigh. Neither of us paid any attention to the fact he was totally naked. It was a normal thing for Lycans to wander around naked or half naked most of the time. It made shifting easier and I'd been dealing with nudity from all my brothers my entire life.

After almost nine centuries one simply stopped being embarrassed by her twin's naked ass being planted on her bed. It was either that or spend my entire life in a constant state of unease. I didn't have the energy for stupid crap like that so I ignored the frequent lack of clothing in our house. He waited for me to speak but I didn't want to tell him what was going on in my head, in my heart. Partly because I was still lost and unsure what it all meant and partly because I suspected what it meant and didn't want anyone to know.

"Talk."

"I'm just a mess, Casper. I don't know what's going on with me lately."

"Well, let's examine. You've been locked up in this house for, what, something around ten weeks now? Your only constant company has been a couple humans, and we know how you feel about them... And mom said dad hasn't spoken to you in weeks."

The knot in my stomach tightened and I had to swallow around the identical one forming in my throat. I'd been hoping I was imagining the last bit and my father had only been busy or even called away somewhere. Apparently he really was ignoring me and the thought killed the last little spark I'd been holding onto. I turned my face into my brother's shoulder and fought back the tears, I wouldn't cry in front of him. If anyone would understand it would be him, but I still wasn't ready to fall even that far. I pulled myself together, pushed away from him and sat up straight, letting his arm fall from my shoulders.

"Yeah, I guess everything just piled up on me. I'm feeling trapped."

I was bullshitting him, just enough truth in my words to keep him from smelling the lie on me. Lycans are the best lie detectors in the world, the change in body temperature and heart rate would be easy enough to detect. As it turns out, the smell the body emits changes when one lies as well, makes it easy for a keen nose to pick out a liar. I had learned to skirt the truth ages ago, never lying but rarely telling anyone everything.

"I get that, you kinda are trapped."

I nodded at that then both of our heads jerked up at the sound of the front door opening downstairs. I narrowed my eyes and tried to remember if my mother had said she'd be by so early in the day. Nothing came to mind and a low growl started in the back of my throat. I didn't like intruders in my home and whoever it was would have to get to the middle of the stairs before I could smell them. Without the identifier they were unwelcome and had better say something quick.

"Casper?"

The growl cut off and I relaxed beside my brother as he smiled, his eyes lighting up at the voice. Casper whistled beside me, the sound carrying through the house and I knew we'd have company any moment. I sighed and leaned away from him, sliding myself up to the head of my bed and propping myself up against the headboard. The solid rap of knuckles sounded on my door frame and I looked up and flashed our guest a half-hearted smile.

"Hey you!"

Casper was off the bed in the span of his excited greeting and had the other man in a tight hug. I almost managed a real smile when the embrace was returned. I took the long moments they hugged to really look at them for the first time in longer than I could remember. My brother was tall at six foot six but was dwarfed by Tristan who stood just shy of seven foot. Casper lived up to his namesake, pale as a ghost with shock white hair and eyes so pale blue they were almost white. He had a rare pigmentation mutation that was a cousin to albinism and it extended to his wolf as well. Tristan on the other hand was as dark as Cas was light. His Jamaican heritage was obvious right through to his black dreadlocks and deep, almost black eyes.

They had met when Casper and I were only twenty, Tristan already well over forty and one of my father's guards. They had fallen for each other instantly and had been together ever since. It wasn't odd for a Lycan to take a same sex partner but no one had seen it coming. Not from Tristan anyway, Casper screamed 'gay' from five miles away. The thought made me grin before I remembered the odds of finding what my brother had. The expression faded as fast as it had appeared and I heaved out a sigh as the pair pulled apart. Tristan glanced in my direction and, as usual seemed to read me without a word leaving my mouth.

"Hey sweetie."

Tristan walked over as he spoke, pulled me to my feet and, in his typical fashion, forced me into a hug. I did the only thing anyone could do in the face of one of his hugs: bear hugged him back. I didn't say anything, I never needed to with him. It didn't matter what was bothering me, only that I was hurting and he wanted to make it better. I appreciated the effort despite the fact it wouldn't work. It was a bit like putting a Band-Aid on a severed limb, heading in the right direction but not quite enough.

"Anything I can do to help?"

"No, but thanks for the thought. I just need some time alone I think."

"Fair enough. I'll get your brother out of your hair then."

I gave him a small smile of thanks as he grabbed Casper's hand and ushered him out the door. I loved my brother but sometimes he liked to be a little too far into my business. If Tristan didn't haul him off now, he'd be on my case all day to tell him what was wrong. I couldn't put my finger on the exact emotion I was dealing with but sympathy seemed to be close. I had gotten myself attached to this human somehow and I needed to figure out how to shut the feeling down.

The boys left the manor and I sat on the edge of my bed, staring at the wall and thinking far too hard about nothing in particular. I stood up and walked to the double doors leading onto my balcony and pulled them open. I stepped out into the late morning sunlight and closed my eyes, glad my mother's wards hadn't blocked out the breeze while holding me in. I took a deep breath, inhaling the scents of early winter. It would snow soon and I lamented being trapped in the house when it happened, I had always loved the snow.

I huffed out a sigh and dropped into one of the wicker chairs near the doors, sulking. I'd been feeling sorry for myself for the last several weeks since being put under house arrest. My mother kept telling me I needed to use the time to reflect on how I had landed in this situation. She was insistent that I evaluate my actions and figure out why I had slipped my bracelet. For the first time in over seven centuries I had felt the need to drop the shackles on my wolf and let her free.

My mind drifted back to the day seven hundred and eight years earlier, back before the bracelet was needed. There had been a time when the runes and wards I had tattooed down my back and the backs of my arms and legs had been enough to chain the wolf. She finally found a way to shake the magic though and the result was horrific. In those days we had only been the ruling species for a few decades and things were tense to say the least. There were sects of rogue humans who opposed us, attacking our weaker ranks during the day while they slept.

One of those assaults landed squarely on our front lawn when a radical militia group stormed the manor at sunrise in my second century. They swarmed our estate, burning our outbuildings to the ground and nearly killed my eldest brother, Marcus. My wolf, being the creature she is, had taken offense and felt the attack was personal against our family. She broke free and, in a single night on the rampage, wiped out six militia groups across four territories. More than two thousand humans lost their lives in one night.

The upside had been the humans who already feared us cowering further and ceasing their resistance. The downside, those militia groups left became so violent we had no choice but to hunt them down and wipe them out. It had been bloody and, if you ask my mother, completely unnecessary. They would have been dealt with eventually, without the need to kill every last one of them. As it was, I'd left them no choice. It was shortly after that when my mother laid down the laws we now all live by regarding humans.

As the oldest Vampire still living, she had total authority and after setting the laws she formed a council. Our ruling elite who decided on everything from estate borders to turning new Vampires to how many humans a given Vampire could keep. It had worked for us well for the last seven hundred years but sometimes I wondered if changes were needed. I stopped to consider my current situation, thinking for a moment that maybe too much change wasn't all good. I supposed I could see my mother's point of view on the matter.

I let out a groan and dropped my head to my hand with the thought. Just what I needed, to start thinking like my mother. I loved the woman and had no doubt she carried a wisdom I wouldn't find for centuries. It came along with being one of the oldest creatures walking the planet. I'd never been able to get either of my parents to tell me exactly how old she was. All I knew for sure was that she and her sisters were the first three of all Vampire kind. They were walking the planet at roughly the same time as Cro-Magnon man. Whether that was an accurate guess of their age or if they had been around before then, no one really knew.

What was known was that every Vampire alive in our modern era descends from one of the three sisters. Alistra and Acacia had been killed centuries earlier with my mother, Ayana, being the sole survivor. All of our kind owed their allegiance to her and sometimes I wondered if that was the only thing keeping me alive after the things I had done. It was with those thoughts rippling through my mind I finally understood something. I was a liability for my mother, keeping her hold on her kingdom tenuous at best. I needed to get my act together, straighten up and start acting my damn age.

I was too often found behaving like a spoiled teenager than the princess I actually was and it needed to halt, immediately. If only the action were as easy as the intent. I dropped my hand from my face and looked out across the expanse of our back acreage. I smiled at the small herd of deer grazing near the edge of the woods and let out a sigh. So what if my mother believed the humans deserved better treatment? Who was I to question her wisdom, her experience? She had been around during some of the darkest times in recorded history.

Humans, before they had known about our kind, when we were still nothing more than myth and legend, always searched for the easiest solution for things. What they called the black plague had been nothing more than a handful of Vampires who had decided they were bored and wanted new entertainment. When turning a human into one of our kind, the human is first bled almost to the point of death and then fed our blood. This forces the change. However, when our blood is consumed by a healthy human, the change doesn't take place.

Instead, other effects take over the mortal human body. In small doses, our blood acts like a drug, causing a safe, non-narcotic high. This led many humans in Asia during the mid 1800's to abandon their opium addictions. They turned to Vampire blood instead, few knowing what it actually was, only that the addiction was much easier to break away from. The only long term side effect presented with constant use, longevity. In high doses however, our blood causes the healthy human body to begin rejecting its own mortality. It shuts down, the skin reacting with sores that weep as the organs fail.

Humans at the time couldn't accept the effects as anything other than a deadly, but very human, plague they decided must be carried by rats. It was labeled and doctors began trying to treat it, many finding their patients stashes of blood and stealing it. This only perpetuated the spread as many of these physicians prescribed small doses of our blood to heal other ailments. The patients would then get carried away, overdose and the plague myth would be carried on into another village. We finally managed to get the phenomenon under control, finding the Vampires responsible for putting the blood out into the mortal population. They were dealt with and the flow of the dangerous substance halted.

My mother had handled the whole ordeal with grace and without overreacting. I could see some need for her way of doing things, even if I didn't always agree. I pushed myself out of the chair and stepped back into the room, pulling the doors closed behind me. Someday I would need to start acting not only my age but like the heir I was supposed to be. Sooner would definitely be better than later. With Vampire society being highly matriarchal and my parents having only one daughter, I would lead someday when my mother finally got bored. I had to make sure I wouldn't completely undo everything she had worked so hard to accomplish.

I wondered as I started down the stairs toward the kitchen if the reason she hadn't stepped down yet was simply because I would screw everything up. She had worked too hard for far too long to have me step in and wipe it all out in a matter of years. Feeling at least a handful of centuries older than I had when I'd awakened earlier, I stepped into the kitchen. I was glad to see both my parents seated at the small table near the end of the island. I cleared my throat to announce myself.

My mother turned to look at me, setting her cup down on the table as my father simply turned the page of the book he was reading. I locked my gaze on the man for several seconds but when he made a point of ignoring me I sighed and looked at my mother. She raised an eyebrow at me as she leaned back in her chair and folded her hands in her lap.

"I'm sorry."

The sincerity in my voice tilted her lips up slightly and caused my father to close his book and finally acknowledge me. I pulled a long breath into my lungs and stepped over to the table. I shifted the third chair back and settled into it, right between my parents.

"I've been acting like a spoiled brat. You've both always supported me in everything I've done, no matter how bad I messed things up for you. I responded to that by continuing to screw you over and make your lives harder. I've threatened the peace you've worked so hard for more times than I can count and I need to cut it out."

My mother's grin expanded until she was beaming a full smile at me, the expression mirrored on my father's face. We sat there in silence for a full minute before my father reached over and ruffled my hair, my mother's hand finding mine and giving it a squeeze.

"Can you forgive me?"

"Already done, none of us are perfect. You just need to remember that your mistakes tend to carry a body count. I'll go this afternoon and have a chat with Xander. I believe we might be able to come to some sort of agreement with him. You've been restricted to the house long enough. You may not get full freedom to wander again but perhaps to the edges of the territory. If we can convince him we can keep you within our borders that is."

"I appreciate it but maybe we should try some extra precautions. The fact is, I can't control the wolf. Maybe another visit with the crafter isn't a bad idea."

My parents looked at each other, carrying on a private conversation no one else had any chance of hearing. My mother finally sighed and nodded as my father turned to look at me. I'd seen the look in his eyes before and it made my heart soar, he was proud of me for the choice I'd made. He wouldn't say it, he rarely did but I knew it and that was enough.

"I'll put in the request. With any luck we can get an audience over the weekend. Don't get your hopes up though..."

"I know. He's a busy man."

He nodded, reaching over to pat me on the shoulder as they stood from the table. I rose as well, knowing there were steps to be taken before I could be released from my gilded cage. My parents left the house to attend to their business as I returned to the second floor and my rooms. The sounds of guitar music reached my ears as it had often in the last few weeks. I had to admit my human was very talented with the instrument. Most of our kind could pick up any instrument they felt the desire to play in a matter of hours but it always lacked something.

The heart, the soul a human put into the music they played and the words they sang was haunting and beautiful. It was also something most of us couldn't hope to find or express, we just lost the ability to show things so strongly after a few centuries. It was the downside of living, well, forever. Life lost its beauty, sadness and intensity. I stood there and listened as I thought about the benefits of keeping humans around as more than food. It seemed my mother was right again and I couldn't help but chuckle to myself at the thought.

I'd had a day full of insight and epiphany, and it wasn't even lunch. I shook my head as I turned to head to my room but then stopped and changed my mind. I walked over to the room Angel occupied and leaned against the wall beside the door. I didn't attempt to open it further, hearing the music from her guitar and the emotion tinged tones of her voice without needing to interrupt her. I leaned there and listened, taking in the emotion of it. The words weren't anything I recognized and it dawned on me that she had probably written it herself.

I smiled to myself, allowing a moment of enjoying having her around without thinking too deeply about it like I had been. I closed my eyes, relaxing and letting the process happen without shame since no one was there to witness it anyway. The door was jerked open a minute later and I jumped at the sudden movement as the newest addition to my home stared at me. I stood there, returning her stare in silence for several silent moments. She finally narrowed her eyes down and put one hand on her hip, the other still holding the doorknob.

"What do you want?"

"I don't have to want anything. This is my house and I'll stand wherever I want."

"Actually, it's your parents' house."

I glared at her, my goodwill and feelings of finding harmony with the humans in my home from a moment earlier shattered. A low growl started in the back of my throat, warning the girl to watch her tone. She had the nerve to roll her eyes at me and my temper flared slightly before ebbing back. She had the uncanny ability to make me sway from feeling terrible for hurting her into wanting to strangle her in minutes. It made no sense to me and I was at a loss to put a stop to either end of it.

"Yes, my parents technically own the estate but it is still my home. Show a little respect."

"Respect? Sorry, I've always believed that's something you earn. Do something that deserves respect from me and you'll get it."

Another flare of my temper and, despite my promise to my mother that I would grow up and act my age I lashed out. My fingers clamped around her neck as I back her into the room and pressed her against the wall. She stood on the balls of her feet, a couple more inches and I would have been holding her off the ground completely. I leaned in and growled in her face, the sound hard, threatening the violence I was barely holding in check.

"You'd do well to remember that I could end your life in the space of a breath human."

She pulled in a ragged breath, made difficult because of my hand pressing on her windpipe. As if to prove my point I leaned a little weight against my hand, cutting off her air supply. Her eyes widened, fear rolling off of her in a cascade of waves that crashed over me. I stared at her, my expression surely devoid of emotion as she struggled against my grip. Her eyes misted over, a single tear breaking free and slipping down her right cheek. The sight snapped something in my head and I blinked several times, the anger ebbing away as I released my hold.

Her feet touched the carpet and she stumbled to the bed, gasping and coughing as she attempted to get air into her lungs. I turned and left the room, my eyes on the floor as I walked and tried to figure out what the hell she was doing to me. I'd always had a temper, passed to me from my father but it had never proven to be so easy to provoke. Something about this girl and the way she spoke to me made me lose the grip I had on my anger. I slammed my bedroom door behind me, turned and leaned back against it, sliding to the floor.

My head fell forward, face pressed into my hands as I listened to the sobbing cries coming from next door. I had come dangerously close to killing the poor girl and I didn't have a good excuse for why. Sure she had ticked me off but many humans hand done so and barely earned more than an eye roll or a shoe thrown in their direction. I couldn't seem to put a finger on why or how she managed to make me react so violently. As I sat there, contemplating my predicament, the sobs from the other room slowed and eased into soft crying.

My heart ached at the sound but I pushed the feeling aside, not willing to allow it any further movement through me. I couldn't get too attached to this human and how I made her feel. They all had one thing in common, exceedingly short lives. The best of our pets might live into the middle of their first century but most died long before then. I couldn't become wrapped up in her pain or it would consume me, warp my judgement. I had to keep her a part of my life but separate from the emotional side of it. Someday, sooner than I cared to think about, she wouldn't be there. When it happened I couldn't allow myself to be in a place where I mourned her or focused on the pain she would likely be in near the end for long.

CHAPTER SEVEN

PAINFUL REVELATIONS

I WOKE up sprawled on the floor, my back aching and my right arm dead asleep where it was curled under my head. I wasn't sure when I had fallen asleep and I didn't even know what time it was. I pushed myself up so I was sitting and leaned back against my door with a sigh. I glanced across the room at the blue glow of my clock, seeing it was almost three in the morning. I grumbled as I crawled to my bed, pulled myself into it and kicked off my shoes. I wasn't in the mood to be awake yet so I rolled onto my stomach and tugged a pillow under my head.

I laid there in the darkness, willing sleep to find me again, not sure how long I had been asleep on the floor. I turned my head so I was facing the clock sitting on the bedside table and watched the minutes pass. After two hours of lying there and getting no closer to sleeping I rolled over and sat up. I took a good stretch, gathered some clean clothes, showered and dressed for the day before heading downstairs. I sat on one of the stools at the island in the kitchen, coffee cup between my hands but completely forgotten.

While the glass mosaic of tiles forming the backsplash above our countertops wasn't exactly exciting it had held my attention for nearly an hour. It wasn't until someone cleared their throat in the doorway that I snapped back to myself. I turned to find my mother standing there watching me. I managed to give her a small smile but knew it didn't reach my eyes. I was lost to confusion, about myself, what I was feeling and the way I had reacted to Angel the day before. My mother sat across from me after getting some coffee of her own.

"What's wrong?"

"Why would you think anything is wrong?"

She gave a single, short nod toward the forgotten coffee held between my hands on the countertop. The now cold contents totally untouched, very unlike me. I sighed as I stared into the dark liquid and shook my head. I couldn't tell my mother what was wrong because I didn't even understand it. I was terrified if I told her the things I had said and done to Angel she would remove her from the house. She was the only steady company I'd had the last few weeks. Despite the fact we didn't seem to get along, at all, the idea of not having her there made a slow panic start to rise in my chest.

I tamped the feeling down, slipped off the stool and crossed the room to the sink. I dumped the coffee, rinsed the cup and set it in the dishwasher. I stood there and stared at the counter for a few breaths then turned and leaned back, the edge of the counter bearing the weight I pressed against it. I crossed my arms over my chest and looked at my mother. She sat at the island, sipping her coffee and waiting patiently for me to decide I wanted to talk. She hadn't answered my question and I knew she wouldn't, she didn't need to.

"I don't honestly know. I wish I could tell you but I'm just... Off lately. I'll sort it out."

"Perhaps your visit from the crafter will help to sort things."

"Yeah, that might be it. Maybe the wolf is restless with the runes acting up."

My eyes went to the bracelet on my right wrist, the runes still glowing the same angry fire red they had turned when I removed it. It was an outward sign the enchantment had been broken. Despite the magic having reasserted itself, after the wards were breached once, doing so again became easier. Until it was fixed, or replaced, I was still a threat and would remain a prisoner to my temper. I hadn't taken that into account when thinking on my reactions to the human. Perhaps it wasn't her after all, I could definitely hope that was the case.

"He will be here tomorrow evening. Xander refuses to back down his stance on the issue until your wards have been adjusted. He doesn't trust you to keep the wolf under control."

"I can't say I blame him. It's fine, I've made it this long cooped up in here. A couple more days won't kill me."

She nodded, finished the coffee in her cup then crossed to mirror my earlier actions. With the cups side by side in the dishwasher she turned to leave the room. We didn't speak as she exited and I didn't move to follow her. Whatever she had to do for the day didn't involve me or she would have had me accompany her. I waited, staring at the wall for ten minutes and then finally pushed away and left the kitchen. I needed to find something to occupy myself, get my mind off things I didn't want to think about.

I took the stairs to the second floor and made my way toward the library. Casper usually left something new on the shelves when he came back from one of his trips. When he had come in to pester me he and Tristan had just returned from Paris and I was sure he must have brought something home with him. I could only hope I was something I hadn't read yet though that was becoming more difficult every year. I had barely stepped over the threshold into the room when the sound of voices pulled me up short. I stopped and leaned against the shelf just inside the door to listen.

One voice belonged to my mother, her smooth sing-song tone unmistakable and the other was one I knew as well. Angel had been crying again, I could hear it in her voice when she spoke and it pulled a frown across my features. I focused, tuning in my sensitive hearing so I could make out what they were saying. I knew I hadn't been invited to sit in on this conversation for a reason but I couldn't help myself. Curiosity killed the cat, guess it was a good thing I was a wolf.

"I just don't know what to do, Ayana."

"Talk to me, what's been happening child?"

"She's so angry, all the time. That temper of hers is out of hand."

"She's always had her father's temper, I'll admit that much."

"Well it's terrifying when it's turned on me. She almost killed me."

"She did what?"

"I said something she didn't like so she pinned me to the wall. She cut off my air, I almost blacked out."

"Is that why you've been crying?"

"Part of it. I just don't know what I've done wrong. I know I can be mouthy but I don't think that deserves violence."

"Of course it doesn't dear."

"Then why? Is it me? Does she just hate me?"

"I don't think so. There's something you need to understand about Silver. She's not like the rest of us. As a hybrid, she's unique. There's not another like her anywhere in the world. Even her brothers only took their father's side of our genetics. All wolves, each one, not a drop of Vampire we've been able to find. We still don't understand exactly how that affects her. What I do know is that she is constantly at war with herself. We've done what we can to quiet it over the centuries but we can only do so much. She hasn't been able to bring a peace between her dueling personalities and it eats at her. I don't even know if she's aware how badly it wears on her."

Silence filled the space behind the shelves for a few minutes and I wondered what, if anything, Angel would say. I had to admit I was a little shocked, I hadn't realized that the wolf was so out of control because I'd let her be, I simply thought it was her nature. I would have to seriously rethink the relationship I had with the other half of myself. I was pulled from my thoughts when Angel spoke again.

"I can appreciate the situation she's in. But it doesn't change the fact that I don't feel safe here with her."

"Understandable if she's done the things you say."

"I can't stay here with her. I barely sleep, I'm always terrified that the next time she gets angry I won't walk away from her outburst. All I do is cry. I don't even leave my room anymore except to eat and only if she's not in the kitchen. I can't talk to her, she's impossible to have a conversation with. At least she is if you happen to have committed the crime of being born human."

"Angel..."

"I'm sorry, Ayana. I just can't do this anymore. Please get me out of here. I wanna go home."

My breath caught and my stomach knotted at the request she made. My brows furrowed down hard as I tried to figure out why I was reacting so harshly. I could always just request another pet and mother would find a replacement. For some reason the thought didn't help, it actually made the knot in my gut worse and caused a tightening in my heart I couldn't explain. I had to admit I didn't want Angel to leave despite not knowing why. I hadn't been easy to live with and I couldn't blame her for wanting to leave but thinking about it happening hurt.

"Give it a week. Please, for me. If at the end of the week she's still making it impossible for you and you want to leave, I'll take you back to the village."

"A week? Seven days and if I still want to leave you won't try to talk me into staying?"

"Seven days and if you tell me you're still done, I will escort you back to your mother myself."

"Okay. Hopefully she doesn't decide to kill me over the course of the week."

"If she goes that far child, believe me she will be dealt with accordingly. She was given her rules before you were brought here. She'd do well to remember them. Perhaps I'll have a talk with her, remind her of the consequences her current course would result in. I'll be in to check on you when I can. Keep your chin up, either things will improve here or you'll be free to leave."

"Thank you."

"You're welcome child. Now go on, Silver should have removed herself from the kitchen by now and you look like you haven't eaten in a couple days."

I started at the sound of chair legs scraping on the wood floor and bolted from the library, heading for my room. I pushed the door closed, crossed the room and sank into the chair facing my desk. I couldn't believe what I'd overheard. I knew I'd been difficult but I'd never actually cross the line and seriously injure Angel. Then again, I doubted she knew as much and as the thought crossed my mind I realized I didn't blame her. She had every reason to fear me and I had no one to blame but myself and my temper for it.

I pushed out of my chair and decided a visit to the gym sounded like a wonderful idea. I shoved open my closet door, grabbed a pair of sweat pants and a plain black tank top. Once I changed I made my way to the gym and, as had become my habit, went right for my hand wraps. They were carefully rewound and replaced on the shelf they always occupied by Ivan. He always made sure everything was exactly where it should be. I worked the poor boy to the bone and he never complained, never talked back and never questioned my motives. He simply did what I ordered because I ordered it.

I paused halfway through wrapping my left hand as the thought struck a chord in my brain. How many years had he served me? It was going well on fifteen now. He had been ten when he was brought to the manor to replace my former valet. The man had served me for almost seventy years before his joints refused to comply any further. He had reached a point where he could no longer function in his position so my mother released him from service. He returned to the village and the next day Ivan had been brought in to replace him.

In all those fifteen years I couldn't remember ever thanking him for the things he did for me. He cleaned up my messes, did my laundry, made up my room and now made sure Angel's necessities were handled. I brushed the thoughts away, finished wrapping my hand and then moved over to the punching bag. The ceiling had been repaired, a new hook in place to hold the bag exactly where I preferred it be placed. I allowed myself a small smile as I stretched then began what I hoped would be a workout to clear my mind of all the weird things fliting through it.

CHAPTER EIGHT

THE CRAFTER AND EPIPHANIES

BY THE time my meeting with the crafter arrived I was a twitchy mass of nerves. I needed to be able to keep the wolf under control. It was the only way I would get any part of my freedom back and I needed it, fast. I sat on our plush couch in the living room, elbows on my knees and my right heel tapping a nervous rhythm on the polished marble floor. I hadn't seen the man I was waiting to meet in just over seven hundred years. Simply thinking about the reason for his visit made my mouth feel as if I'd been chewing on sand. He was bound to be furious with me for my stupidity and I could only hope he would be willing to help me once again.

A heavy knock on the front door echoed through the first floor of the manor and ceased the movement of my foot. My father opened the door and I heard him greet our guest and then explain why he had been summoned. The exasperated sigh released by our guest made my eye twitch as I heard them head for the living room. My parents entered the room, the crafter trailing behind them and I couldn't bring myself to look at any of them. I kept my eyes on my shoes as they approached me, stopping closer than I was comfortable with until I knew how angry he was.

"Silver. I hear you decided to screw up my enchantments."

I couldn't find any anger or reproach in his voice but you could never really tell with his kind. They could be volatile and tempers could flare quickly and for seemingly no reason. I'd never actually known him to lose his but it was a bit of a forgone conclusion that he did given what he was. I heaved out a sigh and waited for the lecture I was fairly certain would follow. I was pleasantly surprised when he went the completely opposite direction instead.

"You know, if you missed me you could have just asked me to stop by. You didn't have to go and throw a tantrum."

His chuckle finally pulled my gaze up to him and I couldn't help the smile that stole across my face. He was still the most imposing man I'd ever laid eyes on, dwarfing even my father by a good eight inches. It was like looking at a darkly tanned wall, his chest easily wider than my entire arm span. His waist length blonde hair was pulled back in a tight ponytail, a slight wave of curl gracing the ends of the strands. He was wearing the most dazzling smile I'd ever seen and it made his emerald eyes sparkle and dance. I couldn't have kept the smile off my own face if I'd tried. For at least the millionth time I wondered how drastically he altered his true appearance for these visits.

I chuckled as I stood from the couch and he let out a laugh that worked its way into every corner of the house, seeming to fill the space with light. I shook my head at the flush of happiness and power washing over me as the sound died away. His emotions were a palpable thing, you could grab hold of them, feel them brushing over your skin. Yet another of the skills his kind possessed, it helped them keep us lower beings in line when needed.

"Hello, Hephaestus."

He closed on me in a single massive step, swept me up into his arms and hugged me tight against his chest. You haven't experienced a hug until you've been sincerely embraced by a God. He dropped a kiss on my temple and then put my feet back on the floor as he took a place on the couch I'd just vacated.

"It's good to see you again dearest. Now, let's see the mess you've made of my work, shall we?"

I blushed brightly and turned my gaze back to my shoes as I lifted my wrist so he could see the bracelet. I was embarrassed I had broken something it had taken him such thought and care to create during what amounted to a temper tantrum. He took my wrist gently in his huge hands and turned it, checking every inch of the silver surface. He clucked his tongue and tsk'd several times as he traced each of the runes with his fingertips. Even at my age I felt like a child being scolded as I stood before the ageless deity sitting in my living room.

The thought struck me as funny suddenly and I couldn't contain the laugh which broke free. He looked up from his inspection and raised an eyebrow at me to which I only shook my head and turned my gaze toward the ceiling. He refrained from commenting as he returned to the task of checking my bracelet. I wondered if he would be able to repair it or if I had done irreversible damage to the magic he'd laid in place so long ago.

"I'm sorry to say that I can't salvage anything of what this used to be. The magic has been tainted and the runes have been damaged beyond repair."

I turned my eyes back to him as he said exactly what I'd been fearing and hadn't wanted to hear. I let out a pained whimper, not sure what to do if he couldn't fix my only barrier. The two finger wide strip of silver was the only thing allowing me to function. It was all that held the beast inside me at bay and if I didn't have it I wasn't sure what might happen. Even in its weakened state it offered me some protection. He reached up and laid a hand gently on my shoulder as his smile turned into something soft, sympathetic and almost fatherly.

"Calm down child. I expected this might happen eventually. Do you really think I would leave you with no safeguards at all?"

"I guess not."

"Of course not. Now, I have a solution that will be a bit more, permanent. It's extreme but it will keep you from being tempted to repeat this process."

I glanced over at my parents and saw a flicker of worry flash through my mother's expression. My father had slipped into the expressionless mask he wore when addressing his guards with orders. The look gave absolutely nothing away. That couldn't be a good sign and I wondered how much this solution would end up hurting me. I refocused on the God seated in front of me and took in a steadying breath, filling my lungs completely before exhaling slowly.

"Whatever it takes."

"All right. First, I think we need to have a talk. Come, let us have a seat on your balcony and chat."

It wasn't ever really a good thing when one of the Gods said they needed to have a talk with you. Typically it meant you'd done something they felt they should scold you for but preferred to do so in private while maintaining their tempers. I didn't have much choice so I nodded and waited for him to stand. I shot a glance at my parents before I followed him up the stairs and into my bedroom. We crossed to the double doors and I opened them so we could step out onto the balcony.

The sun was setting on the other side of the house and it had tinged the sky to the east the most gorgeous shade of purple. I pulled a chair over and settled into it, my eyes locked on the darkening sky since I was terrified to actually look at Hephaestus. He cleared his throat and I swallowed hard, still not wanting to turn and face him. His fingers fell on my right shoulder, the touch feather light and I wondered at the gentleness of his touch for a fleeting moment. It had always shocked me how this giant of a man could be so soft touched and inspire such calm with his mere presence.

"Look at me."

I sighed and finally turned to face him, my gaze ripped from the skyline to settle on the brilliant green of his eyes. He dropped his touch from my shoulder and the chill of the rapidly encroaching night washed over me. I hadn't realized he'd been warming me until the contact was broken but once it was gone I wanted it back desperately. It made me feel safe, protected and with the panic beginning to flood back into my being, I needed it.

"Silver, your wolf is a part of you. A part that you cannot continue to ignore."

"I know but I can't control her. She's wild and bloodthirsty and it scares me. I can't remember the things she does."

"I need you to listen to me, carefully. When I created your father, he was given his wolf as a gift. I forged his soul from the two it began as with as much care as the weapons I make for the pantheon. Of all the things I have created, he has always been the one I'm most proud of. I always knew he would be great, do amazing and wondrous things. I never realized how great the things he would do were until you came along. I never expected that he would be able to fall so completely in love. I didn't dare to dream he would have children."

All I could was nod and keep listening. I knew the story of how my father had been created well, had heard it more times than I could count. I'd always known he was probably even older than my mother but had never had the suspicion confirmed. I wasn't actually sure he even knew how old he really was. The God seated beside me turned to look at the sky, now deep blue over the trees in the distance. He took a deep breath, filling his lungs with the chilled night air, smiled and returned his gaze to me.

"I have children, this much you know but what you may not realize is that I count your father among them. To me, you are family. I don't know if you're aware but my children seem to enjoy producing male offspring. That makes you my only granddaughter."

"I didn't know you thought of me that way."

"Maybe I should have told you centuries ago. How I see you in regards to my family has nothing to do with why I wanted to talk to you other than making sure you understand I want nothing more than for you, and your brothers, to be happy. That said, I feel the need to ask you... Why do you and the wolf fight each other so violently?"

"I don't know. She's always trying to push me back, take control and I know what happens when I let her so I push back."

"Have you ever considered looking at her as something akin to a tiger in a zoo?"

My brow furrowed as I stared at him, not sure what he meant and trying to puzzle it out. I knew if I didn't get it he would eventually tell me, he wasn't the type to enjoy confusing people. After thinking about it for several seconds I shook my head. I couldn't understand how looking at my wolf as a caged animal would help. Of course she was caged, if she wasn't she'd run rampant slaughtering anything in her path.

"Consider this. A wild animal is not meant to live in a cage. It's meant to run free, feel the earth beneath its feet, the wind in its fur. Tigers caged for long spans of their lives often become violent, unpredictable because they have no natural outlet. They are no longer tigers, they are some variation of a being that was once a majestic creature but has been reduced to something to be poked at through bars and have its picture taken."

"And you're telling me my wolf is suffering from those same affects?"

"In a way, yes. She is never free to run, to play and to just be a wolf. Perhaps if we can find a way for you to release her more often in a controlled way, she will relax and be a happier creature."

"Worth a shot. I meant, worst outcome it doesn't work and I have to continue right on like I have for so long."

He nodded as he rose from his seat and I followed, pushing to my feet as he turned to go back inside. We made our way back downstairs, finding my parents sitting at the kitchen island in silence. I offered them a small smile to reassure them I was fine and not in any trouble and then continued into the living room. Hephaestus waved me toward a chair and I moved to sit in it as he gathered a bag I didn't remember him bringing in. Gods could be wily that was, producing things from nowhere on occasion. He sat in the chair beside me, indicating I should turn and sit in mine backwards.

I gave him a strange look but did as he wanted, folding my arms across the top rail as he began unpacking his supplies. I recognized the tools he had used to give me the tattoos that still traced my spine, the backs of my arms and sides of my thighs and raised an eyebrow. He ignored me and continued setting up for whatever he had planned. Once he had everything in order he turned to me with a smile.

"All right, the things we've tried to this point have obviously failed. Therefor we're going to attempt something new and hope it holds. Shirt off."

I didn't consider arguing with him simply pulled off my tank top and dropped it on the floor beside the chair. He positioned me so I was leaning forward slightly, the fronts of my shoulders pressed to the back of the chair and my chin resting against the top rail where my arms had been. I heard the machine buzz for a moment and closed my eyes, waiting for the press of the needle against my skin. I didn't have to wait long but as the ink met my skin I experienced something very different from the last time he had marked me like this.

The searing burn ripped its way from the point the needle was working on my shoulder down my back. I bit down on my lower lip to keep from crying out as the pain worked over my entire body, leaving sparks of white fire flashing against the backs of my eyelids. A whimper broke free and a moment later I heard my father's voice from the doorway between the living room and kitchen.

"Silver, what's wrong?"

"She'll be in pain until I complete this new set. The ink is laced with silver."

I opened my eyes when my father growled, the sound echoing through the room. I slid my gaze up to meet his and gave a barely perceptible shake of my head. The pain was terrible but I could fight through it if it meant having any chance of finding peace with my wolf. I watched the twitch in his jaw stop and saw him relax as my mother stepped up beside him. I focused on the drag of the needle against my skin, trying to imagine the shapes being formed along my skin. Hephaestus wasn't tracing his original runes but instead adding brand new marks on my skin.

I pulled in a ragged breath, trying to relax against the pain and closed my eyes again. I grit my teeth as the progress moved down my back, knowing he would probably line both sides as he had before then move to my arms. I did my best to push my mind elsewhere, not caring where it landed as long as the pain slipped to the background. I reconsidered the thought when my mind wandered to Angel and what I'd overheard the day before. A new pain reared its head, settling over my heart and suddenly the sting of mildly toxic ink was barely worth acknowledging.

My mind slipped back to the first day she'd been in the manor, it was the first and last time I could remember seeing her smile. I remembered how dazzling it was, the cute little dimple that appeared in her left cheek. She'd done nothing but frown and cry since then and I was to blame for it. I'd been terrible to her, treated her so badly I was stunned she had made it so long before asking to leave. I flashed back to what she'd said to my mother. She was ready to walk out, go back to her life in the settlement and never look back. I had to find a way to change her mind though I wasn't completely sure why it mattered to me so much.

In no time at all I shivered as a cool stream of liquid hit my back followed by the excess ink being wiped away. My back cleaned I was moved and repositioned so, as I had suspected, he could work on my arms. I slipped back into my thoughts of the strange, defiant and often infuriating human sharing my space. As if pulled by some unseen force, my gaze shifted up to the top of the stairs. Angel stood there, arms crossed over her chest, watching what was happening in the room below. Her eyes flickered to mine, a scowl crossed her face and she turned to retreat down the hallway. I sighed at the reaction, finally realizing how much she really hated sharing space with me.

Two hours later I was finally allowed to sit up and put my shirt back on, rolling my shoulders to alleviate the stiffness. The new tattoos ran down the inside of my arms rather than the backs so I could get a good look at them. I traced the intricate lines with my eyes, following the flow of the pattern they created. Each one shimmered slightly with the metal in its ink and I knew they always would. The metal would resist being absorbed into my body and would always glitter on the surface.

The patterns were stunning, even more intricate than the original set he'd inked me with so many centuries earlier. They were as beautiful as I hoped they would be functional and I turned my gaze to Hephaestus. My parents had departed sometime during the inking of my arms, leaving us sitting alone in the room.

"I have one other piece of advice to offer you on your wolf."

"Anything you can offer is welcome. I'm at a loss with her."

"Remember that while your wolf is indeed a beast, an animal, it is also more than that. She has always known your emotions, your insight, your fears, regrets and your joy. She feels it all just as you do. When you neglect to let her process these things, and refuse to allow her to express her own emotions, she'll get testy. Perhaps you should pay a little more attention to the things she wants you to feel."

"I was with you up until the end there. Then you stopped making any sense."

"I believe you forgot that physical contact allows me some insight into your emotions."

I narrowed my eyes at him when he mentioned it because I had forgotten he could read me like a book with a touch. The ability was heightened with anyone carrying Lycan blood since he had created us and could therefor get inside our heads. Knowing he had felt the turmoil I'd been dealing with for weeks made me shudder. He chuckled at the movement and reached over to brush my hair behind my ear.

"Relax, all your secrets are safe with me. However, I do believe you need to look more closely at your reactions to your human."

"I've been trying. They don't make any sense to me. One minute I feel bad for making her hurt and the next I have her pinned to a wall choking her."

"Because you're fighting yourself."

"Lost again."

"The wolf is part of you, your other half. Her emotions will affect yours. If what I felt from her is right then I believe, and try to keep calm, she is lashing out at you for refusing to acknowledge her choice for a mate."

My brows furrowed at his words as I tried to make sense of them and when his meaning hit me the reaction was physical. My stomach knotted, chest tightened and I couldn't breathe for several long seconds. When I finally managed to pull some air into my lungs my eyes were watering and the gasps I was taking were ragged. I looked up and met his eyes again then shook my head, refusing to believe it.

"No, not a chance, she wouldn't."

"And why wouldn't she?"

"A human?"

"Why not a human? She doesn't care about your objections to their kind. She only knows what she senses. You deny her feelings for the girl, also denying your own I might add but that's another argument entirely, and when the wolf lashes out at you, you in turn take it out on the human."

I dropped my eyes to my shoes and thought about what he'd told me, hating how much sense it made once he had explained it. I worried at my lower lip as I turned the information over in my mind, trying to find a reason to dispute it. After five minutes I was shocked to realize I didn't want to dispute it, I wanted to embrace it. I knew the feeling had to be the wolf asserting herself now that I had acknowledged her choice. Once I opened myself to her feelings, there was no doubt she wanted the girl.

I decided it was worth at least allowing for the possibility. It couldn't hurt to try and see where things went. It could make all the difference in the way I treated Angel and maybe, just maybe, could convince her to stay. I looked back up and offered him a smile then rose from the couch and moved to hug him. He returned the gesture gently, careful of the still healing fresh tattoos.

"Work through things, have a chat with your wolf. Let her know she's not forgotten, stop ignoring her. These can't be taken off like the bracelet so they will never be able to fail. However, the magic they are imbued with is different. They do not cage the wolf, they calm her, help to ease the suffering between times you allow her to run free. The more she is allowed out, the more her anger and rage will fade. You two will learn to find a balance, some kind of harmony. Working out your feelings for that girl will help you with that."

"I'll do my best, I swear it. I should probably find my mother and see if she'll allow me a run. I think the wolf needs some attention."

He nodded and then followed me to track down my mother, who initially put her foot down on the idea of my wolf roaming free. She rethought her stance when Hephaestus himself offered to follow and keep an eye on me. Being our creator he could force my wolf back with a few words if she got out of hand. Feeling I would be safe and in good hands, my mother finally relented and agreed to let the wolf out for a run. It was with a smile on my face that I followed her to the front porch, my heart rejoicing as she wiped away two of the runes on the rails.

The barrier breached, the magic dropped away and I felt the

pull. I stripped off my clothes and glanced over at my guardian for the evening. He smiled and gave me a small nod before he turned his gaze toward the woods in the distance. I took a running start, leapt off the stairs and headed for the gates. I reached deep within as I ran, not so much calling the wolf to me this time as telling her the night was hers. The shift was, for the first time, instant and completely painless, slipping my human form in the span between strides.

My wolf senses were aware of Hephaestus running beside me and I was shocked to realize, while I didn't have control, I was present. She hadn't locked me out this time and she seemed happy, something I hadn't felt from her in longer than I wanted to admit. I knew in an instant these new runes would work and I would find some kind of harmony with the other half of myself.

CHAPTER NINE

CONFESSIONS

I STARED at the ceiling fan, a new hobby of mine lately I had noticed, watching it spin in the darkness of my room. I'd fallen into bed after my run with Hephaestus left me exhausted but even after running myself ragged, sleep was being elusive. I was pointedly avoiding my parents since getting mother's okay to run. I knew they would ask about my conversation with the God, what advice he had given me. I would have to tell them the wolf had to come out more, which might end well after my singularly uneventful run, but there was no telling. They would no doubt know there was something else. I would end up spilling everything I'd been feeling lately, right along with everything I'd been avoiding feeling.

I sighed and rolled over onto my stomach, my mind racing as I tried to figure out how to handle things with Angel. I had to find a way to convince her to stay, to give me a chance to prove I wasn't a complete jerk. If she left the manor and went back to her family there was a high likelihood I would never see her again. The humans called the settlement my parents controlled a 'village' but the term was really misleading. As high queen, my mother controlled the largest territory of any Vampire alive. Her stock consisted of well over two million humans settled over more than a thousand square miles.

She couldn't leave, not if what the God had told me was true, if my wolf had decided this girl belonged to her. I would just have to stop acting, well, exactly like I had been acting. My behavior had to change completely. I had no clue how to work on keeping my temper under control around her though. So far she had gotten my hackles up far too easily and figuring out a way to turn the reaction off was proving puzzling. A soft knock on my door made me turn my head toward the portal and I could already feel my mother's energy on the other side. No doubt she knew I was awake and had come to check on me.

"Come in." I rolled over onto my stomach as I spoke to the wooden portal, settling in as I heard it open.

"I figured you were still awake. Is everything okay? You disappeared on us after Hephaestus left."

"I'm, actually I don't really know. Confused, I think."

She walked over and sat on the edge of my bed, the faint light from the hallway lending more than enough light for both of us to see clearly by. I let out a soft sigh as she reached over and rubbed my back. She had done it so many times when I was young and something was bothering me but she hadn't repeated it recently. It was comforting and I felt myself relaxing.

"What are you confused about? I thought your run went well and the new runes worked?"

"It did, and they work wonderfully. It's just some things Hephaestus said while he was here."

"Do you want to talk about it?"

"Yes. But I don't know where to start and I don't know that you'll like what I have to say."

"Why don't we start from the same place he did and see how I feel about it after you get through it all? Sound good?"

"Yeah. Okay. Well he told me these new tattoos weren't for caging the wolf. They're for calming her so I can let her out more often."

"Really? Is that how you were able to let her run free for three hours without incident?"

"That's what he said and the run made me believe it. Apparently by keeping her locked out of the world for so long I've actually turned her into the crazed monster she is. He claims if she gets out more, she'll feel some relief, feel needed and she'll settle down."

"I suppose that makes sense."

"Yeah. I'll just have to figure out how to do that without going nuts and murdering people again. I mean, it worked this time but he was also right there. Maybe if I only run with someone else for a while."

She let out a soft laugh and I smiled at the sound. I knew she and my father would find a way to make it work, make it happen and give me whatever I, and the wolf needed to be at peace. The next part was harder to admit though. I wasn't looking forward to what she might think of my wolf's choice in possible mates. I could admit she seemed to have good taste as far as looks went but the attitude the girl had shown left something to be desired. I let out a pained whine at the thought of telling her the truth about what I had been feeling for Angel. She gave my shoulder a squeeze and turned to shift her legs onto my bed, leaning back against the headboard.

"Tell me what's on your mind. I can tell you don't want to share but maybe it's better if you do."

"It is, I'm just worried you'll think I've lost it."

"Try me."

"It's about Angel."

"I see. I thought that might be the case. What about her?"

"It seems my wolf has chosen her. I've been fighting it, she's been lashing out at me mentally and I've been taking it out on Angel."

"I see."

Those two words gave me pause and for a moment I worried she was about to go and haul Angel back to the settlement herself. The relaxing aura I'd been settled in evaporated in a flash and I tensed again, waiting for the worst. I wasn't sure what I would do if she made the choice to take Angel away. I had been warded into the house again after Hephaestus left so it wasn't like I could follow, or even go find her. I was suddenly scared she would be gone by morning and I felt the urge to haul myself into the next room and confess how I felt.

The thought took me by surprise, I hadn't thought of confessing how my wolf felt but rather how *I* felt. I examined that during my mother's silence and a small half smile tilted my lips as I realized it was true. My wolf wasn't the only one who had developed an attachment and feelings for the spirited human. I couldn't imagine the manor without her in it. She drove me crazy with her defiant attitude and her unwillingness to cower to me unless I physically forced her to do so. That said, I was absolutely head over heels for her and the fire she showed in my presence.

"So what are you going to do about it?"

"What do you mean?"

"Well I suppose in light of that you'd prefer she not leave in five days like she's thinking of doing." She said it like she knew I'd already heard it and I guessed she probably knew I'd been listening.

"I'd honestly prefer she didn't. So you knew I was listening in?"

"Of course. I can pick up your energy from the woods at the edge of the property. I always know where you are when you're on the grounds."

"Beautiful. Guess I should have figured as much. What I need to know is how? How do I keep her from leaving this place and never looking back?"

"That I can't really help you with sweetheart. You know her much better than I do I'm afraid."

"You're right. Hopefully I can figure something out before she's gone."

"You will. Now I need to go check on your father, he's on patrol and you know he forgets to eat."

I chuckled and nodded as she gave my shoulder one last squeeze and then pushed off my bed and left my room. As if hinting that I shouldn't wait any longer than necessary she left my bedroom door open. I heard the front door open and then close again and forced myself to roll off my bed. If I was going to do this I probably shouldn't wait, I would only talk myself out of it. I stepped into the hall and walked the few feet to Angel's door, pausing and staring at it for a few long seconds. I finally raised my hand and rapped on the wooden portal hard three times.

I heard movement from inside the room and waited for her to answer. The door opened and her expression dropped into a glare the instant she saw me standing on the other side. Wow, I had really screwed up and my chances of fixing it in five days were slim. I had to try though and the process had to start immediately.

"Are you knocking on my door at midnight for a reason or did you just want to stand there and stare?" I bit back the snarky response to her attitude and took a slow, steady breath. Strangely, the wolf didn't press this time, seeming to understand what I was attempting. She calmed and I felt the agitation ebb away completely. I realized all I wanted to do was apologize, fix things and beg the human standing in front of me to stay.

"I wanted to apologize."

Her eyes widened but then narrowed a split second later, a skeptical look crossing her features. I couldn't blame her for not trusting anything leaving my mouth, I had given her no reason to believe or trust me. I would have to hope I could convince her I meant it and she would give me a chance to make it right.

"What for?"

"For everything. I've been nothing but rude, pushy, demanding and hurtful since you set foot in this house. I treated you like dirt and expected you to be fine with it and cave to my whims."

"That much is true. So you're apologizing for being an ass to me?" I actually smirked at the comment and chuckled a little, she really was something else. My reaction seemed to catch her off guard and she shifted away from me slightly, a confused look on her face for a moment before it slipped away.

"Yes, I am. I know it'll be hard to forgive me until I prove I can be different and I understand. Just, please give me a chance?"

"Give me one good reason I should, Silver."

"I could give you two but I doubt you'd like them."

"Never hurts to try."

"I've been getting physical with you because my wolf has been pushing me to understand something I was refusing to listen to."

I knew I didn't have to explain my relationship with the animal half of myself. Humans understood Lycan genetics and the relationship with their animal well after so many years living alongside them. I watched her expression change, slipping into something less guarded and more curious. She stepped away from the door and nodded me into the room. She walked over to a set of double doors identical to the pair in my room and pulled them open. We stepped out into the cool night air and I took a deep, calming breath, the familiar scents of dried leaves and impending snowfall easing my nerves. She walked over and sat as I took the chair opposite her.

"Okay I'm listening. Explain."

"She has this idea that... Well see, wolves they..." I was lost for exactly how to say it so it made sense and decided just saying it was probably best. "She wants to claim you. As her mate."

"Come again?"

"Our wolves know their mates when they meet. Destined souls or whatever. She's convinced you're hers."

"Is she now?"

"Yeah."

"Yet she's been letting you treat me like the dirt under your boots and almost let you choke me to death."

I winced at the reminder I had almost killed the poor girl and I had to force myself to meet her eyes. Mine were misty with tears I had been refusing to shed around anyone. I hated myself for the way I had been treating her and I wanted to knock myself senseless for it. I knew part of the feeling was coming from the wolf but some of it was decidedly mine. I was attached, I cared and I didn't know how I had treated her so badly.

"Believe me, she's plenty pissed at me for that, all of it. And, I'm pretty pissed at me for it too. I can't believe I hurt you. I feel horrible for letting myself act that way."

"Then why did you do it?"

"When I started denying her feelings, pushing them aside and refusing to acknowledge them, she got angry. She had every right. She started taking her anger out on me, mentally of course. I, being the apparent jerk I am, turned around and took it out on you rather than dealing with it. That just made her worse and the cycle continued."

"And now you think that will stop?"

"Just the fact that I'm in here saying this to you makes her pretty happy. I have to admit I already feel a lot calmer and more centered than I have in weeks."

"Okay. Well, say I believe you that your wolf thinks I'm meant to be hers or whatever. What else?"

"Huh?"

"You said you had two reasons and that was only one. What's the other?"

I'd hoped the news of my wolf wanting to claim her would have made her take more pause and forget I'd said I had a couple reasons. I wasn't sure I could handle telling her how I felt, the wolf was easy enough. Even though she was a part of me it was somehow easier. Admitting my human side, or rather, the Vampire side had feelings for her as well was a lot more difficult. I finally took a deep breath and decided to go for it, lay it all out on the table and see what she said.

"That's the kicker. Despite fighting it and denying it even to myself, the other part of me, this woman sitting in front of you... I feel the same. I think I started falling for you the moment I saw you but wouldn't admit it."

CHAPTER TEN

SHOCK, AWE AND ACCEPTANCE

THE SILENCE had stretched on for well over ten minutes and I was beginning to believe I'd thrown her into a very real state of shock. I'd been trying to figure out what else I could say to bring her back to a normal state and get her talking. Nothing even remotely helpful came to mind so I sat there, silent and waiting for her to snap out of it. I considered reaching over and putting a hand on hers but she pushed out of the chair suddenly. She crossed to the railing and leaned on it, looking out over the field behind the manor.

"So what now?"

I was infinitely glad she was speaking but I honestly didn't know how to answer her question. I rose out of my seat and moved to join her at the railing. I left a few feet between us and kept my eyes on the landscape. It was a difficult prospect, I wanted nothing more than to look at her but I refrained. She would need time to process everything and having me staring at her couldn't possibly help. I sucked in a breath, pushed off the rail and turned to lean my lower back against it. My arms moved to cross over my chest as I turned my eyes up to the windows on the third story of the manor.

"I wish I knew. My hope is that we can find a way to fix everything. I know I've done some serious damage with my behavior and I don't blame you for hating me. I can only cross my fingers you'll forgive me and let me try and make it up to you."

"I don't hate you, Silver."

Her words were soft, almost a whisper but they reached my ears and made my heart skip a little all the same. I forced myself to breathe as I shifted my gaze to my left and saw her turned toward me, hip rested against the rail and arms crossed like mine. My eyes met hers and I felt my heart jump and my stomach lurch as she stared back. The eye contact didn't seem like defiance anymore, no longer struck me as rude or confrontational. We stood there for several long seconds and just looked at each other before I remembered her words.

"You don't?"

"No, I wanted to and believe me I tried. I was terrified of you, no denying that. But hate? Never. I was hurt that the interest you seemed to show that first day just vanished."

"Caught that the first day you were here, huh?"

I chuckled and she let her own small laugh out as she nodded and I wondered exactly how transparent I'd been that day. Obviously it had been visible enough for her to catch it so my mother had probably seen it as well. Things had gone straight to hell after the first day and I wondered how she would feel about trying again, starting over. I wanted the chance to express all the things I'd felt those first few minutes, all the things I'd been denying these last few weeks.

"How about if we start again?" I swear it was like she was in my head and I found I liked believing she might know what I was thinking.

"You read my mind. I was just about to ask you if that would even be possible. I know I've done things that will be hard to forgive, even harder to forget, but I hope we can work past them."

"I think if you can keep from repeating them it would go a long way in helping me forget they happened."

"I can do that. I wish you could feel how happy the wolf is right now, just with the fact I told you. Even if it takes years for you to feel anything for her, or me, she's happy with today. She's finally happy with me. The new runes help with that I'm sure."

"I'd noticed these."

She reached over and traced a finger over the shape of one of the runes near my elbow. I smiled and closed my eyes at the contact, realizing it was the first we'd had since her arrival that wasn't violent. I allowed myself time to enjoy her touch as she traced her way over several of the marks. Her hand moved slowly toward my wrist and she seemed to realize what she was doing suddenly. Her hand fell away from my arm. I opened my eyes and looked over as she pulled her arm back and turned her eyes toward her shoes.

"They're beautiful."

"Thanks. Hephaestus does amazing work."

"Is that who was here? Seriously?"

Her eyes had snapped up to meet mine again and I chuckled at the expression she wore. She was looking a bit awestruck and I couldn't blame her. I'd had the same look the first time I'd met one of the Gods. She seemed to realize how she'd sounded and her cheeks tinted pink as she reached up to cover the blush. A full laugh escaped me as I reached over and pulled her hand away from her face. I thought her blush was cute and I wanted to see it.

"Yes, seriously. You'll probably see several others if you're here long enough. Athena stops by to chat with my mother sometimes and Hermes likes to pester Casper when he has some downtime."

Her eyes widened and her jaw dropped open at the mention of their names and I shook my head with a grin. Sometimes I forgot that the human population worshipped the pantheon because we decreed it but few knew they were real.

"I had no idea."

"You'll get used to it. Now, the more pressing issue. Are you still planning on leaving?"

"You knew about that?"

"Yeah. I overheard and I admit it brought me up short. I couldn't bear the thought of you not being here."

"Well, I say it still depends in the next few days. I do appreciate your apology, really. You have no idea. But I need to know how much you mean it. It sounds good standing here right now but I need to see proof that things are going to change. I'm tired of being scared, Silver."

"I know. I'm done threatening you. Fact is, if you really are her mate, *my* mate, then you have every right to be defiant sometimes. Our mates are meant to keep us in line, tell us when we're being stupid and keep us from making the wrong choices. Standing up to me is apparently your right, and your place. You'd know how true that is if you ever get to watch my father completely deflate when my mother puts him in his place." We both laughed at the comment and from the look she was wearing I had the feeling she'd seen it already in her time at the manor.

"Glad to hear it. I do know I was over the top and crossed the line more times than I should have the last few weeks. I should have learned to keep my mouth shut but when I get scared I tend to fight back."

"Not the 'flight' type, eh?"

"Nope, fighter, that's me. Guess I just didn't have the brains to not get testy with our princess." She smirked at me and I couldn't stop the laugh that broke free. I shook my head and turned so I was facing her, hip leaned against the railing, left hand reached down to brace on the top of it. I sobered a bit, the laugh dying as the smile slipped from my face.

"Yeah well, try not to use that too much. I try to forget what I am."

"Why?"

"Do I honestly strike you as the princess type?"

She kept quiet for a moment and gave me a solid once over. I knew she was taking in my ripped black skinny jeans and dark purple tank top. I usually wore combat boots and a black leather jacket as well but I'd been in for the night so had removed both. My still shoulder length black hair was pulled back in a loose ponytail, a few strands having fallen loose and hanging to frame my face. Piercings graced both ears, my right eyebrow and my nose as well as my tongue. Add to the look the strings of tattoos, both old and new, lining my arms and I was rather alternative. She grinned and shook her head as her eyes returned to mine.

"No actually. You don't look like any princess I've read about."

"Exactly. I'm just me, just Silver."

"Well, just Silver, maybe we should try this starting over thing we talked about. See what happens, where it takes us. I know I'd like a chance to replay that first day. I have the feeling you would too, give it another go, say and do what was really in your head before things went south."

I nodded in agreement and she smiled as she pushed away from the railing and turned to walk back into her room. I took one last soothing lungful of night air and then followed her inside, intending to bid her goodnight and leave her to get some sleep. I closed the doors and turned to face her as she stepped over a few feet from me. She offered me her hand and I grinned as I gave a small shake of my head and took it.

"Hi, I'm Angel Kent. Nice to meet you, glad to be here, looking forward to getting to know you better."

She had been right on the mark, I did want to replay her first day, do what had been on my mind then. So I did exactly that, what had been running through my head when I'd seen her standing in the kitchen weeks earlier. I gripped her hand harder, pulled lightly to bring her over against me and wrapped my other arm around her waist. I didn't want to give her the chance to freak out about what I was doing so without hesitation I leaned in and kissed her.

The second our lips met I regretted waiting so long to follow through with the urge. Heat flared through my body, a rush of sparks flickering through me and setting my nerve endings on fire. The reactions only intensified a few seconds later when she relaxed, melting against me and returning my kiss full force. My heart soared and a deep rumble vibrated up from my chest, the closest a wolf can get to purring. Her arms came up around my neck and I pulled her as close as I could, holding her tight against my body. I was lost in the feelings the contact was sending through me and decided to push my luck.

I chanced tracing her lips with my tongue, surprised but very pleased when she only hesitated a moment before opening to me. Our tongues met and fireworks exploded through me, making my knees weak and drawing a whimper from me. It wasn't my first kiss by any means, that event had occurred when I was fifteen. This made that first seem like a fumbling failure as far as kisses went. I'd lost my virginity at nineteen but even that didn't compare to what Angel was making me feel. Every other time, every other woman faded into the background as our contact intensified and deepened.

I finally pulled away and leaned back a few minutes later, finding we were both breathing hard. I licked my lips and let my eyes meet hers, finding the sparkle they'd lost weeks before firmly back in place. I reached up and brushed her hair back behind her ear, my thumb ghosting across her lower lip before I dropped my hand. My brain kicked in as the blood flow returned to it and I cleared my throat. I forced words out despite the fact that talking was very low on my list of things to do right then.

"Hi Angel, I'm Silver. It's *really* nice to meet you."

"That's what you wanted to do the first day we met?" Her voice was as husky and forced as mine had been and I felt a small swell of pride at the fact I'd caused the reaction in her.

"Pretty much."

"Wow. You should have, would have saved us a whole hell of a lot of fighting and hostility."

"Yeah, probably."

"No, definitely. Talk about a tension reliever."

I laughed and she smiled at me, the sight melting any lingering anger hiding in the corners of my mind. I no longer had the desire to assert myself or force her to submit. My wolf chuffed happily in my mind and I could feel her rage toward me evaporate completely. The anger and fear I could once feel rolling off the human in front of me was gone, replaced by other emotions. I gave myself a moment to hope I had changed the tide of Angel's choice. With any luck she would definitely be staying at the manor with me now.

"I'm gonna do better Angel. I promise."

"As much as I probably shouldn't... I believe you."

"Thank the Gods for that. Its progress and I'll take it."

She dropped her arms to my hips as she leaned her forehead against my shoulder for a moment, exhaling a soft sigh. When she looked back up she dropped her hands and took a step back. She put a hand on my stomach and stood there looking at me for a few beats. Her eyes seemed to be searching mine for something but I wasn't sure what. I stood there silently, allowing her the time she needed to look for whatever she was hoping to find. I figured she saw whatever it was when she gave me a small smile and dropped her hand.

"It's late. I should sleep and so should you. Get out of here and rest, we'll see what tomorrow brings."

"Okay. I'll see you tomorrow."

I dropped a light kiss on her forehead then forced myself to walk away. It was hard, but she was right, we both needed sleep and she needed time to decide where, if anywhere, she wanted this to go. I made it to the door as she dropped onto her bed and turned to look over my shoulder.

"Sweet dreams, Angel."

"I think they just might be for the first time in weeks. Goodnight, Silver."

"Goodnight."

I left her room and returned to my own, my heart fluttering in a way it never had and my stomach tied in a tight knot. I wondered if I'd manage to get any sleep after what her kiss had done to my insides. I dropped onto my bed and closed my eyes, the contact replaying in my mind. A smile spread across my face a moment before I shivered. Goosebumps broke out over my body as the muscles low in my abdomen tightened and heat pooled between my legs. I let out a low whimper and forced my eyes open against the images playing in my head. It was going to be a very long night.

CHAPTER ELEVEN

STARTING OVER

I ROLLED out of bed the next morning to find a note from my mother taped to the inside of my bedroom door. I tugged it free and carried it to the bathroom with me, leaving it on the counter as I got ready for the day. There was a spring in my step and a lightness to my movements which had been missing for longer than I cared to remember. I felt like I might actually have something worth looking forward to every day, a reason to get out of bed. It was a good feeling and I held tight to it as I showered and dressed for the day. I picked up my mother's note as I left the bathroom and finally read it.

Silver,

Your father and I have some business to attend to in Rome. I'm not sure how long we'll be, you remember how Yalena can be, but we're hoping to keep it to two weeks. Casper, Tristan and Ferris are coming with us. We've left Marcus behind with strict instructions to take you out for a run whenever you need. You have a full squad of guards to watch your back and keep you in line. If you doubt their ability to keep you from losing your control, contact Hephaestus. He said he would be happy to come run with you whenever he has the time. Xander has relented after a spirited visit from Hephaestus and agreed your house arrest can be lifted. The wards have been removed and you are free to wander the grounds again. Be safe, be honest with yourself and your wolf. Take care of each other. See you soon.

Mom

I smiled as I set the note aside and pulled open my door, my positive feeling only growing after the news. I trotted my way down the stairs and turned into the kitchen, my smile widening when I saw Angel seated at the island reading. She looked up from her book, saw me standing in the doorway and ventured a small, hopeful smile. The reaction made my heart leap and I crossed the room to where she was sitting. I brushed my hand up her arm as I passed her, heading for my morning coffee and I felt the slight shiver my touch elicited.

"Morning." Her single word was soft, almost like she had fought herself about saying it and it had simply slipped free.

"Morning to you too. Sleep well?"

"Better than I have in weeks, actually. You?"

"Not bad." I fought a grin as I pulled down a mug and filled it, replacing the pot and reaching for the sugar. I spooned some into the steaming liquid as she spoke again.

"Just not bad?"

"Had some, uh, interesting dreams that kept waking me up."

I turned, mug in hand and leaned back against the counter, catching the smile on her face as she stared into her own mug. To my eyes it looked just a little smug and it made my own tip into something a bit more on the sly side.

"Interesting, huh? How so?"

"From that grin on your face I'd wager you know."

"Caught me."

"Question is, how?"

She fought to return her expression to something more neutral, her eyes locked on her mug as she tried for a straight face. She finally lost, let out a giggle and then covered her mouth and cleared her throat.

"So you talk in your sleep."

"I do not. Do I?"

"You do. I admit I wonder if I could live up to the standards my dream self apparently set for you. Must have been quite a set of dreams, given what I heard from your room."

She finally looked at me and my face heated as a blush crept into place causing her smile to widen. The playful twinkle in her eyes made me forget the blush even as it darkened on my cheeks.

"Well then. Guess there's no point trying to pretend I'm okay with it ending with one kiss."

"Nope, pointless. I'm onto you."

I chuckled and moved to take the stool beside her and she

surprised me by turning, leaning back in her own stool and propping her legs across my lap. I laid my left hand on her knee, keeping the other hand on my mug, not about to waste my morning coffee. We sat there in silence for a few minutes, drinking our coffee. I was a little shocked to find the silence between us had lost its tension and no awkwardness remained. It was comfortable, companionable and was free of fear or panic from her end. It felt wonderful.

"Oh, my parents had to go to Rome. They might be a couple weeks. I know my mother promised she'd check in and take you back herself at the end of the week if you wanted to leave but I imagine the matter was too pressing to put off."

"It's fine. I have the feeling I won't be leaving. Maybe I'm being overly hopeful but, a girl can dream."

I gave her knee a squeeze through the pale denim of her jeans and raised my mug to take a long drink. Once I settled it back on the counter I glanced over at her again and took the time to really look at her. Minus the initial zing of lust our first meeting had caused and the turmoil the last several weeks had left me in I had the chance to really see her. I'd thought she was stunning the first time I saw her and even now she was absolutely gorgeous. With the old sparkle back in her eyes they shimmered like perfectly cut sapphires and I found myself getting lost in them.

"Silver? You okay?"

"Huh? Oh, yeah. Sorry, got lost in thought there. You know you have gorgeous eyes?"

"Wow, you know that's the cheesiest thing anyone has ever said to me?"

She smirked and I chuckled as I shook my head, it had been very cheesy but I hadn't been able to help myself. I thought it and it had needed to be said so it had left my mouth. I rarely filtered the things I said and anyone who dealt with me on a regular basis knew if it was in my head it was typically out of my mouth.

"Leave my cheese alone, it's allowed."

"I didn't say I didn't like it, just that it was cheesy. Thank you though. Yours are, odd. In a good way but at first it was a bit unnerving. Your mothers are gray but yours, they're like molten silver."

"That's how I got my name. Was born with them. I always thought my mother's were the same though, kinda molten looking."

She shook her head as she drained the last of the contents of her mug and pushed it away so she could lean on the edge of the counter. She stared at my eyes, concentration etched on her face and I somehow knew she was remembering Ayana's eyes.

"No, to me hers just look gray. They're still stunning but, not like yours. Oh and that blush you just got makes them even brighter."

She giggled a little as I felt said blush heat and darken, knowing it was creeping to the tips of my ears. I wasn't normally the type to blush but somehow she had become a champ at making it happen. She deserved a medal for it, not that I was in a rush to tell her she was the first female in over two hundred years to cause the reaction. I wasn't ready to give her an ego quite yet, she would get there on her own I was sure.

"Thanks. And I'm glad you seem so sure you'll be staying now. You were still on the fence when I left your room last night."

"I know. I just needed time to process. Honestly, between my reaction, the change in the energy in this house since last night and this conversation, I'm not in a hurry to run anymore."

"Good."

"Oh, your chatter during your dreams helped too."

"You couldn't resist could you?"

"Nope."

"You're not gonna let me live that down any time soon are you?"

"Not a chance in hell."

She laughed and I shook my head, taking in the musical sound of her laughter and wondering how I had survived without hearing it for so long. It made it impossible to keep the smile off my face. The gentle curve of my lips became more pronounced when she reached over and brushed my hair behind my ear. Her fingertips feathered over the crimson tinting my cheeks and I turned my head slightly, brushing my lips over the inside of her wrist. Her sharp intake of breath pulled my gaze to her face as she pulled her lower lip between her teeth and bit down.

"You okay?"

I whispered the words against her wrist and watched her jaw tense slightly. I wondered at the reaction for a moment until she released her lower lip, swallowed hard and nodded.

"Fine."

I felt my smile twist into a wicked little smirk at the breathy way the single word came out of her mouth. She cleared her throat, shook her head and returned her eyes to mine, catching the expression on my face. She narrowed her eyes, a smile firmly in place on her lips and used the tips of her fingers against my temple to shove my head playfully. I laughed and caught her wrist in my hand before she could pull it back and tugged so she leaned in closer.

"Hey, don't be mad because you can't resist me. Not my fault."

"You're a jerk."

The laugh present in her voice and the grin on her face said she thought I was currently being anything but a jerk but I simply shrugged. I leaned in the last couple feet and kissed the tip of her nose, making her go cross-eyed before she giggled and wiped her nose with her palm.

"So. Have you ever seen one of us in wolf form?"

"Not that I can remember. Then again, I don't think I'd be able to tell the difference between one of you and a real wolf. Wouldn't have ever been close enough."

"True. Well, my restrictions have been lifted and I'm allowed to roam again. I was thinking a run sounded great. I can call Marcus and you could come with us."

She seemed to think about it for a minute and I wondered if she would agree. I wanted her along, partly because if she intended to stay, she would be around the wolf eventually. I also knew I needed to let my wolf interact with her sooner rather than later. She was pushing to get her own time with the human we were claiming.

"Okay. Call him, let's do it. You won't take off and leave me stranded in the woods though, right?"

"Never, I'll be right by your side the whole time. Neither of us will be willing to stray far from you."

The words made her smile widen and she responded by leaning over and kissing my forehead. I returned her smile, pulled out my phone and dialed my oldest brother. He answered on the second ring and agreed to head right over with a handful of guards. I explained about Angel tagging along and made sure he would bring guards who would behave around humans. With the call taken care of I removed her legs from my lap and slid from the stool.

I downed the last of my coffee, grabbed her mug and deposited them both in the sink then made my way toward the living room. I stepped through the door and pulled my shirt off, dropping it to the floor and starting to remove my bra. A gasp pulled me up short and I started to turn around, stopped by the feeling of fingertips trailing over the tattoos on my back. I smiled at the touch, closing my eyes and letting out a soft sigh.

"I didn't realize how many of these you had. Are they anywhere else?"

I nodded and rather than telling her where, I popped the button on my jeans, lowered the zipper and tugged them down over my hips. I dropped them to the floor, revealing the older set of runes matching the ones down the backs of my arms. These hadn't been added to and so were just the flat black of the original tattoos, minus the silver infused into the newer set. They ran across my lower back, just below where the waistband of my jeans sat then curled and weaved their way down the outside of my thighs.

The feather light touch of her fingertips traced the band across my lower back and I swallowed hard against the sensation. The contact was threatening to throw me into overload and she seemed to sense it as she dropped her hand and took a step back. I forced a deep draw of air into my lungs, exhaling slowly as I moved to continue undressing.

"Just gonna strip down right here in the living room?"

"Yeah, you'll get used to it. Nudity is a fact of life with Lycans."

"Well I guess I'll just have to cope with seeing you naked then."

The tone of her voice told me she would be doing a lot better than just coping with my nudity. She was enjoying it, despite the flicker of nerves I felt from her direction. I dropped the last of my clothes to the floor on top of my jeans and considered turning and facing her. I decided to take pity on the poor girl and not overload her on the first day we were actually getting along.

"This might be weird the first few times you see it. Should be over relatively quickly though."

"Wait... Am I okay here? I mean, will I be safe without the others around?"

"They won't be with us to protect you, they'll be there to protect everyone else. The wolf would never hurt you. Now that I've accepted what you are to me, I wouldn't either. You're safe with me Angel, I promise."

"Okay. Then I'm trusting you. You'd better not be lying to me."

I shook my head and then gave up control, letting the wolf come forward and the shift took me quickly. It was over in a few seconds and I turned around, looking up at Angel with a wolfish grin on my face. I'd seen myself in this form before and as I took in the widening of her eyes and the way her mouth fell open slightly, I knew what she was seeing. My wolf was about waist high to her, a gleaming silver in color fading into a rich copper on ears, muzzle, legs and tail. My silver eyes sat in the canine face, perfectly matched to the fur surrounding them. When my father described me as unique in this form, he'd been all too right.

"Oh my Gods. Silver you're, beautiful."

I padded the few feet to her and poked her in the stomach with my nose, making her laugh. My tongue lolled out in the best approximation of laughter a wolf can manage then I barked at her. The deep tone of my canine voice made her jump a little but then she smiled and scratched just above my nose. I waited for her to finish and then moved to press my shoulder against her thighs. She knelt beside me and ran her hands through the thick, silky fur on my sides. I let out a happy rumble at her touch as her hands moved back toward my head.

Without asking what I might enjoy or pausing to think it through she reached up to rub one of my ears. The sensation made me close my eyes, sit down and lean heavily into her, a happy little chuffing telling her she'd picked a good spot. I was impressed with her seeming knowledge of my suddenly canine anatomy and I wondered if she'd ever owned a dog. It would explain a lot. The thought was ripped out of my head as her other hand came up under my chin, scratching lightly and causing my tail to thump loudly on the floor. She laughed and then moved to sit on the couch.

She patted the spot beside her and I jumped up and laid down, dropping my head right into her lap and sighing happily. I was a very content wolf in that moment, both halves of myself in complete agreement, this girl was the one. Now that I'd admitted my feelings and allowed this side out around her, there was no place left for doubt. She was my mate, the one destined for me to meet. I shifted around so my massive canine self was curled up beside her, my chin rested on her left thigh. She flipped on the TV to wait for my brother and the guards, her fingers absently playing and tracing patterns in my fur.

CHAPTER TWELVE

PARENTAL INVOLVEMENT AND MATE CLAIMING

I WAS leaning against one arm of our couch, my left knee up, leg propped against the back cushions as my right foot tapped on the floor beside the furniture. Angel had stretched herself out on the seats, her head resting on my chest, my arms wrapped around her. She was staring at the TV, her fingers tracing along mine and leaving a smile on my lips. Things had changed drastically between us in the two weeks since the kiss we shared in her room and I let out a sigh as I thought about it.

"You okay?"

The concern in her voice made my heart flutter as I turned my head and pressed a kiss to her temple. I had stopped being a violent, controlling bitch and she had started trusting me. More than trust, she cared and her concern for my wellbeing was proof of it.

"I'm great. Just thinking."

"Oh yeah? About what?"

"How much things have changed in the last two weeks."

She let out a small laugh and I looked down at our hands as her fingers slipped between mine and she tightened her grip. I brought both of our hands up and pressed a few light kisses against her knuckles. She responded by turning her head to nuzzle my neck and my eyes slid closed as I pulled her closer against me. We sat like that for a minute before she shifted around, turning so she was pressed against me and releasing my hands so my arms could wrap around her.

My palms settled on her lower back as her lips found mine and I let out a happy rumble as her arms slipped around my neck. I pressed her closer, one hand moving up between her shoulder blades as she took control of the kiss. I let her have it, not fighting her for dominance the past week since we'd settled into our new relationship. Her tongue tickled across my lower lip and I smiled before parting my lips for her. Our tongues met and the fireworks I'd fully expected to disappear by now set off through me again. I was still amazed at how I reacted to her kiss, wondering how I'd react to more and suddenly needing to adjust where she was pressed between my legs.

"Well this is a lovely change from last month."

My eyes shot open as we broke our kiss suddenly, both turning to look toward the door. My parents were standing there, my mother smiling at us. I grinned right back at her and managed a nod as I caught the pink tint creeping across Angel's cheeks at being caught making out on the couch. She was too damn adorable when she blushed and she knew I thought so. She put her back to me again and as much as I missed the previous contact, my self-control was thankful. It was getting harder to leave her in her clothes with every day that passed.

"We worked things out."

"Meaning your daughter has stopped being an insufferable ass." Angel had apparently recovered enough to be her usual snarky self. My parents both tensed at the words as they left her mouth but the laugh I broke into eased their stances slightly.

"That I have. It's amazing how much of that was denial. Once I stopped fighting with myself, I stopped taking my anger out on Angel because there was no anger."

"And you aren't losing your temper at every little thing any longer I see. Since your human just called you an ass and you laughed at it." My father had a small grin on his face as he spoke, knowing me well enough to understand how I would normally react to such a comment.

"An insufferable ass, get it right. Yes, she did call me that and I deserved it. I was one, I'm more than old enough to admit it. Besides, as my mate it's kind of her place to inform me when I'm acting like said ass."

"So you've claimed her then?" Angel showed no sign of being embarrassed by my father's question so I decided she didn't know exactly what he was asking.

"Yes and no."

"Meaning?" One eyebrow went up to punctuate his single word

and I chuckled a little as I glanced down and watched Angel's brow furrow.

"Accepted she is my mate and stopped fighting it. Yes. Actually *claimed* her. No. Not yet."

"And why not?"

"Oh Gods dad. I'm so not discussing my sex life with you, seriously."

I knew Angel had suddenly grasped what he really meant when she launched into a coughing fit and had to go for the glass of water on the coffee table. I rubbed her back as she drank half of it and gave her an apologetic smile when she turned a glare on me. The expression was stern but lacking any anger, she was simply confused.

"What is he talking about?"

""Oh Silver, you haven't even told her?" My father did exasperation better than almost anyone.

"Told me what? Someone had better start talking, quick."

"No dad, I hadn't told her. Two weeks ago I thought she hated me so I was a little nervous about bringing it up. For obvious reasons. Angel, come with me. We need to talk and this isn't something I want to discuss in front of my parents. My father might be comfortable chatting about my sex life with me but I'm not quite so open."

She nodded as I stood and took my hand when I offered it to her, letting me pull her up off the couch but I dropped her hand as we started for the door. I glared at my father as we passed, making him chuckle and causing my mother to smack him on the shoulder. I heard him mutter a 'what?' at her, watched her finger poke him center mass on his chest and caught her responding 'cut it out' as I opened the front door. His laugh carried through the house as I closed the door and turned to Angel. I reached out to her and she didn't hesitate as she slipped her hand into mine. I eased my fingers between hers, gripped lightly, headed down the steps then started across the grounds.

"I probably should have had this discussion with you earlier but I was worried you'd spook and take off. After the things I've said and done to you, the idea of risking what I'm about to tell you is a lot to expect."

"Why not tell me and let me decide?"

"Claiming is a Lycan thing. Something the wolves do when they take a mate. We're very monogamous creatures, did you know that?"

"I didn't."

"Well we are. When we mate, it's for life."

I glanced over and saw the smile on her face, glad she was happy about something I was telling her. I wasn't so sure she would enjoy the rest of it as much so I allowed a moment to bask in the contentment flowing off of her.

"That sounds nice actually."

"It is, once we pair, we're loyal. It's the perk of pairing with a wolf. We never stray. Even thinking about doing it hurts us pretty deeply."

"Already? Or after whatever this claiming thing is?"

"It'll be stronger after that but it already hurts. Just the thought of either one of us with anyone else makes my heart ache."

"I think I like that part. So what's the part I might not like?"

"The claiming itself can be intense, even for another wolf. With you being human and me being half Vampire, we can't say what might happen. It forms a bond, a telepathic link and a very physical unity. You'll be able to have conversations with me even in my wolf form. The bond itself, it can't be easily broken. Once I claim you, that's it, you're mine. For the rest of your life."

She thought about it in silence and I let her, knowing it was a lot to consider. Humans didn't look at pairing the way we did, they dated casually, married and divorced on a whim. I'd known plenty who changed partners more often than I fed. It was why our kind rarely bonded with them, they were far too easily distracted and fickle. I worried she wouldn't like the idea of being with one being, me, for the rest of her life. She was young after all and had decades ahead of her.

"I guess I'm not understanding how that's a bad thing."

"You're young, Angel. Eighteen is really early to be tied down. I know enough about humans to know how your age group tends to behave."

She turned that glare on me again but it was coupled with a small smile and I knew she was telling me I was being stupid.

"You know you sound like an idiot right now don't you?"

"Do I?"

"Yeah you do. Look, I know how my age group typically behaves but I thought we had established that I'm nothing like most humans."

"Very true."

"So then why should I be judged by their bad behavior? Did it not cross your mind that I might actually want this?"

"Not really. I just assumed the thought of being permanently bound to one person would terrify you."

"The thought of ever losing you terrifies me."

I stopped dead and turned to face her, not sure she'd actually said the words I'd just heard or if I'd imagined them. She paused when she realized I wasn't moving and stepped back beside me, turning toward me. I searched her expression and her eyes for any hint of deception and found nothing but the truth staring back at me.

"You really mean that don't you? Even after the way I treated you?"

"Even after that. I'm a forgiving person and you've proven yourself to me. I understand the inner demons you were fighting that made you act the way you did. You've been absolutely perfect since you told me you'd change."

She stepped in, closing the small gap between us and reached up to wrap her arms around my neck. My hands found her hips, squeezing lightly as she smiled at me. I was in awe of this human, never having met another like her and internally praising my wolf for her choice. She was strong, confident, proud, determined and occasionally completely maddening. Through all of that I was a little stunned to realize my fall was complete, I was totally in love with her.

"I would do anything for you."

"I honestly believe you would. So why would I mind being bound to you?" One of her pale, perfectly sculpted brows quirked up with the question.

"I guess you might not. I just wanted you to be able to choose it. I wasn't about to force it on you."

"Well I appreciate that. Now you've told me and I've given you my answer, I want this. I want you." She dropped her eyes to my lips and my brow furrowed as I watched her wrestle with something. When she looked back up there was a look on her face I couldn't identify but the emotion I felt from her was nervousness tinged with hope and the fear of rejection. "I love you."

The world ground to a halt around me, the Earth falling away beneath my feet. I hadn't allowed myself to dream she would ever feel the same way I'd found myself feeling for her. Hearing it threw me completely out of my element and I lost my powers of reasoning and speech for several seconds. The world stopped its free spin around me and I processed her words finally. I pressed a gentle kiss to her lips, lingering for the span of four quick heartbeats then pulled back and sighed happily.

"I love you too."

Her face lit up as she leaned her forehead against mine, those beautiful blue eyes glimmering with unshed tears. I was glad they were there out of happiness this time. I was finished hurting her, done causing her pain and I hoped she knew it.

"I was worried I'd lost my mind and was saying it too soon. It still feels almost too fast but I couldn't deny it anymore."

"I've been in the same boat. This is how it happens though."

"Really?"

"Really. My mom said she fell completely in love with my dad in the space of two days. He claimed her the next day and they've been together ever since. Few thousand years now."

"Holy cow."

"You're telling me." We both laughed at my comment and I kissed away a single tear as it fell down her left cheek.

"So now we can stop playing games and pretending we're okay sleeping in separate rooms?"

I couldn't help but laugh again, glad she'd been having the same thoughts on the matter I had. I wondered if it had been as hard for her to stay in her own room every night as it had been for me. I'd ended up in the hallway outside her door at least five times in the last two weeks. Every time I had scolded myself before I'd worked up to knocking on her door and gone back to my room. I was tired of sleeping alone with her right next door.

"Definitely. Being good and keeping my hands mostly to myself has been killing me. I'm shocked I have anything resembling willpower left at this point."

"You? Imagine how I feel every time you strip down to shift!" I realized then that I had done exactly as she said at least four time over the past fourteen days.

"Damn, sorry about that."

"As you should be. Thank the Gods you were kind enough to my state of mind to keep your back to me every time. If you had turned around I don't think I could have held myself back."

I smirked at her and she blushed, the pale pink creeping over her cheeks rapidly. I moved one hand to brush my thumb over her cheekbone lightly. I pressed my lips to hers, not lingering for fear of pushing us too close to the edge out in the field. I wanted her, had every intention of claiming her as mine before the night was out but an open field being patrolled by roving Lycans was not my ideal setting. I slipped my hand into hers and nodded back toward the house, hoping my parents assumed the best of the situation and cleared out. The claiming process could be rough, painful and noisy in the best cases, with a human involved, there was no telling what might happen.

I led her back to the house, glad to find it empty as we ascended the stairs to my room. I pushed the door open and stepped inside, tugging her in after me. She kicked the door open and in a move that impressed the wolf in me, yanked my shirt over my head before I even realized she had moved toward me. I raised an eyebrow at her and she only smirked at me in response. I decided to leave the comments in my head where they belonged and pulled her shirt off, dropping it on mine. I got hold of her hand again and pulled her against me, my lips finding her neck.

She whimpered at me and my wolf grumbled happily at the sound, recognizing the desire it represented. She went for the hooks on my bra but I stopped her long enough to disengage our bodies and flip a light on. She looked at me in confusion, brows furrowed, head tilted ever so slightly.

"I don't want us hiding in the dark. I want to be able to see you for this."

Her expression changed as she smiled and stepped back up against me, her hands returning to their previous task. I didn't stop her this time, letting her unhook my bra and slide it off my shoulders. She dropped it and took a half step back, sucking in a sharp breath as she let her eyes drift down my upper body. I grinned at her reaction then crooked a finger at her, ordering her back over within my reach. She complied and I mirrored her previous action, dropping her bra on the pile.

My eyes raked down over her chest, my lips tilting up into a little smirk when my gaze found her skin marked. A sapphire blue water-like tattoo swirled its way down her left collarbone, between her perfect breasts, across her stomach and disappeared below the waistband of her jeans. I had the urge to trace it with my tongue, find out where it trailed to lower on her body. I reached out and traced its path with the tip of my index finger, sending a shudder through her when my caress drifted over her navel.

I tugged the waistband of her jeans, popping the button fly open in one pull and slipped my fingers under the fabric near her hips. I pushed gently, edging the garment off her hips and down her thighs then letting the denim pool at her feet. She responded by stepping out of them and kicking them aside as she worked my jeans off. I kicked them out of the way as she registered my lack of underwear. Her smile turned a bit devilish as her eyes locked between my legs.

"I never wear anything under those jeans. Too tight."

"I'll make sure I remember that." Her voice had already dropped half an octave and it brushed over me, making me shiver.

"You do that. Like what you see?"

"Oh yeah."

"Good. Now drop those."

My eyes flickered to the barely there underwear she was wearing and she complied, slipping the purple lace off her hips and down her thighs. She stepped out of them and I took a deep breath to keep myself from pouncing on her as she added them to the pile. My eyes went to the place her tattoo had disappeared into her jeans and continued following it. The swirling pattern the same color as her eyes followed the curve of her right hip, trailed across her lower stomach and then terminated where her pubic hair would have started if she'd had any.

A growl rumbled through me and I wasn't sure if it was from desire or the thought of someone else seeing so much of her. It didn't matter that she hadn't known me when she'd had it done, she was mine and the idea of someone else seeing her, touching her, made me possessive. She seemed to understand the dual nature of the growl I'd let loose and she stepped over and ran her hands up my stomach. I shivered at her touch as she pressed her body against mine. A whimper replaced the growl and I wrapped my arms around her.

"Relax. My cousin was the artist. No one else who matters has touched me."

"Good. Mine."

She smiled at the words and nodded as she kissed me, not fighting when I took control. She seemed to understand I needed to affirm my hold on her and so let it happen. I bent my knees, pressed my hands to the backs of her thighs and pulled as I stood up again. She moved with me, pushing off just enough so I could lift her off the floor. She wrapped her legs around my waist and I turned, walking to my bed as we kissed. I dropped us to the mattress and we moved together into the middle of the bed as I pushed to deepen the kiss. She opened to me without hesitation and those fireworks I was still getting used to rocketed through me as our tongues met.

I worked a hand between our bodies, tracing smooth skin with my fingertips and feeling wetness already gathered there. There was no doubt she wanted me as much as I wanted her now, I could feel the evidence slicking my skin. I broke the kiss, my hand cupping between her legs and looked down at her. I didn't want to stop but she needed to know what was coming. I refused to leave her in the dark and cause her more pain than was necessary.

"I have to bite you. This is going to hurt. I wish I could make it less painful for you but I have to break the skin, leave my mark. Before I do, I need you to remind me you're okay with this one more time."

She nodded quickly then pulled me back to her lips without a word. I decided it was all the answer I needed and continued where I'd left off. My middle finger slipped between her lips, pushing over her clit and she cried out, the sound muffled by our kiss. I teased the sensitive little bundle of nerves until her hips picked up a rhythm against my hand. She finally pulled away from my lips and let out a little growl at me. The sound caught me off guard but I couldn't deny the throb it sent straight between my legs.

"Stop teasing me."

I shuddered at the commanding tone in her voice and nodded, my fingers already on the move by the time she finished speaking. Less than two seconds after the last word left her lips I shifted my weight and pushed two fingers into her. She cried out as she threw her head back against the bed, her hips rising to meet my hand. I slid my fingers out then pushed them back in, eliciting a moan from her. I picked up a rhythm after that and she quickly matched it, her hips thrusting down against my hand to push me deeper.

I let her ride it out for a minute but then got hold of one of her wrists with my free hand and guided her hand down between us. She opened her eyes and locked them onto mine with a grin and I returned the expression. It was wiped right off my face a second later when she slid two fingers into me, making my eyes flutter closed. We moved together for the next few minutes, the sounds of whimpers, moans and ragged breathing filling the room around us. Finally, her walls twitched around my fingers, the muscles in her stomach fluttering and I knew she was close.

I wasn't far behind and as I picked up my pace to push her over the edge, she did the same. I pressed my lips to the soft spot at the base of her neck and timed the next step perfectly. I bit down as she climaxed, breaking the skin as she screamed my name. Her blood hit my tongue and the taste pushed me over right behind her, tearing my mouth from her skin as I cried out my own climax.

CHAPTER THIRTEEN

BOUND

MY SENSES of hearing and smell came back to me long before I felt the need to open my eyes. Two things were obvious, the birdsong outside telling me it was morning and the very unique scent of Angel wrapping around me. I smiled and buried my face against the back of her neck with a happy grumble as my arms tightened around her body. The movement pulled her closer against me and she responded by wiggling as close as she could get and letting out a soft sigh.

We laid there in the silence of the morning and let the feeling of waking up together settle over us. I had never awakened with another body beside me and I'd thought it would be awkward. Instead it felt so normal it probably should have freaked me out. I refused to let it do so, it was meant to be and I wasn't fighting it anymore. I finally couldn't ignore my bladder any longer so I dropped a kiss on her shoulder and pushed out of the bed, leaving her with a growl to punctuate how unhappy I was with it.

I dealt with my morning routine, including brushing my teeth since I was already in the bathroom and returned to the bed. She slipped out as I climbed back in to go do the same run and I chuckled as I settled in. I was awake but that didn't mean I was ready to be up, I intended to spend a good portion of the day curled up in bed with my new mate. She returned two minutes later and crawled right back in with me. She pushed me over onto my back and cuddled in against my left side, her head resting on my shoulder and her arm draped across my stomach.

"Morning."

I chuckled at the raspy word she released against my shoulder and hooked a finger under her chin to lift her face. I smiled down at her, earning one in reply before I dipped my head and caught her lips in a soft kiss. She hummed happily against my lips until I pulled away and pecked the tip of her nose.

"Morning beautiful. How'd you sleep?"

"Wonderfully. You wore me out."

I grinned, rather proud of myself for the feat and got comfortable, closing my eyes against the sliver of sunlight breaching the curtains. The rise and fall of her ribcage along with the soft brush of breath against my chest settled into an even rhythm. I thought she had slipped back to sleep until her arm moved, her hand easing down to rest on my hip before she gave it a gentle squeeze. She cleared her throat and her next words were a bit clearer.

"So do I get to move my things over to this room now?"

"You better. I'm never letting you sleep in that room again."

I could feel it when she smiled against my skin and it pulled one across my own lips. She turned her head and rubbed her face against my shoulder then nuzzled up to my neck. I closed my eyes against the light kisses she trailed up to the soft spot at the back of my jaw. I grumbled out a low, happy noise when she nipped at my ear. I didn't attempt to stop her, letting her have the freedom to do as she pleased, I was hers now and I wanted to make sure she knew it.

She nibbled at my ear for a bit longer then rolled onto her back to stretch. I eased over onto my side to watch her, taking in the amazing view with a grin on my face. I let her finish her stretch before I reached over and brushed her hair away from her shoulder. I eased my fingertips gently over the mark I'd left behind the night before and she winced as she took a sharp breath.

"Sorry, baby."

"It's okay, just sore."

"I know, it will be for a few days but then it'll heal. You'll always have a scar though."

"I don't mind that a bit. Let it scar."

I smiled at her words as I leaned in and pressed my lips lightly to the wound, already scabbed over thanks to her new link with me. I wanted to test the other parts of our bond but I didn't want to scare her first thing in the morning. I decided to wait until we had been awake longer, or maybe a couple days, I'd feel it out. I nuzzled at her neck and she shuffled around, turning her back to me and moving so she was pressed against my body again. I wrapped her in my arms, right where she'd been when we woke up earlier and held her close. The situation was such a contrast to just over two weeks ago it left me reeling somewhat. I wouldn't have believed it was possible had I not been living it myself.

"What ya thinking about so hard back there?"

"Huh?"

"This is gonna sound weird but I can, I dunno, feel you thinking." Maybe waiting wasn't best after all, seemed she was already finding pieces all on her own.

"Doesn't sound weird at all. That's part of the link we established last night."

"Really?"

"Yep. You'll know when I'm thinking hard about things, not what I'm thinking about, just that I'm concentrating on something. My emotions will get easier for you to read. Eventually you'll learn to tell the difference between your feelings about something and mine. And I can't lie to you, you'll know it."

"Sounds handy. Wait, you can't lie to me? Does it not go the other way?"

"It does, but you couldn't have lied to me before. Lycans are walking lie detectors, definitely with humans."

"Ah, that's neat. Well seems like some good things for the pros column." She grinned and I laughed, nodding against her shoulder.

"It'll take some getting used to for both of us, but we'll adjust. We can learn it all together."

"Learn it, huh? So you've never been through this before?"

"Nope, never."

"Over eight hundred years and you've never taken a mate?"

I pulled in a slow breath, exhaling heavily and knew there was no way I could keep this part from her. She had a right to know and if I'd been less of a chicken, I'd have told her earlier, before we'd bonded.

"Remember when I told you wolves mate for life?"

"Yeah, I remember it vividly."

"Well that also means they only mate once in a lifetime. One mate, ever. If we... Lose that mate, we spend the rest of our lives alone."

Silence claimed the room as my words settled around us and the only thing I could hear was the steady rhythm of her breathing. I kept quiet, letting her absorb and decide on her own when to speak and what she wanted to say. She eventually eased my grasp on her waist and turned over to face me. Her hand moved to rest on my cheek, her thumb tracing my lips. The sadness I saw in her eyes made my heart tighten in my chest.

"So once I'm gone?"

"That's it. You're my one and only." She swallowed with some effort and I reached up to brush a tear from her cheek before it could finish falling.

"That seems really unfair. You'll outlive me, there's no question there. Then you just have to spend the rest of Gods know how long lonely and missing me?" I nodded and pulled her in, pressing a kiss to her forehead and hoping she would understand that I was okay with the situation. "Gods, Silver if I'd known."

"Would you have rejected me?"

"No. I wouldn't have been able to. I was drawn to you from the moment I saw you. Gods know I tried to fight it for weeks."

"Then it wouldn't have mattered. At least this way I know you went into this bond without any 'what if's' running through your mind. I need you to understand, I'm okay with it. Losing you, when it happens, will probably be the worst pain I've ever had to bear, but it'll be worth it. After almost nine hundred years I had just about given up on finding you. Every minute I get is worth whatever pain comes at the end."

She snuggled in closer to me and held on tight, her nails dug sharply into my hip but I didn't mention it. She needed to hold onto me, reassure herself of what she had done and why so I would let her. When she finally released me, I felt the marks her fingernails had left bleeding but refused to tell her. It wasn't until she raised a hand to run it through my hair and caught the crimson under her nails that she realized what she'd done. She flipped the blanket back and moved to check my hip, brushing her hand across my bare skin, her palm coming away red.

"Shit. I'm sorry. Why didn't you say something?"

"Don't worry about it. You needed a minute to freak out so I let you have it."

"Thank you."

"You're welcome."

"You still should have said something."

"Why? They're barely worth mentioning. Look." She glanced down, the tingle across my hip telling me the marks she'd left were already healing. She raised an eyebrow and watched as they closed and disappeared.

"Nifty trick."

"Isn't it? You'll gain a little of that as time goes on. It won't be as drastic obviously but you'll heal faster than humans usually do."

"And another nifty trick."

She managed a small laugh and I smiled, knowing she would be fine once she processed the last twenty-four hours. I pulled her back down to the mattress and wrapped her in my arms again. It had been a weird and crazy day and night and I wanted to stay right where I was and hold her a little longer. She cuddled up and breathed out a heavy sigh as I closed my eyes. I had no intention of falling back to sleep but that intention hadn't been communicated from my brain to the rest of my body.

CHAPTER FOURTEEN

FALLOUT

WORD OF my claiming of a human traveled fast and within a month of the event dozens of Vampires from all over the world were requesting meetings with my mother. Being the type of woman she is, she granted them but made sure they wouldn't be meeting with her at one time at an official meeting of the council. She had always hated repeating herself and grouped them together whenever she possibly could. I wasn't looking forward to the gathering. Angel and I had no choice but to be present for the ordeal since it was about us. My mother wanted to be sure if it came to it, I was given the chance to defend myself.

I stepped out of the shower and dried off, toweling my hair as I stepped into the bedroom. Angel stood in front of the full length mirror on the back of my closet door messing with her hair. I gave her a once over, something I typically did several times a day. I had managed to convince her she didn't need to dress up for this event, it wasn't formal by any means. Since it might take hours it would be best if we were comfortable. In light of my advice she had pulled on her dark blue jeans, my favorite pair that hugged her perfect ass just right. She had paired it with a black baby tee, the cut showing off both my mark on her neck and just enough of the tattoo across her stomach to tease me.

I smiled and crossed the room, still stark naked and not giving a damn. She was so intent on her hair she didn't realize I had moved up behind her until I slipped my arms around her waist. She started slightly but then pulled her hair to one side and leaned back against me. Her arms dropped, her hands finding mine so she could link our fingers together. I nuzzled her neck, pressing a lingering kiss over my mark. My wet hair fell across her shoulder and she shivered then opened her eyes and looked in the mirror.

"Are you seriously still naked?"

"Mmhmm. Shhh."

I disengaged the fingers of my right hand from hers and slipped my hand under the waistband of her jeans. My eyes drifted to the mirror, watching her as she pulled her lower lip between her teeth, closed her eyes and leaned her head back against my shoulder. I could feel her fighting herself, knowing she should tell me to stop so we wouldn't be late but wanting what was happening as much as I did. In the end I pushed at the edges of her mind with my own and flooded her with every ounce of the desire I was feeling for her.

She whimpered and let herself relax back against me, her now free right hand slipping around the back of my neck. I pushed my hand lower, meeting the warmth between her legs and finding her ready for me, as always. I growled from deep in my chest, pulling a low whine from her as I eased my finger over her clit. She let out a moan and pressed her hips forward against my hand as I sucked the skin on the side of her neck between my teeth, biting down lightly. I had every intention of leaving a less permanent mark on her.

Her breathing had kicked up to a ragged panting when a knock sounded on the bedroom door. I growled and released her silky skin from my grip with a huff. The noise she made when I pulled my hand from her jeans told me she was as unhappy about the interruption as I was. I walked to the door and yanked it open, not giving a damn I was still lacking clothes. My mother stood in the doorway, one eyebrow raised at me and a knowing smirk on her face.

"I understand the two of you qualify as newlyweds but you cannot be late for this meeting."

"Fine. Let me get dressed and we're on our way. Okay?"

"Angel, can I see you in the kitchen for a moment please?" I growled, knowing full well she was removing my mate from the room so I couldn't distract her, or myself, again.

"Uhm, sure." She brushed her hand over my very bare right ass cheek as she passed and leaned in to kiss my cheek. *Later love.*

I flashed her a wicked smile as her words filtered into my mind. She was getting better at using the link our bond offered us every day. I winked at her, she returned the gesture and then stepped into the hallway with my mother. Once they were gone I dug into the closet and pulled on a pair of jeans and my usual tank top. I stuffed my feet into my boots, not bothering to tie them and made my way downstairs, finger combing my hair as I went. When not distracted by a certain sexy blonde I could be ready in a matter of minutes.

I found the two women in my life standing near the front door chatting and slipped up beside Angel, my arm curving around her waist. She smiled and leaned her head against my shoulder, giving my mother a small nod. I looked between the two of them a few times, wondering what they had been talking about. I almost opened my mouth to ask but then thought about it and grinned as I focused on Angel.

Everything okay?

Yeah. She was just letting me know that I should probably keep quiet during this thing unless they speak directly to me. She hasn't had time to brief me on all the rules yet and I'd hate to offend someone and cause problems.

All right. Seems like a decent plan, I'll probably do the same honestly. Unless they piss me off.

And we both know how hard that can be. I could hear the laughter in her voice through the link and I raised an eyebrow at her.

Oh shut it. She actually laughed out loud at my last comment and my mother cast her gaze from my mate, to me and back again before she rolled her eyes.

"Already taking advantage of the link your bond created I see."

"Of course. Keeps people out of our conversations." I winked at her and gave Angel a squeeze as they both shook their heads. My mother refrained from commenting again as she ushered us out the door.

Since we had Angel with us, we opted to drive to the hall my mother used for these meetings so we all piled into my father's SUV. I settled into the very back and pulled her against me as my parents climbed into the front seats and my father steered us down the drive. I hugged her to me, silent but brushing my lips back and forth over her temple. She relaxed so fully that by the time we pulled up to the hall half an hour later, she was dead asleep. I ran my fingers through her hair and gave her a light shake to wake her.

"Baby. We're here."

Her eyes fluttered open as she sat up and stretched, apologizing through a yawn for falling asleep on me. I waved her off, crawled out of the truck and helped her down to the pavement before shutting the door. I dropped my hand into hers, offering a reassuring squeeze when I felt her anxiety filtering through to me. She had nothing to worry about, I was sure the whole ordeal was just a formality, something my mother complied with to keep the barons of the council from turning into nags.

We stepped into the hall, finding half of the barons already present and I gave Angel's hand a light tug so she would follow me. I led the way to a padded bench settled in front of the semi-circle created by the council seats. I dropped onto it and patted the space beside me so she would sit. She lowered herself to the seat next to me, her eyes on the Vampires already present. She was nervous, I could feel it pressing in on me. I dropped my arm across her shoulders, closed my eyes and reached down to find the calm within me.

Once I had hold of the emotion, I reached out to Angel, my mind finding hers as I pulled her close against me and let my calm security wash over her. She signed as her eyes slid closed and then leaned against me. After a few beats she sat up again, opened her eyes and looked over to smile at me. I returned it with a smile of my own and swept her hair back behind her ear.

"Thank you. I was freaking out."

"I know, I felt it. You're welcome. Relax, I'm sure everything will be fine."

She nodded as the doors of the hall opened and the last of the barons entered the room. They took their seats, my mother took hers and the meeting was called to order as my father took his place just behind my mother.

"This meeting of the Council of Barons has been called because the majority of you requested meetings with me regarding my daughter and her new mate. Being a majority request, an official inquiry was believed best for handling the situation and any issues you all may have with it. I ask that those children and thralls of the barons present please remain quiet and in their seats. I open the meeting to question or comment."

"If I may?"

My mother turned to face one of the older barons, one I had figured would be the cause of the most noise about our mating. She nodded to him and he stood, clearing his throat before he began earning an eye roll from me he couldn't see.

"I personally found this pairing to be one of great concern. As our princess and the future leader of this council, taking a human as a partner shows a certain fondness for them that we cannot risk becoming a part of our future. With all due respect Ayana, a change in the outlook on humans and our connections to them could cause leniency and could very well lead to another uprising."

A murmur of agreement went up through the group and my eyes narrowed. I couldn't believe what I was hearing, apparently these old bloodsuckers didn't know me very well if they thought every human I met got the kind of treatment Angel had been receiving. My mother held up a hand to silence the group and once they had settled down she scanned their faces.

"Before I address Ryland's claim, anyone else care to voice an opinion?"

"Yes, please. If I may?"

"Of course, Xander. The floor is yours."

I held my breath for a ten count, needing to calm myself before he opened his mouth. Xander McCallum had never liked me and had been out to make my life miserable since the day I was born.

"I have to wonder. Does dear Ryland have any idea what opinion of humans or dear princess actually holds? He speaks as if she adores the lot of them and would love nothing more than to see them sharing meals with us and playing in our front yards."

"Isn't that the case?" My gaze was ripped from Xander when Yvonne spoke up and I dared a glance at Angel. She held my eyes, her hand finding my knee and giving it a tight squeeze. She remembered my opinion of humans well and knew she was the exception to a very unpleasant rule.

"Why not ask her?" Xander turned toward me and my gaze flickered to my mother who gave me a small nod. I drew in a breath and gave Angel's shoulder a squeeze before I stood.

"Silver."

"Yes Ryland?"

"Do tell us your opinion of the humans in your territory."

"Which lot? The lapdogs or the culls?" Another murmur went up through the group gathered and I could almost feel Angel wince behind me. *I'm sorry love.*

Don't be. I knew your feelings before I was brought into the house. It's just been a while since I heard you talk like this.

"Both."

"Pets are simply entertainment. Creatures to keep us from being bored for a while until they outlive their entertainment value and are replaced. And the other, well, they're just food aren't they? As a matter of fact, I seem to recall my own mother laying the back of her hand across my cheek only a few short months ago for calling them cattle."

"Is this true Ayana?" My mother sighed and turned her attention to Yvonne, rising from her seat with a solemn nod.

"It is. You all know my opinions on our humans. While they feed and entertain us, they deserve some measure of respect. My daughter has always been less than thrilled with this outlook."

"And Silver, how has your human mate colored your opinion?" I turned to face Yvonne when she addressed me, not waiting for my mother to okay my response to her.

"I find myself easing slowly toward the same opinion as my mother. But it is slowly I assure you. I have no desire to run out and stop the culls for love of humans. That would be genocide for our own kind."

"Then why take a human?" I laughed at the question, I couldn't help it since it was so ridiculous.

"You ask that like I had a choice in the matter, Grant. I'm not like the rest of you. You're all Vampire, with the ability to choose your mate should the opportunity present itself. I have far too much of my father's wolf in me for that. Their mates are destined, chosen for them by the Gods. Mine turned out to be the same. I won't claim that I don't love her, I do, with everything I have in me. But the initial choice of mate was not my own. You can ask my parents or Angel herself, I fought the choice hard. Hard enough that it threatened to end me if I'd kept going. Now I regret having pushed her away for so long but the fact she is a human was what kept her at arm's length for me for as long as she was held there."

"Ayana, Ianos, this is truth?" My parents both nodded to Ryland and he heaved a sigh as he sank back to his seat.

"Council members. Any concerns you may have regarding my daughters choice of mate are poorly placed. She will be a great leader one day, I have no doubt. Until then, she deserves some semblance of respect from the lot of you."

"Regardless of how safe and unbiased you believe her choice to be Ayana, I move the pairing be severed and the human removed to another territory at once."

My mother turned a heated glare on Grant, my father growling at the room as a chorus of agreement went up from close to half of them. My heart felt as if it was being squeezed in a vice as I sank to the bench beside Angel. So many being in agreement was never good, majority would rule if it came right down to it. Panic rose in a steady wave, my breathing hitching as tears stung the corners of my eyes. I stared at the floor, telling myself it wasn't happening, that they couldn't do it. If they forced the bond to be broken it would leave me shattered.

"I move for a vote, Ayana. Majority rule as always."

"Very well, Grant. Anyone second the motion?"

"I do."

"Fine. Grant has called for a vote on the matter, Yvonne seconds the motion and it carries. As usual, votes will be cast by stone, white to agree with the motion and sever the bond, black to stay the motion and allow the pairing to stand. Voting opens now."

I was in the midst of a full on panic attack as the first of the council moved to cast their votes. In a matter of minutes they could rule to sever something the Gods had called into place. The thought calmed me and I closed my eyes with a deep breath. My mind centered on the only one I could think to call to my aid. *Hephaestus hear me. You told me if I ever needed you that you would be there for me. I need you now. My destiny is in danger of being ripped away from me. I stand to lose the only one I've ever loved. Please, help me.*

I knew Angel had heard my plea when she nudged her way under my arm and wrapped her own arms around my waist. I pulled her close, my eyes closed tight and held onto her. If they thought there was any chance I would let go of her without fight, they were sadly mistaken. I didn't care what their ruling was, she was staying with me even if I had to kill every one of them. The thought bolstered my confidence slightly and I managed to open my eyes, still not daring to look at the jar used to cast their votes.

CHAPTER FIFTEEN

THE DIE IS CAST

AN HOUR later the hall had erupted in a firestorm of a fight, with several people shouting at one another. I was one of the ones shouting but I decided I had every right to be angry and showing it. The council had voted to sever my bond with Angel. In all their wisdom, term used lightly here, they had passed judgement on my relationship with her, simply because she was human. Deep down, I could appreciate the irony of the whole thing. After all, wouldn't I have felt the same about one of them taking a human partner only months ago?

That didn't change how I felt or the fact I thought they were overstepping their bounds. It was that belief that had started the shouting match. They were demanding Angel leave with them, the bond be severed and she be relocated. I was having none of it. She wasn't leaving, no matter what they had decided on the matter. I had her behind me, her arm around my waist as I growled at any of them stupid enough to get near us. They would have to kill me if they wanted her.

"Ayana, get your daughter in line! The council voted and the motion carried, the girl has to leave with us. Now."

My mother stayed silent at Yvonne's words, but I could tell from the fire flashing behind her eyes that it wasn't because she agreed with them. She didn't want to lose her temper with the group and she was holding on by a very thin thread. She was saving her energy to deal with that and leaving me to handle the crowd control. I had it dealt with for the moment, as long as they were mostly talk. Only a couple of them had dared to come anywhere near Angel and I and they retreated quickly when met with my wolf anger. What I hadn't expected was for Xander to step up between the two of us and the crowd, blocking them from any further advances.

"Why are you helping me? I thought you hated me."

"I never hated you, Silver. I was terrified of you. You could be seriously out of control and it caused devastation. Ever since you settled in with your human though you've been calmer, less angry and haven't been losing control. If being with her helps keep you in check and helps keep you from rampaging through my land killing people, I'm all for it."

I couldn't help it, I smiled at his comment and was glad we had at least one supporter in the bunch. He wasn't saying he was fine with the human mate thing, but he was willing to admit she was good for me. Angel's forehead touched the back of my shoulder and I could feel how tired she was. I got hold of her hand and gave it a squeeze as I bit back the whimper trying to break free. It wouldn't help either of us for me to show them weakness right now. I took a slow breath in, exhaled it in a huff and eyed the group, ready to take them on to get us out of the hall if needed.

I started for the door, Angel still in contact with me as we moved together. Our path was blocked by Yvonne, a glare on her face as she kept us from the door. I glared right back, toning down the growl I let loose but not tamping it out completely. She flashed me a devilish smirk, like she knew something I didn't and lunged for Angel. The sound that left me as she got a hand on my mate was pure predator. She didn't make it far before I had hold of her wrist, my hand tightening around it. I felt the bones shifting under the skin and watched her brow furrow as she looked from the wrist in my hand to my eyes.

"You would do well to remember who I am and release me pup."

"I know damn well who you are. It won't matter if you don't let her go."

"Now, now, Silver. We're family, no need for violence."

"Then you need to listen very carefully, I won't say this again before things get ugly, Yvonne. Let. Angel. Go."

Each of my last three words was punctuated by a throaty growl that lingered in the air around us. The older Vampire glared hard at me, defiance in her gaze. My grip tightened, tendons and ligaments threatening to pop if I pressed any harder. She seemed to realize I wasn't kidding and finally released her grip on Angel. I dropped her wrist and turned to my mate, pulling her a few feet away and raising her arm. Her wrist was red and angry, already swelling and I had the feeling the bruising wasn't far behind. I closed my eyes and took a deep breath, willing my temper to ease off some before I exploded.

Taking my cousin's head off in the council hall wouldn't be my finest idea and would land me in a world of hurt. Despite my earlier threats, I wouldn't be able to inflict more than some minor injuries on her without serious repercussions. After a few deep breaths I got my temper to a bearable level, rubbed Angel's wrist gently and then turned toward the door again. I was intent on getting us the hell out of this hall and back to the house. I needed her somewhere safe, somewhere I could keep an eye on her. In a room of angry Vampires who wanted to take her away was not the place.

"Enough!"

The voice that pierced through the shouting and chaos was a deep, rumbling bass and reverberated off the walls of the space. Everyone stopped where they stood and turned to the new presence in the room. No doors had been opened to admit him, in true fashion for a deity, he had simply appeared. I smiled and pulled Angel close as I looked up at him where he stood beside my parents.

"What are you doing here? This has nothing to do with you, Hephaestus."

"This has everything to do with me, Yvonne."

"I disagree. This is a Vampire matter. The wolves are your lot, not us, we do as we please without your interference."

"Ah, normally I would agree with you. However, in this case you have decided to venture into wolf territory."

"How have we done that? We have insisted that one of us, our princess as a matter of fact, not be allowed to keep a human partner."

"But, you have to stop and ask yourself, which part of your princess claimed the girl first?"

"I don't understand the question. What do you mean?"

"It has been made very clear that Silver's Vampire half isn't exactly fond of humans."

"Apparently."

"This claim on the human was made by her wolf half. The Lycan in her chose its mate, against her own wishes initially, I might add."

Yvonne turned her glare on me, giving Angel and me an

appraising once over before she turned back to the God in our midst. I pulled Angel closer, feeling how scared she was as I held her tight against my side, her head resting on my shoulder. Hephaestus held his head high, one eyebrow arched slightly and a knowing smirk on his face as she considered his information.

"Either way, the pairing is an abomination to our kind."

"Be that as it may, since the bond isn't a Vampire partnering but a Lycan claiming it isn't your place to decide to sever it. There are only two ways a claiming bond can be severed. Either one of the two mates must request it and begin the severing themselves or the Lycan elders may choose to dissolve the bond. No other ruling entity may sever a Lycan claiming bond." I was glad he'd left out the third option, Angel dying, I doubted I would fare well if that happened.

"A loophole. The girl is human, the laws were never meant to protect humans. Besides, Silver is a Vampire princess, not a future Lycan alpha."

"Actually, she's both."

My father's voice turned my attention in his direction and pulled a smile across my face. I doubted any of the Vampire council had really considered my future place in the hierarchy of both groups. My mother had named me princess and future leader of the clan council when I was sixteen. What the old Vampires didn't realize was that I had been named future elder for the Lycans the year before. I smiled and pressed a kiss to Angel's temple, thankful the God had stepped in. I would never doubt his claim of being there when I needed him again, this day had more than proven that fact.

"It doesn't matter. She's subject to our laws and we have decided the pairing cannot stand."

"Yvonne, answer something for me if you will?" She turned her gaze to my mother, her eyes narrowed down defiantly but nodded for her to continue. "Are you willing to continue arguing right and tradition with a God and risk all-out war?"

The Vampire seemed to pale even further but then regained her composure and ran her fingers through her long black hair. She seemed to be thinking it through thoroughly and I hoped she would see reason and drop the whole thing. Then again, she had the family stubborn streak and would regularly fight about something just because she refused to admit she'd been wrong. It was a horrible trait mother and I attempted to stamp out but still fought ourselves. I watched her take a breath, about to answer when another voice cut her off.

"Well, isn't this just bloody adorable. What are we fighting about now, kiddies?"

I turned toward the owner of the voice, eyes narrowed as I took in his familiar appearance. His black hair was trimmed to just above his ears with that 'just rolled out of bed' look that took an hour to get right. His red eyes filled with fire but also gleaming with the mischief always lingering just below the surface. His usual leather pants and vest were in place, finished off with a pair of studded biker boots. I also noted that at some point over the three hundred or so years since I had seen him last, he had adopted a British accent. It wasn't working for him, not that I would be the one to tell him as much.

"Hades. What brings you here?"

He turned to me and grinned, the expression full of all the disdain he felt for his current location. He hated coming to Earth. Over that he really hated dealing with our issues so if he was here then things could be headed in a very bad direction.

"Well love, as it turns out, Hephaestus informed me that some of my kids here were about to start some serious shit if left to their own devices. Yvonne?"

"Yes?"

"Why would you go meddling in the affairs of the wolves?"

"I assure you this is a Vampire matter." The laugh the deity let loose washed over the room and every occupant, except Hephaestus, shivered as it hit them. He would never be accused of being warm and friendly.

"I assure you that it isn't, love. Drop this, leave it to the wolves. Let them sort it."

I couldn't help the smile that stole over my features, it was smug and more than a little cocky but we had won. Yvonne looked as if she was about to argue but the look Hades turned on her wilted her anger almost instantly. She heaved a sigh, nodded her defeat and then glared at me and turned to leave.

"Oh, and Yvonne..." She stopped with one hand on the door and glanced over her shoulder at him. "I encourage you to leave this alone entirely. The human is off limits to my children and should anything happen to her at the hands of one of you. Well, I would be desperately disappointed to have to put any of you down myself. You know how I hate trying to clean blood out of leather, such a pain."

I watched the muscles in her jaw tick several times before she nodded and then exited the room. The others who had backed her followed over the next five minutes, each earning a glare from Hades as they went. With the majority of the council vacated from the premises, he gave us an over-exaggerated bow and was gone. I shook my head and managed a laugh, relieving some of the tension which had built up over the past hour. Angel wrapped her arms around me, buried her face in my shoulder and broke down, sobbing into my shirt.

"I'll call a meeting of the elders. They should be able to get here within the next few days. Once they rule this a legitimate claiming, no one will be able to attempt this again." Ianos said.

"Thanks dad. And Hephaestus..."

I trailed off as I turned to look at the God in question and he smiled, lighting up the dim room with the action. I offered a small, forced smile in return as he crossed the room. He laid a hand gently on Angel's back and her crying slowed and then stopped completely. She looked up and I wiped the lingering tears from her cheeks with my thumbs before dropping a gentle kiss on her forehead. She managed a tiny smile and then looked at the God, my gaze followed.

"Thank you too. Somehow I knew you'd hear me."

"Of course I heard you, I always will. And I told you that if I could come, I would. This was too important to leave to chance. You two cannot be separated, and hopefully your canine family will understand this."

The way he said we could not be separated made me wonder if he knew more about our bond than he was letting on. I almost questioned him on it but then he hugged my father, whispering something to him before he embraced my mother and was gone. I stood there in silence as my parents spoke, not hearing a word of it as I replayed the last two hours in my mind. It had been an intense day and it wasn't over. I turned my gaze toward my mate when she tugged on my shirt and offered her a warm smile.

"Can we go home now?"

"Sure. Come on."

I wrapped one arm around her shoulders and led her toward the door, knowing my parents would follow shortly if we walked out. Sure enough, we had barely loaded into the backseat of the SUV when my mother climbed into the driver's seat. I raised an eyebrow at her in the rearview mirror and she chuckled as she turned and looked at me over the back of the seat.

"Your father is making calls. He didn't want to put of gathering the elders so he's trying to get them here by tomorrow night. He'll shift and run home when he's finished. Let's get you two back to the manor, it looks like poor Angel could use at least two days of sleep."

I nodded, agreeing with the sentiment as my human snuggled against me and sighed softly, already drifting off. The day had been a lot to handle, even for me so I could only imagine how her mental state had fared. I would make sure I got her talking about it after she had rested and recovered physically. The mental and emotional scars of something like what we had been through were often deeper and took longer to recover from. My mother pulled away from the hall without another word and turned us toward the manor.

CHAPTER SIXTEEN

A MEETING OF THE ELDERS

MY FATHER had scrambled a last minute meeting with the Lycan Elders, but given their large territories it took three days to gather them all at the manor. Over those days, we had dealt with a messenger from Yvonne once a day and had also received one from Grant and another from Ryland. All had been sent back to their masters with messages to leave us be or action would be taken. We were halfway through day four and hadn't seen another, but with a woman like my cousin that didn't mean much. Angel and I sat on the back porch of the manor, staring out over the sprawling fields beyond.

We were joined by my parents first, followed at short intervals by each of the other nine alphas that made up the Elders. I noticed Angel's foot tapping nervously on the redwood deck and reached over to take her hand in mine. She glanced over, our eyes meeting and the fidgeting stopped as she smiled at me. I pushed gently and let my calm wash over her, eliciting a soft sigh and a small nod of thanks. I lifted a hand to brush her hair behind her ear and winked at her as the last of the Elders took his seat.

"Welcome. Thank you all for coming on such short notice."

My father's deep voice greeted the group and a chorus of "You're welcome" and "don't mention it" went up around the group. I smiled as I looked at the old wolves present, the youngest of them at least twice my age. I scanned their faces as I took a calming breath, leaving the bond open and allowing my emotions to wash over Angel in a steady wave. This was bound to be terrifying for her after the incident with the Vampires having happened so recently.

"I apologize for the distinct lack of information I could manage to give each of you over the phone. I can imagine you understand not wanting to repeat myself nine times." They all chuckled and several responses of "hear, hear" sounded from the gathered group. "Our situation is this. Silver, as some of you may already know, has taken a mate. The girl happens to be human."

A murmur went through the group, punctuated by a few nods but no one lost their temper or made any rude remarks. It was a start and I could only hope things continued down the same path. The wolves tended to be more accepting than the Vampires since they didn't use humans for food. As a species able to hunt regular game off in the woods, they had always lived peacefully side by side with humans. It was in our favor they did such since it meant their outlook on the species was more tolerant.

"The Vampire council recently ruled in favor of severing the bond and removing the girl. They attempted to follow through with it and only Hephaestus and Hades stepping in stopped the meeting from becoming a massacre."

"So someone decided to stand against their ruling?" I looked at Desdemona with a grin and she smirked right back at me. She was the closest to my age and we had spent several summers together before she became alpha of her pack.

"I did. I wasn't about to let them take her without a fight. I would have fought them to the death of I'd had to."

"I don't doubt that in the least. You always were a spitfire with more guts than brains, girl."

I flipped her off and she barked out a laugh, the sound followed by a similar noise from several other members of the group. Angel grinned and looked between the two of us then ventured a glance around the group. I could feel the hopeful energy rolling off of her, she was beginning to think this meeting would go much better than the last. I could have made sure she knew it would, even my minor nerves were more geared toward having so many alpha wolves in one place. We could get rowdy around other dominant wolves and things sometimes got out of hand.

"So, what do you need from us, Ianos?"

"Well, Griffin, we were granted a reprieve when Hades declared the bonding a Lycan matter and told the Vampires to stay out of it. We are to decide what happens to the girl and to her bond with my daughter."

"Well that seems an easy enough decision to make. Silver?"

"Yes, Des?"

"Did your wolf choose the girl?"

"She did."

"And the other half of you? She's okay with the choice?"

"She's more than okay with it."

"Obviously." She gave me a knowing smirk and I flipped her the bird again, causing another round of laughter to erupt for a moment before she waved it off to silence everyone. "And she's been... Properly claimed?"

To that I raised an eyebrow at her and she gave me the knowing smirk again, now she was just being an ass. As a former lover she was trying to get a rise out of me and I knew it. Instead of rising to the occasion I simply reached over and pulled Angel's hair out of the way. The tank top she had on showed the scar from my bite perfectly. The members of the group all nodded and my father stood and addressed them again.

"So, Elders, what say you to the claiming of Angel Kent by Silver, my daughter, your second, future leader of this Elder group?"

An Elder named Kurt spoke first. "I say the claiming stands. It appears she followed our laws and claimed the girl properly. Both are over the age of consent and I assume, from the way she's clinging to your daughter, the human went into the claiming knowing what she was doing and wanting is as much as Silver did."

"Believe me, I did." I turned a smile on my mate and she flashed one back at me, sending a chuckle through the group.

"I agree with Kurt. After Ianos, he's the oldest of our number and if the two of you old farts are accepting enough to allow the claim to stand, who are the rest of us to argue?"

I raised an eyebrow at Griffin for his comment as my father slowly walked over and playfully cuffed him on the side of the head. Everyone else laughed as Griffin closed one eye, jerked into a forward curl and held the side of his head. We all knew the strike hadn't hurt him, he was being dramatic but he was good at it. I looked around the group as each member nodded their agreement with the decision and with each one my smile grew. The wolves were unanimous, my claim on Angel would stand and she would remain my mate. I gave her hand a squeeze as I rose from my seat, only dropping the contact when the first of the Elders stepped up to hug me.

I returned each embrace warmly, having known every one of these wolves since I was just a baby and glad they were accepting of my pairing. Something deep down had told me they would support us but it was nice to have the conformation. Each member offered their own words of encouragement as they embraced me then moved to shake hands with my parents. Last in line was Desdemona and I gave her a half-hearted glare when she stepped up and grinned at me. She held her hands up in truce and I dropped the look, my expression softening into something much more friendly.

She stepped into me and pulled me into a tight hug, holding on for longer than she probably needed to. After a final squeeze she let out a heavy sigh that held more emotion than if she had actually told me she missed me. I knew her well after so many decades spent dancing around each other and our attraction. After that came more than three centuries of summers spent exploring my territory and hers as well as each other. The summer long visits had ended abruptly when her father was killed by a rogue bear and she had stepped up to take control of the pack. An alpha didn't leave their territory for long periods and definitely not on a yearly basis.

"Angel's gorgeous, Silver." The words were whispered against my neck and I couldn't help but smile as I whispered back.

"I know she is."

"She's a lucky girl. I hope she knows that."

"I do know it."

The comment from my right made Desdemona drop her hands to mine and flash a glance in Angel's direction. She was standing there watching us, her arms crossed over her chest and one brow arched in question. The look on her face left no doubt as to what was running through her head, it was an all-out challenge, through and through. Part of me wanted to back her down, there was no way she could take on an alpha female and survive. Then again, she was staking her claim on me with the other woman, letting her know she'd overstepped her bounds and crossed into territory she wasn't welcome in.

"Well that's very good to hear. Makes me happy Silver has someone."

Angel's eyes flickered to where Des was still holding my hands and I swear she growled as she looked back up, meeting the alpha's gaze and holding it.

"So glad you're happy. You can get your hands off my mate now."

I bit off a laugh by tensing my jaw as Des dropped my hands, held them up in front of her in surrender and took a step away from me. She chanced a smirk in my direction and then winked at me and turned, walking away from the confrontation she could easily have won. I shook my head as Angel stepped over to fill the space the other woman had just vacated. I had just taken a breath to say something about it when she knocked the air from my lungs with a pulse-altering kiss. All words forgotten in the moment, the only thing that escaped was a needy whimper. She smiled against my lips, held the contact for another three minutes and then pulled away and took a step back.

Once my eyes focused, I turned a stupid look on her, smiling as I tried to make my brain work again. As if wanting to tell me exactly where the action had come from, she stepped beside me. After she slipped a hand into my back pocket and shot a look toward the corner of the manor, where Desdemona had stopped. She was watching us, a grin on her face, both eyebrows raised in humor. The blood flow returned to my head and I glanced down at her, a grin firmly in place.

"You just had to make your point, didn't you?"

"Mmhmm. I saw the way she was watching you, the way she hugged you. She needed a reminder that you're mine."

I couldn't help it, I chuckled and shook my head at her. "She could tear you limb from limb before you could take a breath."

"I know. I also know you wouldn't let her."

"Never. I'd rip her apart before I'd let her touch you." She smirked up at me for the comment and I rolled my eyes as I pulled her closer and kissed her forehead. "You're something else, you know that?"

"Yeah, I'm a pain in the ass, I know."

"Yeah well, I love you anyway."

"Good thing." She winked at me and then pressed a light kiss to my lips. "And for the record, I love you too. But don't think that gets you off the hook. I expect a full explanation of whatever relationship you may have had with that woman."

I let out a groan at the thought of explaining centuries of sexual encounters with another woman to my human partner. Things could get very ugly, very fast but I knew she deserved to know. I would get around to telling her before the week was out. For the time being, we had the best news we could have asked for and the ultimate positive outcome of the meeting we'd just been part of. We needed to celebrate and I knew just how to go about that process. I turned a wicked grin on her, picked her up and tossed her over my shoulder, both of us laughing as I carried her into the house and up to our room.

CHAPTER SEVENTEEN

BETRAYAL

I HAD walked Angel through my history with Desdemona and she had taken it better than I expected. I knew she wouldn't ever trust the alpha around me, but she wasn't hurt or irrational about the situation either. She accepted that I had a past, and a lot of it with so many centuries under my belt, and let it go. I was thankful for it every day since I'd told her because it meant I didn't have to spend the next several weeks, or months, defending things I'd done before I knew her. With the outcomes of both meetings put behind us, we settled into a kind of routine.

My parents were spending more time closer to the main hub of the settlement, leaving the manor in our hands most days. I appreciated the privacy and I suspected they knew it though they did stop in every couple days to check in on us. My father brought my brothers with him once a week and we would all go for a run. My wolf was happy and calm thanks to all the time she was spending romping in the woods and we'd been living in harmony for a while without incident. It was just after one of these runs almost ten months after the meeting with the Elders when all hell broke loose in my world.

I pushed through the front door after an exhausting run with Casper and Tristan one night and barreled up the stairs. Angel was sprawled across our bed on her back, her e-reader held above her and she was reading intently. Ivan was perched on the seat in our bay window and I walked over and stared over his shoulder at what he was reading. He realized I was there and turned to grin at me. Things with my other human had improved since I'd claimed Angel as well. I was showing more appreciation toward Ivan and everything he did for me.

He'd become like a younger brother to me and the three of us often spent afternoons sprawled around the room reading, watching movies, or just chatting and goofing off. I gave the ends of his sandy hair a tug and took his book from him. He raised a brow at me and I nodded toward the door, he smirked as he took the hint, stood and vacated the room leaving Angel and I alone. She hadn't moved since I'd come into the room, despite knowing I was there and having heard Ivan leave.

I grinned as I watched her for a bit longer, sometimes just taking in the sight of her feeling so relaxed and at home in what had once been my space. It really was *our* home now and she had settled in perfectly. I moved to the bed and crawled up over her, plucking the reader from her grip and flipping it closed. I dropped it on the floor beside the bed and pressed my lips to hers as I eased down onto her. She turned her head, breaking the contact and pushed me away with a giggle as she scrunched up her nose.

"Ugh, you reek. Go take a shower."

"Why bother? I'll just be covered in sweat, and other things, again in half hour." I waggled my eyebrows at her playfully and she rolled her eyes at my thinly disguised innuendo.

"Well, be that as it may, I refuse to get naked with your nasty ass until you go clean it."

"Oh really?" I cocked an eyebrow at her as I popped the button on her jeans and slipped my hand under the denim. A wicked grin crossed my face as my fingers pressed between her legs, finding no underwear to slow my progress. Her eyes fluttered closed and she pulled her bottom lip between her teeth, her hips rolling, rubbing her already slick heat against my hand. I leaned in, pressing my weight over her as I let a breath out across her ear. "Because this doesn't look like refusal to me." I should have known better than to push my luck by teasing her and she responded to the comment by opening her eyes and narrowing them at me.

"You jerk. Get off." She planted her hands on my chest and shoved hard, flipping me off of her as I giggled lightly.

"I thought getting off was what I was aiming for? Seems to me you're the one hindering the process." A pillow hit me in the face and the small giggle I'd had burst into a full on laugh.

"You're terrible! Go take a shower, then we'll revisit this scenario, Casanova."

I rolled my eyes with a dramatic sigh and slid off the end of the bed, heading for the bathroom. I really did smell and I couldn't blame her for wanting me to clean up before anything transpired. I also knew she would never blame me for trying, it was proof I still wanted her. Even after a year together, I caught hints of doubt from her every now and then. She was still holding onto some disbelief that I not only wanted her, but needed her in my life. I did the best I could to remind her how much I loved her every day and the doubt had started to fade away slowly.

I flipped the water as hot as it would go and stepped under the steaming spray, wincing a bit at the sting it left on my skin. I got used to the heat a minute later and set about getting properly clean so I could go back into the bedroom and get dirty all over again. The thought pulled a grin across my face and I used the visuals flickering through my mind to push me through my shower in record time. I shut off the water, grabbed a towel and stepped out into the chilly room with a shiver. It felt good and even the icy press of the tile against my feet did nothing to ease the heat burning low in my body.

Very little could interrupt my ache for Angel once it had settled in. The sound that ripped through the silence of the space as I pulled my robe on definitely did exactly that as it sent a flush of ice water through my veins. I couldn't have said if the scream my mate released was verbal or in my head but it spurred me into action. I bolted from the bathroom, finding the room a mess. The dresser had been knocked askew and our desk was turned over, papers covering the floor. My heart rate skyrocketed as my eyes flickered over the room and then landed on the bedroom door. It hung limply from the top hinge, the other two ripped from the frame and the center of the solid wood portal splintered almost in half.

I growled and followed the unfamiliar scents of two men down the stairs, seeing them dragging my mate down the front steps of the manor. I let out a roar as she fought to try and free herself and tore down the stairs. I was fast enough that I should be able to catch them before they reached the dark SUV parked in the driveway. Her struggling slowed them down and I was glad they had left her conscious. I was down the stairs in seconds and launched myself at the door. I was brought up short as I hit an invisible wall, the force of the sudden stop knocking me flat on my ass. I growled and got to my feet, reaching out and contacting a barrier in the doorway.

My eyes flickered to the frame and widened when I saw the

string of familiar runes drawn on the wood. They had warded me into my own home, allowing them to get away with my mate. My gaze moved back to the two men as one opened the back of the SUV and they tried to toss Angel in. She fought them hard and the bigger of the two apparently got fed up. He pulled an arm back and brought his hand down on the side of her head, knocking her out cold with a single blow.

"Angel!"

The scream that left my lungs was filled with rage and pain as they threw her into the back of the vehicle. In seconds, they had climbed into the front seats and pulled out of the drive so fast they kicked up gravel and dirt behind them. I beat my fists against the barrier several times then threw my entire body weight at it, knowing my attempts were futile. The vehicle had been out of sight for more than ten minutes by the time I leaned my forehead against the invisible wall, tears streaming down my face. I dropped to my knees, crying because I was unable to do anything else.

I finally thought to go for the phone, finding my cell signal jammed and the wires for the home phone cut, the line dead. I couldn't even call for help and I had no idea when my parents would stop in to check on us again. Dread settled over me, pain and hopelessness on its heels as I pounded on the barrier absently. The sound of tires on the gravel out front reached my ears but barely registered until the barrier fell away and I slumped onto the porch. My senses returned a little at a time and the first thing I registered was my mother holding my hand in one of hers, the other stroking my hair.

The world around me came into focus and I noticed I was dressed, the sudden realization snapping me into full awareness. I sat up and looked around the room, hoping I'd only suffered from the worst nightmare of my life. The looks my parents and Marcus were giving me told me I hadn't been dreaming and the tears started up again. My mother wiped them from my cheeks, giving me a minute to cry before she shushed me and forced me to look at her.

"Silver. What happened?" I told them what I remembered and the three of them exchanged looks before they all focused on me again. There was something they weren't telling me and I didn't appreciate being kept in the dark.

"What?"

"Pull yourself together enough to get a good, deep breath over here near the door."

I took a few calming breaths, grabbed a tissue to blow my nose so I could have a hope of smelling anything at all and pushed off the couch. I wiped the last of the tears away as I crossed to the door and narrowed my eyes as I tried to place the scent. My eyes widened as I placed it and I turned on my father with a growl.

"Vampires."

"Unfortunately, we don't know who they were or who sent them. Their scents aren't familiar." I turned and glared at my mother for her comment.

"I would think it's obvious. Yvonne sent them."

"Silver, I know you're angry with her for her role in what almost happened with the council but you can't..." My growl cut her sentence off as I pulled myself up to my full height and stood nose to nose with her.

"I can't what, mother? Accuse her of kidnapping my mate? I think I can, I think I have every right and I think I'm spot on actually. Who else would be so bold, so stupid as to defy you and Hades?"

She didn't seem to have an answer for that as she let out a heavy sigh and shook her head. Thinking I'd won the argument I turned for the door and started toward the porch. A hand on my arm stopped me and I turned on the older woman again, another growl slipping free. Her grip tightened and she pulled me back as my vision bled into a kind of clarity which only came when I shifted. Her brow furrowed and her eyes narrowed at me as she held me there, watching the beginnings of my change.

"Silver. Stop it. Right now, stand down." My father's words were an order and as much as I wanted to ignore him, I couldn't. As my alpha, he could control my wolf when he could see me and with his command she slid back beneath the surface. I whimpered at the loss and my shoulders sagged in defeat as my mother released my wrist.

"Honey, you can't just run off into Yvonne's territory without some proof." That got my hackles up again and I straightened up and snarled at her.

"Like hell I can't. I know she's behind this."

"And if she is, she'll be dealt with. Until we have proof it would only be your word against hers. I hate to be the bearer of bad news here but, she still has the backing of more than half the council."

"Fuck the council!"

"Silver! Whether you like them or not they have a purpose. I know the two of you have never gotten along but just this once, try to remember that she's your cousin. We're family."

"I don't care what bloodline we may share, she's not my family. Family doesn't do this shit to each other. I can't just sit here and do nothing. I have to find her, Gods know what they'll do to her." I was crying again and I didn't care how weak it might look.

"Silver..."

"Please mother. Don't make me drop this, I'll follow whatever leads there are and if they don't point to Yvonne, I'll drop her as a suspect. But you can't expect me to stay here and let everyone else look for Angel."

"No, I don't suppose I can. Okay, you can look but please, honey, try to give your cousin the benefit of the doubt here." I nodded and then grabbed my jacket and keys from the hooks by the door, pulling the leather covering on as I left the house. I paused on the porch, just at the top of the steps and looked over my shoulder at my parents.

"Regardless of whether it was her or not, it was a Vampire. Someone defied direct orders from Hades. We both know they'd be better off if I find them first, at least I'll make sure they die relatively quickly."

My parents both nodded, it was well known that those who defied the God of the underworld often ended up punished with an eternity of torture. I descended the stairs, climbed into my jeep, started it and peeled out down the winding driveway. I opened my link with Angel as I drove, pushing my mind out to touch her own and praying she was alive, awake and could answer me. A startling nothingness greeted me, ripping a whine from me and threatening to start the tears all over again. I pushed the pain down, knowing I needed to keep my mind as clear as I could in case she came to and established contact again. She was alive, not only because she had to be for my sanity but because I would know it if she wasn't, I'd feel it.

CHAPTER EIGHTEEN

THE SEARCH...

DESPITE THE promise I had made my mother I knew exactly where I would be starting my search for my mate. I slammed on the brakes as I pulled into the lot at the private airstrip, leaving skid marks and the smell of burnt rubber behind. The dark blue, restored 1986 CJ-7 I'd been driving for years rocked with the sudden halt in motion and I jumped out, thankful for the lack of doors, and a roof. I pocketed my keys and stalked across the space toward the office. I slammed the door open, letting it hit the wall and leaving a dent in the drywall. The small man behind the desk jumped about three feet and then his gaze settled on me and he let out a sigh of relief.

"Oh Silver, thank the Gods it's just you. You scared the piss out of me!"

"It's warranted James, trust me. I need to get to Paris like, an hour ago."

He went wide eyed and then fumbled with the phone on the desk and started dialing. I recognized the tones of the numbers and slapped a hand down on the base, cutting off the call before it could connect. He stuttered at me as he looked between my hand on the hook for the phone and my eyes. I knew he was weighing the outcomes. Would it do him more damage to defy me and alert my father or to cave to my demands and have Ianos to deal with later? It seemed he couldn't decide as he let out a pained whine and I shook my head.

"You can blame me when my father comes down on you. Tell him I threatened to beat you unconscious and take the plane. He knows I can't fly by myself but that, given the circumstances, I would damn well try."

"Would you beat me and take it?"

"Consider this your one warning. Get your ass in gear or I'll lay you out and handle this myself."

"That's enough of a threat for me. What's going on?"

"Angel was kidnapped this morning. By two rather intimidating Vampires."

His eyes went wide in shock and then narrowed in anger as a growl slipped from his lips. Without another word he dropped the handset into the cradle and snatched up the keys to the plane. Our pack had all grown fond of my mate over the last few months and anyone that hurt her had the whole of them to deal with. He went through his takeoff checklist, made sure we had the fuel we needed and then made a call to approve our flight plan. With everything taken care of, we climbed aboard and I settled into the co-pilot seat. I couldn't take off to save my life and my landings left something to be desired but I could manage in the event of an emergency.

Minutes later we were in the air and on our way to Paris though I wished we could move faster as I looked at my watch. The kidnappers had a four hour head start on me and I knew all too well that every minute was precious in this scenario. I slipped into my head as we flew, still trying to establish contact with Angel. Every minute that ticked by in silence worried me and ratcheted the fear settled in my gut up another notch. I didn't know how much more of the silence I could handle before I lost my mind. I needed to hear her, to know she was unharmed, the not knowing was fraying my nerves.

Time had slipped into something foreign to me as we crossed the seemingly endless expanse of open ocean below. The sun had set at some point, though I wasn't even sure what time it was. The only indication of what was below us were the occasional flickers of bioluminescence my heightened vision caught here and there. I had slipped into a kind of heavy despair after hours on end of silence, my hope for a response from Angel wearing thin. I was so tired from my attempts and the rotating anger and pain which had been flowing through me that I almost dismissed the soft whimper I heard in the back of my mind.

Angel?

Silver, is that you?

Oh thank the Gods. I've been worried about you. Are you okay?

I'm... I hurt Silver.

They hurt you?

Beat me up pretty good. My head is throbbing, my lip is bleeding and I think I may have a couple cracked ribs.

I whimpered and James shot me a look, I only waved him off and pointed to my temple, a signal he understood as a mated wolf himself. He kept quiet and let me concentrate on the reestablished contact with my mate.

Did they do anything else? I swear if they touched you I'll...

No. No they didn't. Just beat me up and left me here.

Where are you?

I'm not sure.

Can you see anything?

Not really. It's dark but it smells like a basement. I can't hear anything, like traffic or anything and there's no light at all, not sun or street lights or anything.

Damn. Well hopefully I'll be able to sense you once we land.

Land?

Yeah, I'm coming to look for you. The two men who took you are Vampires. Something tells me they're Yvonne's.

I'd be willing to take that bet. Where do you think I am?

Paris. Plane should be landing in the next half hour. I'll be looking for you as soon as I'm back on the ground. I'll tear the city apart if I have to.

I know you will. I'm really tired, Silver. My head hurts.

I know love. Sleep, heal. I'll find you, I promise.

I know. I love you.

I love you too.

The silence returned but this time I didn't feel the panic rising to meet me at the dead space. I knew she was alive and even though she was hurt, it could have been a lot worse. With any luck I would find her within a couple days and we could deal with Yvonne for her betrayal. The plane touched down on time and I was out of the cockpit as soon as it was safe. I was down the stairs onto the tarmac before the jet engines even stopped spinning. I bolted through the small building that held the offices for the private airstrip and stumbled onto the street out front.

I closed my eyes and reached out with my mind, searching for Angel's energy, hoping to find it nearby. I couldn't cover the entire city from where I was, I would have to make my way through the streets and search in sections. I would eventually run across her, I had to believe it, she had to be here. No one else had been angry enough to pull something this stupid and think they could get away with it. I knew Yvonne was banking on my mother being her aunt to save her ass when everything went pear shaped. I could only hope she would be wrong about having Ayana's support in this insanity.

After dropping my clothes in the nearest wooded area and searching all night in wolf form, skirting the edges of the city I still hadn't found her. I was beginning to get light headed and knew I would need to stop and sleep eventually. I had just begun searching for a cave to slip into for the night when I heard a bark behind me. I turned and was met with the snow white form of my twin brother, his concern apparent even on the canine features. I hung my head as he trotted over and licked my muzzle with a whine. In that moment I knew he understood what I was doing and he was here to help me, not to scold me and bring me home.

I huffed softly and let out a yawn to tell him I was turning in for the night and he gave me one sharp nod of his head to tell me he agreed with the plan. I nuzzled under his chin and then turned and picked up the path I had been on before he'd stopped me. It wasn't long before we found a cave big enough for both of us, kicked some grass and leaves into the space and settled in for the night. I curled up, my twin curled around me with his head resting across my shoulders protectively. My mind was a tangled mess of worry and doubt after a night of nothing but I was so exhausted I was asleep in minutes.

CHAPTER NINETEEN

...CONTINUES

ELEVEN WEEKS later I was on the verge of losing my mind, the hope I'd been clinging to of finding Angel somewhere in Paris fading fast. I hadn't been able to sense even a trickle of her energy anywhere in the city. I had circled the outskirts four times in wolf form with Casper's help and then walked the streets in human form for three weeks. I could contact her, we were talking most days but I couldn't seem to find her. I had begun to wonder if she really was in Paris or if I had been so ready to assume it had been Yvonne that I'd blocked all other possibilities.

I had started another circuit of the inner city when I crawled out of the hotel bed I'd been passing out in for the last month and a half. The four hours of sleep I'd allowed myself were proving they weren't nearly enough. I hadn't bothered with breakfast and had only eaten lunch to get Casper off my back before picking up the search again. It was now quarter past eight in the evening and I hadn't stopped for food since just before noon. My stomach growled at me and I ignored it, not wanting to waste time stopping to eat.

"You need to eat sis. You won't be any good to her even if you do find her in this condition."

"My head knows you're right Cas but I just can't convince my heart to take the time. Every day she sounds weaker. They're barely giving her enough to keep her alive. Why can't I find her?"

The last question came out on a growl and my brother's hand fell on my shoulder to calm my temper. I didn't have the energy to waste getting angry if I wouldn't stop to eat. I heaved out a sigh and shook my head, a single tear sliding down my cheek and leaving a dark spot on my pale tank top. I was running out of ideas and knew I should give up on Paris and try some of the other home ports. Ryland and Grant had been just as outspoken. I should let Paris be and check their home territories, Belfast and Berlin had plenty of hiding places.

Silver?

I'm here. The weakness I could hear in her voice even through the link was heartbreaking. They were killing her slowly and I didn't know how much time I had left to find her.

They brought someone else in today so they moved me. I saw runes I didn't recognize on the walls outside the room they had me in.

Can you show me? I felt a push on the link we shared and closed my eyes, getting flashes of the runes on the walls and recognizing them instantly.

Do you know them?

I do, they were blocking your energy signature so I couldn't find you. Is the new room warded as well?

Not that I saw, just the last one. If they had me warded in how could we still contact each other?

They were mocking me. Allowing me to talk to you without being able to find you. They were making me listen to them starve you to death. Apparently they think I won't figure out where you are if they've given up on the wards. Silence greeted me for a minute after my comment and I worried I'd upset her too much.

So that's gone at least. But now what do we do?

Did you see or hear anything when they moved you?

No... Wait, yes. The guys who moved me, they were going on about some livestock fair. Complaining about the local wolves holding up traffic with their cattle trucks.

My pulse jumped and a smile took over my face seconds before the expression dropped into a glare. The news was all at once exactly what I needed and the last thing I wanted to hear. I took a steadying breath, eased my pulse back into a normal rhythm and schooled my mind. I needed to be calm when I contacted her again. The last thing she needed to do was panic, she didn't have the energy left for it and if I was in a panic when I connected with her, she would feel it and react to it.

Silver?

I'm here.

Do you know where I am?

I think I do. Give me a little time to get to you. Stay strong.

I'll try.

I eased back out of the connection and went for my phone, swiping into my contacts and tapping the top number. It rang a few times before I remembered the time difference and tried to calculate what time it was in Dallas. Before I could do the math, there was a click on the line and the sound of someone clearing their throat.

"Hello?"

"Hey, dad."

"Silver? Is everything all right?"

"Better now. I think I know where Angel is. Can you and mom get to Ghent as soon as possible?"

"Belgium?"

"Yeah. I have the feeling Lars has Angel but somehow I doubt he acted on his own."

"I think you're right on that one. I'll get some guards together and we'll be there as soon as we can."

We hung up after that, I didn't need to thank him, he knew I appreciated everything they did to help me. I turned to Casper who already had the keys to my rented jeep in his hand and nodded. We ran full out to the lot we had left it in, jumped in and he peeled out. We made astonishing time into Ghent from Paris, only stopping to gas up the jeep. Casper made me eat at each stop and I didn't fight him on it. If I was going to have the energy to take on several Vampires and save Angel, I needed food in my system. By the time we hit the city limits we had plans to meet my parents when they landed but I knew the waiting would be tough.

I sat in the jeep at the tiny air field, the runway little more than a poorly kept strip of pavement in what had once been a thriving farm acre. My foot had been tapping impatiently for longer than I cared to think about and I was on the verge of just barreling in on my own. Thankfully, my parents chose that moment to land and the minute they were off the plane we picked them up. We had rented a second vehicle at the last stop we'd made, an SUV with Casper at the wheel.

My parents, Marcus and the second oldest of my brothers, Ferris climbed into the jeep with me. My twin brothers Gabriel and Liam along with Tristan, two more Lycan guards and two of my mother's Vampire guards filled the SUV. The minute everyone was in and doors closed, we were off toward our destination. We needed answers if we had any chance of finding Angel alive and all those involved had better pray to the Gods she made it. If I lost her because of them, the pain and chaos my wolf had rained down on the human militia seven hundred years earlier would seem like a child's birthday party compared to what they would suffer.

CHAPTER TWENTY

THE FINAL CLUE

I SQUEALED to a stop in front of a massive castle that dwarfed our manor, standing at least three times larger. I wasn't impressed in the least as I jumped out of the jeep and started for the front door. I had the best of my parents' guards behind me and not a soul attempted to stop my progress. I kicked the front door in and followed my nose, the unique scent of Lars leading me right to his parlor. He was leaned back in an overstuffed wingback chair, his alligator loafer -feet kicked up on the antique mahogany desk. He swirled the scotch in his glass and looked up at me when I entered as if he didn't have a care in the world.

I crossed the room, grabbed him by the lapels of his blue velvet smoking jacket and hauled him out of the chair. He scrambled to get his feet under him as he sputtered and dropped his glass. Thanks to the century he'd been born into, he was a short man and I had five inches on him. I held him up so we were nose to nose and saw fear flicker through his eyes before he bolstered himself and flashed me a cocky grin. He was bluffing, pouring on false bravado trying to throw me and I'd let him, for the moment.

"You'd do well to remember where you are and put me down you impudent pup!"

"You would do well to examine why it is I'm here you inconsequential bloodsucker."

He paled at the threat my tone held and seemed to remember who, and what I was. It sobered him quickly and he stumbled over his words trying to get them out of his mouth. I waited a moment as he stammered, trying to give him the opportunity to get it out himself before I'd had enough. He was wasting my time and every second spent trying to get something useful out of him was longer Angel spent enduring whatever torture they had been subjecting her to. I could feel our link unraveling one thread at a time the weaker she got and it was tearing me apart inside.

I shook the man hard and he sucked in a sharp breath, his eyes closed tight against the anger in my eyes. He exhaled a shaky breath, shuddering as it left his body and opened his eyes again. He put his hands over mine, seeming to remember for a moment what he was and met my eyes. I let him hang there with our eyes locked for thirty seconds before I raised an eyebrow and smirked at him. He was trying to roll me, to influence my mind and he actually thought it would work.

"You can't do it, Lars."

"Do wha...wha...what?"

"Roll me. I'm immune you waste of space."

"I wasn't... I just thought... Shit. Fine, fine, what do you want to know?"

"Where is the girl?"

"I don't know."

"Damn it all Lars! My patience is wearing very thin." My jaw tensed as I lifted him just a little higher, stepped toward the wall and then slammed him hard against it. His head bounced off the drywall and he winced. Vampires could take some serious pain, but I could deliver more than he could tolerate.

"Honestly I don't know! I only opened my borders. I don't know where she put the girl!"

"Who?"

"Yvonne!" I dropped him with a growl and turned, stepping right into my mother's space, anger altering my vision as I huffed in her face.

"Still intent on defending her?"

She sighed, dropped her eyes to the floor and shook her head as she reached up and touched my cheek. She looked back up into my eyes, her brow furrowed in concern, the sorrow for what I was going through etched on her face.

"No. I'm sorry, Silver. I should have trusted your gut. You knew it was her all along."

I deflated slightly as I exhaled, my vision bleeding back to normal as I gave her a small nod, squeezed her hand then walked out of the room. We needed to get to Yvonne and get some answers, find out where they were holding Angel before she lost the struggle to hold on. I hopped back into the jeep as the rest of the group left the house.

"Silver, wait." I paused with the key in the ignition and looked at my mother. "Casper and I will go back to Paris with you. Your father and the others will remain here so we can relay her location when we get it out of your cousin."

I nodded and waited for her and my twin to load into the jeep and then turned over the engine and peeled out. I raced back toward Paris, pushing the jeep to its limit and only stopping to fuel up and make sure Casper and I ate. The drive felt like it took years and I eventually let Casper take over driving after he promised to speed the entire way so I could maintain contact with Angel. She was weaker each time she answered me and it was getting harder to get a response every time. I was losing her.

We screeched to a stop outside Yvonne's manor in Paris and I was out of the jeep before Casper had the key out of the ignition. I barged up the steps but my mother's hand on my shoulder stopped me before I could break the door down. She pulled me back and handed me off to my brother who wrapped his arms around me as she knocked roughly on the door. I glared at the back of her head, hating her at the moment for taking my anger fueled entrance away from me.

The door opened a minute later and Yvonne smiled at my mother before noticing Casper holding me back behind her. I could feel the wash of power flow off my mother as she snapped her fingers in my cousin's face to regain her attention. The smug look she'd had moments earlier was wiped clear when she locked onto my mother's features. Her expression wasn't even remotely friendly and that made me relax a fraction.

"What a surprise! I hadn't expected to see you Aunt Ayana. And Casper, and Silver, how lovely. Can I help you with something?"

My mother pushed the door open all the way and brushed past my cousin without being invited in. She waved my brother in behind her and he dropped his hold on me, making sure I wasn't going to charge Yvonne before he stepped away. We followed my mother into the manor, Yvonne on her heels the whole way to the parlor, flustered and trying to find out why we were at her home. My mother stopped in the middle of the room, turned suddenly and caught Yvonne across the cheek with the back of her hand.

The smaller woman stumbled back a few feet, braced herself on the edge of a decorative table to keep from falling on her ass and glared at my mother. She started to open her mouth to say something and I growled at her. The sound rumbled up from somewhere deep inside me and cut her words off before they could leave her mouth.

"I think you need to tell your cousin where her mate is before something bad happens to you, Yvonne."

"Why, Aunt Ayana, I haven't the foggiest what you're talking about."

"Enough lies, Yvonne. Lars gave you up."

The younger Vampire frowned and let out a sigh as she shook her head. "You just can't find good help these days. All so eager to stab you in the back. Oh well, no use crying over what might have been. Why don't you join me for a drink?"

"Yvonne. You better start talking. Now." I was just barely holding the wolf back, she wanted me to set her free so she could tear the woman apart, but we didn't know where Angel was yet.

"Oh cousin, resorting to threats? Please. If you hurt me, you'll have to answer to Hades. He may have given his little order but at the end of the day, he wouldn't choose a filthy human over one of his own. You know how much he loves adding to his collection of souls."

My jaw tensed, the muscles ticking rapidly as I fought to maintain control. I attempted to ease the anger by reaching out to Angel. I was greeted with silence as I faintly heard my mother arguing with Yvonne. I pressed the link harder, searching for my mate but finding only stillness. I came back to the room around me, confusion settling in my mind as I tried to figure out why she wasn't answering me. I opened my mouth to say something to my mother about it when I was hit with a shock I hadn't been expecting.

A flash of pain shot through my head, like someone had jammed a red hot poker into my skull. I let out a scream and dropped to my knees, my hands on my head. Seconds later the pain shot through my body, threatening to stop my heart and dragging tears from my eyes. I dropped onto all fours, my hands supporting the weight of my upper body as my stomach purged itself of its contents on Yvonne's carpet. The pain slipped away after a few minutes but was replaced by the most horrific emptiness I'd ever experienced.

I suddenly had an idea what had happened and rage boiled

through me as I looked up at Yvonne. My vision bled into its wolf clarity, my heart pounding against my ribcage as I gathered my strength. My mother registered what had happened just as I let out a primal roar and pushed myself off the floor. She sidestepped out of my way just in time. I launched past her, grabbed my cousin by the throat and slammed her hard against the wall. The drywall smashed behind her, the foundation shaking and the wall cracking all the way to the ceiling from the impact.

"You bitch. You killed her!"

Fear flooded Yvonne's eyes as my nails lengthened into claws, the tips pressed hard against the sides of her throat. I snarled in her face and watched the little color she had drain from her features as she stuttered and stammered over herself. I leaned in hard, cutting off her airway and wishing she actually needed to breathe to survive. My thumb claw nicked her jugular and a thin rivulet of crimson slid down to her collarbone and over her chest.

"No, they shouldn't have. Not yet!"

"Silver, release her, love."

I turned my glare on Hades where he had appeared behind me and growled. He waved off the motion and walked over to me, placing a hand on my shoulder and squeezing lightly. My muscles relaxed and I dropped Yvonne to the floor, watching her as she cowered. I wasn't sure if she was scared of me or Hades, but I would take either at the moment. His influence had calmed me enough to allow him to handle the situation. He knelt in front of her and reached out, placing two fingers in the middle of her forehead.

"I told you to leave the girl alone. That you dared to defy me while believing I would support said defiance is blasphemous. Now, where is the human, Yvonne?"

"Wa...ware...warehouse. Th...th...three miles sou...sou...south of Lars' estate."

"Good girl. I do hate to do this, your nature is such a riot for me to observe when I'm bored. I did lay down a direct order however, which you chose to ignore. Do say hello to Persephone when you arrive, she does love having new visitors to her torture chambers."

With that he flicked his wrist and she vanished with a terrified scream. I knew she would be subject to so much more than I could put her through at his hands, but it didn't feel nearly as satisfying. I dropped to the floor, my vision as well as my hands back to normal. I sobbed, the crimson carpet below me tinting a shade darker as blood mixed with normal tears. Broken didn't begin to describe how my heart felt. Shattered, devastated and lying in ruin all came to mind before being swept away on the tide of emotions tearing through me. Hades stepped over and placed a hand on my shoulder, his other hand moving to lift my chin.

"Stop fretting, little one. Your human lives, but just barely. You need to get to her, soon."

"I... She's...? Are you...?"

"Sure?" I nodded and he let out a sharp laugh at the inquiry as if I'd told a joke. "Love, I rule the underworld, someone dies, I know about it. She is weak, so weak your bond is almost completely severed but your human will live if you hurry. Save her and the bond will mend in time."

I was off the floor and tearing through the house before anyone could register that I'd moved. I hit the jeep, only pausing long enough to jam the key in the ignition, giving my mother and Casper a chance to catch up. The back tires kicked up gravel as I tore out of the driveway and fishtailed out into the street, narrowly missing a tree. I wasn't in the mood for careful, I just wanted to get where I was headed and save my mate. My mother was already on the phone, giving directions to my father, with any luck they would have her with them by the time we made it back to Ghent.

CHAPTER TWENTY-ONE

THE RESCUE

I HAD become a champion at covering the almost three hour drive from Paris to Ghent in right at an hour and fifteen minutes. The engine on the jeep protested the one hundred and thirty miles per hour I was subjecting it to, but I couldn't slow down. All that mattered was getting to Angel, my world having narrowed down to the single task. Everything had become a blur around me and I only focused when we hit the edge of the city. I had to be sharp to get to the right place, even if forcing my mind to work was making my heart ache.

Now that we had reached the city, I could feel the pain Angel was in, it was faint, just a twinge in the back of my mind, but it was there. I fought the tears that kept threatening to start again, I didn't have time to cry. I could break down later, once I knew she was safe and would live through the night. I left rubber on the pavement as I slammed on the brakes outside the warehouse Yvonne had directed us to. I jammed the jeep into park and jumped out, leaving the engine running as I covered the space between the vehicle and the door of the building.

"Silver!"

I paused, my fingers hovering inches from the handle on the door and shifted my gaze to my right. My father was kneeling on the pavement just a few feet away, Angel in his arms. I was in motion the second my eyes registered it was her. I closed the gap and took my mate from him, cradling her against my chest. She was cold and her heartbeat was so faint it was hard to hear but Hades had been right, she was still alive. I had to get her somewhere else, anywhere else and the best place I could think of was home.

"James is already on his way with the plane. If we get her loaded up and head out we can meet him when he lands."

I gave a small nod, the only indication I had heard my father at all and started toward the SUV. I wasn't about to put her in the jeep, it was open to the elements and even I was feeling a chill. No, that couldn't be right, I always ran hot thanks to the Lycan blood. I was filtering from Angel, feeling the cold that had settled into her. I let out a whimper and it sounded pathetic and broken even to my own ears. I hated seeing her like this and not being able to fix it.

I stood beside the SUV for a minute, unable to get in while holding the woman in my arms but completely unwilling to let her go. I finally handed her to Casper as I climbed in and situated myself against the arm rest on the other side of the vehicle. My brother and father worked together, one inside the truck and the other standing beside it, to get Angel into the backseat. I pulled her against me and held her close, letting my body heat begin to warm her. My mind shut out everything else as Marcus got the vehicle moving, not caring where we were headed as long as the destination got Angel the help she needed.

She let out a whine and I winced at the pain in the sound then finally allowed myself to really take in her appearance. She had lost more weight than she could afford to and looked like she'd only had a matter of hours left had we not found her. Her face was covered in bruises, a deep gash slashing across her forehead and splitting her left eyebrow. It had thankfully missed her eye, her eyelid unmarred other than the bruising present but picked up again on her cheek. The angry red wound ran down to her jawline and then terminated just below her left ear. Her upper and lower lip were both split on the right side, swollen from the hit she had apparently taken.

Another angry looking gash marred her right cheek over a bruise so deep it was almost black. Several of the bruises had already started to lighten to browns and even that sickly pale green I'd seen too often. Her arms were layered in bruises of various colors, all in different stages of healing and most looking like hands and fingers. She had been held down several times. I pushed down the anger trying to bubble to the surface. I couldn't lose my temper, not until I knew she would survive and she wasn't out of the woods.

Once we got her home and I had the chance to get her cleaned up I would likely find more wounds that would set my anger off. I did my best to not think about it, just wrapped her gently in my arms and leaned her head on my chest. I pressed my face against the top of her head and whispered to her the entire drive. I told her all about my search and everything we had been through trying to find her. I didn't have a clue if she could hear me or not but it kept me calm which kept her calm.

We pulled into the small airstrip just as James landed the plane and worked together to get Angel loaded as he refueled and did another inspection of the plane. We all settled in once she was onboard and I tuned out the conversations going on around me. I was focused on my mate, nothing else mattered despite the fact they could probably use my input on whatever they were discussing. We departed and within minutes of taking to the air, I dozed into a light sleep, Angel resting against me.

I was jarred awake an hour later by a violent shaking and as the world came into focus and I registered the voices around me I realized Angel was having a seizure. We eased her to the floor of the plane, clearing the area around her and I sat with her head in my lap. I didn't have the energy left to fight the tears so I let go and cried as the waves of the episode passed. She was barely hanging on but there was nothing we could do until we made it back to the manor.

Most Vampires didn't bother with major health concerns for their human populations and so didn't have facilities to treat them. Ours was the only territory to have the supplies needed to medically house a human for any length of time. We had no choice but to make sure she survived until we could reach home. I leaned back against the seat I'd been in a few minutes earlier and pulled Angel up into my arms again. I curled her into my lap, getting as much of her against me as possible, still trying to raise her body temperature some.

I was exhausted, mentally, physically and emotionally and I didn't know how much more I could take. I was holding it together for Angel and if it hadn't been for her I'd be a mess. I gave in and let my mind wander, a small smile taking over my face as I thought about the manor. It had been my home for my entire life, almost nine centuries yet somehow, it had never felt like a home. I lived there, I played there growing up and I learned there. I had family gatherings and the like but it had always been just a residence to me.

That had changed when I accepted Angel and her role in my life. She had made the manor really feel like home and it would never be the same once she was gone. My heart tightened at the thought of her ever not being there. The idea of coming home from a run in the woods and not having her there to greet me, tell me I was sweaty and gross and to go take a shower hurt. Another set of tears slid down my cheeks, wetting her hair where I had pressed my face against it again. I'd known the moment I decided to accept her as my mate that I would lose her one day, much sooner than I liked.

I hadn't let myself think about how it would feel, what it would put my heart through. Now that I'd gotten a taste of it, I decided it was a feeling I never wanted to repeat. I had to find a way to keep her with me but the prospect was a terrifying one. There were multiple options but the ones that didn't have rules and laws set against them had side effects I would prefer to avoid. I sighed and shook it all out of my head. All of it could be dealt with later, once I made sure she would survive.

Her temperature had gone up a few degrees and she had stopped shivering against me. One good sign out of around a hundred I would need to make me feel okay about her condition. The major ones wouldn't present themselves until she was awake. The mental and emotional scars of what she had been through would last longer than I cared to consider. I would do what I could to ease the pain she would feel long after the cuts and bruises healed, but even I couldn't take it all away. I dozed off again, the hectic schedule I'd been keeping the last few weeks catching up to me.

CHAPTER TWENTY-TWO

THE WAITING GAME

WE'D MADE it home and gotten Angel set up with all the medical supplies we had to help her. We made sure she got nutrition and fluids. Medications eased the pain I could sense she was feeling even through the darkness that had claimed her. She had fallen into a coma and six weeks after pulling her out of the warehouse in Ghent she had yet to wake up. Her mind was cloudy and I hadn't been able to find anything to latch onto so I could attempt to bring her out of it. I sat by her bedside, her left hand gripped in both of mine and my forehead on the mattress by her thigh.

I was crying again. I had discovered that even someone as hardened and loath to show emotions as me could turn into a whimpering fool when faced with the one they love in pain. I forced a slow, deep breath into my burning lungs, urging the tears to subside with the action. The energy in the room changed, becoming heavier around me but not making me feel trapped. Then calm settled over me and I knew Casper had entered the space. The second chair in the room was dragged across the carpet and situated facing mine if the orientation of the legs I could see was an indication.

I heaved out a sigh, expelling the air I had just taken in and sniffed when I felt his hand on my back. I'd been short with him the last few weeks, his usual antics fraying what little was left of my nerves. I was in no mood for joking and playing around like we were kids given the situation. I expected more of the same from him as I lifted my head and turned to look at him. I steeled myself, ready to tell him to screw right off if he intended to be himself but stopped when I saw his expression. It was softer, lacking the humor it normally held and his eyes reflected a sympathy I'd never seen in them before.

"I'm so sorry, Silver."

I didn't know what to say to the comment. He hadn't shown even the slightest understanding for what I had been going through since we'd returned from Belgium. I had actually reached the point of wondering if he could grasp how it felt. I didn't have the energy to explain it to him so I hadn't bothered to ask. Sometimes I wondered how Tristan put up with him, he acted like such a teenager all the time. I needed him to grow up, act his age and be my brother, care how I was feeling but he hadn't so I gave up hoping.

"For what?"

"I haven't exactly been helping, have I?"

"Not even a little."

"I guess I just thought if I could take your mind off the situation, make you laugh, it would make it easier. That's not what you need though is it?"

"No, it's not. Normally it would help, when I'm just in a bad mood but, this is so much different, Casper. I'm not cranky, not just having a temper flare up. I'm falling apart inside."

"I know. I didn't get that. Tristan caught your blow up at me the other day and when I started ranting at him about how cranky you were he laid into me about it."

"He did?" My eyebrows shot up at the thought of even tempered Tristan blowing up at anyone, let alone Casper.

"Yeah he did. He told me I needed to stop being selfish and understand what you were going through. He asked me how I would feel if it were him in that bed and me sitting there, waiting for him to wake up and not sure he ever would."

"Got through to you, did it?"

"Oh yeah, intensely. The minute my brain registered the thought my entire body started shaking. Just thinking about coming so close to losing him threatened to rip my heart out."

I glanced back at the still form of my mate, tubes and wires snaking off of her from multiple points, monitors beeping around us. "Yeah, I know the feeling. Intimately."

"I honestly didn't mean to be so unsympathetic about this sis. I guess I hadn't considered how deeply you'd be hurting."

I only nodded as I sighed and gave Angel's hand a squeeze before I got up from my chair. I stretched my arms over my head, popping my back and working the tension out of my sore muscles. I'd been sitting by her side every moment I could manage since we'd returned. I left long enough to shower and eat daily and to get a run in with my father once a week. The way my emotions had been swinging back and forth lately, I couldn't afford to let my wolf feel ignored. I'd done my best to remember her needs but I could tell she felt the same worry I did. She refused to go any further than the very edge of the woods, always keeping the manor in sight.

"Have you eaten today?"

"I can't remember. I don't think so. I need a shower though, I feel rank."

"Why don't you go get cleaned up and I'll go make some food? Meet you back here in a half hour?"

"Sounds good. Thanks Casper."

"No problem. Sorry it took me so long to get it."

"It's okay, I'm used to your thick skull by now."

I shoved the side of his head and he responded with a small smile as he headed for the door. I rummaged through the closet and realized I desperately needed to do some laundry in the next few days. Only a week before Angel's abduction I'd released Ivan from service, he deserved to be with his family, not waiting on me hand and foot. I found a clean outfit in the chaos and moved to the bathroom, tossing the clothes on the counter as I turned on the water. I kept hoping the showers would help clear my head, they always had in the past. Of course, the past hadn't been filled with the love of my life lying in our bed in a coma for weeks. I stood with my forehead pressed against the cold glass of the shower door focused on breathing.

After standing there for fifteen minutes, I gave up on the idea of actually making it into the shower and turned it off. I turned toward the counter, faced with all of Angel's clutter scattered over its surface. I had picked on her endlessly about all the girly crap she'd started using after moving into the manor. She always took my joking and turned it right back on me, ribbing me about my overly monochromatic wardrobe. I choked out a sob, wondering if I'd ever get to hear her picking on me again. Ever get another chance to hear the laugh I loved so much wrapping itself around my soul.

I reached over to the counter, picking up the first object my hand fell on and leaned back against the shower door. I slid down the glass panel until I hit the tile floor then pulled my knees up and rested my chin on one. I held the brush I'd grabbed just in front of my legs, my fingers pushing through the bristles absently as my gaze searched the wood grain of the cabinets for nothing in particular. The longer Angel stayed locked in the stillness that had taken her, the deeper into depression I fell. The lack of the connection I'd established with her over the last year wearing down my tough façade.

A light knocking sound drew me out of my own head and shifted my gaze to the bathroom door. I furrowed my brow at it, trying to remember when I'd come in, what for and who would be knocking. It came back to me slowly, the fog I'd slipped into ebbing away a little at a time. I remembered Casper coming to talk to me, his confession and that I had forgiven him for his blasé attitude. He had gone to make food and I, my brain sought the answer until it flickered out of the murk. I'd been off to shower. That hadn't ended up happening judging from the two-day-old clothes I still had on.

"Come in."

"Hey, sis. I thought you were gonna get cleaned up. What happened?"

"I don't know. I just... Didn't really care, I guess."

"Come on, I made you some dinner. You need to eat."

I nodded and he pulled me off the floor, pausing to eye the brush in my hand before putting an arm around my shoulders and leading me out of the bathroom. He walked me to the chair I'd vacated such a short time earlier and eased me down into it before taking the one beside it. He looked me over, I assumed trying to decide if I'd finally snapped and had a meltdown. I turned my head and looked at him, giving him a sad smile.

"I'll be okay, Cas. I'm just a mess emotionally. I don't know how much longer I can hold it together through this."

He nodded, handed me the sandwich he'd made for me and kept on me until I'd managed to eat most of it. He sat and stared at me for a while after we'd finished eating and I knew he was trying to decide if he should get me talking. He seemed to decide against it, gathered both plates and the two empty cups and vacated the room, leaving me sitting alone beside the bed once again. I wasn't sure how long I had been there alone staring at Angel's frail form in the bed before I was joined by another presence. This one was just as familiar but a little less expected.

A cool hand fell on my arm as a tall, lanky body settled into the chair beside me. I glanced over and took a minute to really look at the only other human in my life. Ivan looked like he hadn't slept in days, pain and sympathy clearly etched on his features as he gave my arm a gentle squeeze. We sat there and looked at each other for what felt like ages but was more than likely only two or three minutes. He finally took a deep breath, sighed and spoke.

"I'm so sorry. Is she doing any better?" I glanced back to the still form of my mate and bite back another wave of tears.

"Not really. She's moved a little here and there. Finger twitches and such but she doesn't seem any closer to actually waking up."

"Don't lose hope. She'll wake up."

"I wish I was still so optimistic."

"Silver, she loves you too much to quit fighting to get back to you. I honestly think that girl would walk through hell to come back to you. And probably put Hades right in his place while doing it."

I actually managed a small chuckle at his comment but it broke at the end as a tear slipped free and I sniffled sharply. I heaved out a deep sigh and shook my head, realizing he was right and turned back to him.

"Thank you. I don't know if I ever apologized for how badly I treated you those first years Ivan. Hopefully I've been doing better."

"By leaps and bounds. I'm not terrified of you anymore. I'm here helping you because I want to be these days, not because I'm worried you'll kill me if I don't. She's been good for you. I won't linger, I just wanted to check on both of you. Keep your strength up, she'll need you when she comes around."

I nodded as he pushed up from the chair and left the room silently. His words prompted me to return to the bathroom and finally get the shower I so desperately needed. He was right, I had to be as close to my best as I could manage when she woke up. She would need me for the fight she had ahead of her. Once I was cleaned and redressed I returned to my vigil at her bedside, her hand in mine as I dozed in the chair.

CHAPTER TWENTY-THREE

BREAKING THROUGH THE FOG

AS IT turned out, I managed to keep a strained hold on my sanity just long enough. After almost three months of Angel missing and another ten weeks in a coma I teetered on the verge of giving in to my depression. She had healed physically, the bruises faded, breaks and fractures mended and open wounds healed, several scarred. The pain I could sense from her had eased away over the last three weeks so we'd been able to remove one of the tubes she'd been connected to. The removal had allowed me to slip into the bed beside her, given me the chance to hold her again if even she might not know I was there.

I had to believe it had been that development, coupled with continued encouragement from Casper and Ivan which had kept me holding on as long as I had. I was thankful for it when I woke up before sunrise one morning to a whimper beside me. I had trouble focusing at first, my emotional and mental states having directly affected my sleep and leaving me foggy. Once I registered the sound and its source, my eyes shot open fully and I propped myself up on my elbow, looking down at the woman beside me.

"Angel?"

She stirred, the slight movement barely registering but there all the same. A hopeful smile edged onto my face as I reached up and brushed the hair from her forehead. The smallest flicker of finger twitches fluttered against the palm of my free hand that held hers. My heart surged and it took everything in me to keep still and let her work her way out of the haze. She has shown more small movements over the past ten days but she hadn't made any noises.

The whimper she'd released made me cross my fingers and pray it meant she would be awake soon.

My brow furrowed as I watched her for any small sign she was trying to open her eyes. The attention paid off when her eyelids fluttered a couple minutes later. I pressed my palm to her cheek, my thumb brushing her lower lip and bit my tongue. She didn't need a shock as she came out of this, she needed to ease out of the darkness in her own time. That time came and her eyes opened slowly, a little at a time and I stopped myself short of whooping in excitement. She seemed lost and dazed for a minute but then her pupils dilated in the dim light of the bedroom and she focused on me.

Her mouth moved and I realized she was trying to speak so I touched my fingers to her lips to stop her. She'd been out for a while and there was a good chance her throat and vocal chords would need to be eased back into speaking slowly. I turned enough to reach for my cup of water on the bedside table, found a spare straw in the top drawer and moved back to face her. I tilted the cup enough for her to reach the straw and let her get a drink. She coughed a few times then tried again, managing to get a few small mouthfuls down before nodding at me.

"Hey." The sound of that single, raspy syllable ripped a sob laced laugh from me as I brought her hand up and kissed her palm.

"Hey yourself. How do you feel?"

"Weak."

"I'll bet. You've been out for a while."

"How..." A harsh cough cut her off before she could finish what she'd been saying and I brought the cup back, letting her drink a bit more before she tried again. "How long?"

"Were you out?" She nodded and I took a deep breath, knowing I couldn't lie to her, she'd know. "About two and a half months."

She blinked at me a few times as if trying to process the time frame I'd given her and then shook her head. She apparently didn't realize how badly she'd been hurt, how close I'd come to losing her. I swallowed hard against the lump forming in my throat and chewed my lower lip for a few long seconds.

"You were in a coma baby. You came really close to... I ummm... I almost lost you." I was fighting all the emotions I'd been reeling through the last few months and speaking wasn't easy.

"How close?"

"For a minute there, I actually thought you were dead."

My shoulders jerked a couple times then sagged as I fought to keep from crying, not sure I'd be able to stop if I started. The gentle pressure of Angels lips against the palm I'd had on her cheek broke the dam. I put my head on her shoulder and let the floodgates fall, setting the last of the pain I'd been holding so tightly free. The soft twitch of her cheek against my hand told me she was smiling and I couldn't help but look up at her through the tears.

"I just told you that you almost died and you're smiling? Do you have a head injury we missed?" She let out a soft, slightly pained laugh at the comment and shook her head.

"No, I was just thinking about a couple years ago." The rasp in her voice was easing away a little at a time but her words were still strained.

"Couple years ago?"

"Mmhmm. That night you just about choked me to death right next door."

"And that made you smile?" I frowned at her, my brows knitting as I pushed the memory away, I hated thinking about that night.

"The comparison did."

"Comparison?"

"If someone had told me after you left my room that night that we would be here just short of two years later. Sitting in your room, you crying over me almost dying, I'd have checked *them* for a head injury."

I chuckled a little because I had to admit this had seemed the least likely outcome at the time. She thought I hated her and I was too stubborn to admit I was in love with her. How time could change things and I was thankful the change had been for the better for the two of us. I couldn't imagine my life without her anymore and the fact I'd almost had to actually experience it still hurt too deeply to shake off.

"I was pretty terrible, wasn't I?"

"Terrible? You were downright evil most days, sweetheart."

"I can admit that. Not that I'm not enjoying this trip down memory lane but, you aren't hurting anywhere?"

"No, not beyond feeling a little sore and stiff, but I imagine that's from being in this bed for weeks on end."

"More than likely. I was worried they'd done permanent damage."

"I was worried they would, too."

"You remember some of it?"

"Almost all of it. How long did they have me?"

"Close to three months."

"Gods, it felt like years."

I leaned over and kissed her forehead, not having anything to say in response to the comment. I could imagine every minute they'd held her had seemed like days. She had no sense of time and nothing to focus on, to keep her mind off of what they were putting her through. I had behaved myself in the weeks since we'd found her. I left my mother and the council to deal with Lars and all of Yvonne's henchmen and stayed out of the way. The reminder of what she'd been through sent a wave of anger through me and my whole body tensed a fraction.

"Shhh, I'm okay, Silver. Relax."

She raised her arm slowly, her muscles not wanting to respond after weeks without use and she brushed my hair back. Her hand fell onto my shoulder and I closed my eyes, letting her mind press in closer as a soothing wave of her calm washed over me. I relaxed, the tension easing from my muscles and leaving me pressed against her. I caught myself before I put too much weight on her, not wanting to cause any further pain. Her hand slid down my arm until her fingers found mine, slipping between them to link our hands together. I nuzzled my face into the side of her neck and breathed in, drawing her familiar scent into my lungs, letting it calm me further.

"I'm trying to let the anger go. I really am, it's just so hard."

"I can imagine it is. If it had been you, I would have done whatever it took to get you back."

"I almost killed her."

"Who?" I leaned back and looked at her, glad Hades had stopped me from crossing the line and ripping the vile woman's throat out.

"Yvonne."

"Don't take this the wrong way, but I'm glad you didn't."

"Honestly, so am I."

She nodded in understanding and then her eyes slid closed. Her exhaustion edged against my mind and I took a minute to be excited about our bond strengthening by the minute. She needed to get some sleep and I was more than willing to shut up and let her. Now I knew she would wake up in a few hours and be able to respond to me. It was the only thing that mattered to me right then so I pressed a kiss to her temple and brushed my nose across her ear.

She shifted some and I helped her roll onto her side, cuddling against her back. She pulled my hand up under her chin and held on like she was afraid I'd leave. It put a crack in my slowly mending heart and I held her as tight as I dared for fear of hurting her. She snuggled back against me as close as she could and I trailed my lips over her shoulder.

"Sleep. You need it. I'll be here when you wake up."

"Promise?" Her voice already held an edge of sleep, her word punctuated at the end by a small yawn that turned up the corners of my lips.

"Yes, I promise." I leaned my forehead against her jaw, my nose and lips pressed against the side of her neck as I finished my promise on a whisper. "Every day for the rest of your life... My Angel."

CHAPTER TWENTY-FOUR

SCARS

I STEPPED out of the bathroom to find Angel standing in front of our full length mirror in just her jeans and a bra. I knew instantly what was going on, having discovered her in exactly the same situation several times recently. She'd been awake for six weeks and, thanks to the rapid recovery of our bond, had been back on her feet for almost four of it. During those past four weeks she had worried herself over the scars her ordeal had left behind.

She had many to choose from, one of them marring the beautiful lines of her tattoo where it twisted across her hip. That was the worst of them and would take a while to fade, if it ever did. The rest were faint, already even with her skin tone rather than the angry purplish-red of the one on her hip. The two which seemed to bother her the most were on her face. The split down her lower lip extended down her chin and left a slightly raised but thin scar behind.

The other held most of her attention though from where it started on her forehead and stretched down through her eyebrow and across her cheek to her jaw. She hated it and I hadn't been able to convince her it wasn't as bad as she thought. I buttoned my jeans and pulled the tank top over my head as she traced her thumb along the pale line. With a soft sigh I stepped over and reached up to grip her wrist, stopping the progress of movement over her cheek.

"Why do you put yourself through this?"

Our eyes met in the mirror and her brow furrowed as she asked, "Through what?"

"Staring at them so much. Why don't you just try and ignore

them?"

"Why should I?" Her eyes narrowed down with the snapped question.

I puffed out my cheeks and exhaled slowly through my nose, trying to put my words together before I opened my mouth. She hadn't been sleeping well, our nights punctuated by nightmares and flashbacks of her time in captivity. It had left her moody and on edge and I had to remind myself that she wasn't angry with me, she was only tired and testy. I still didn't want to set her off if I could avoid it.

"Why shouldn't you?" To my credit I had soothed any hint of temper and my words were gentle.

"*You* have to look at them. *You* can't just ignore them." Her gaze dropped away, breaking our eye contact and I suddenly understood.

I stepped up beside her, put my hands on her shoulders and turned her to face me. I reached up and eased my fingers over the scar on her face. It would probably fade in a year or two but I honestly wouldn't care if it was there forever. The problem was that she seemed to think it would change things. I had to alter her thinking about it, immediately. I ran my fingers through her hair, making sure it was pulled back from the entire scar and leaned in.

I dropped a gentle kiss on the spot where it cut through her eyebrow and then let my lips trail over her cheek and down to her jaw. She shivered against me and tried to pull away but I wrapped my other arm around her, my hand pressing into the small of her back. I leaned back, looking right at her as my fingers moved back up the line my lips had just followed. The touch was feather light all the way to the tip of the raised skin on her forehead. When I had traced the whole of the scar I settled my hand against her cheek, my thumb brushing her lips.

"Angel. I don't want to ignore them."

"How could you not? I mean honestly? Silver, look at me."

"I am." She tried to look down but I stopped her by moving to catch her chin with my thumb and index finger. "Do you remember the day we met?"

"Of course."

"You shocked the hell out of me."

"I did?" She locked eyes with me, holding my gaze and not looking away and I smiled as I nodded.

"You did. I had spent centuries believing that if I did ever meet the one person destined to be mine, she would be either Vampire or

Lycan. I never thought humans were beautiful. Not terrible to look at, I didn't mind some but I hadn't met any that knocked me off my feet, left me reeling. Then I saw you standing in my kitchen."

She blushed and I gave her a smile for the reaction as she asked, "Really?"

"Really. I still didn't like humans and obviously it didn't make me treat you any better back then. But I still thought you were gorgeous. And you know what?"

"What?"

"I still do. Every morning when I wake up with you beside me I wonder how I got so lucky. I was horrid to you, bad enough that even I would have walked away from me. But you fought through it, gave me a chance and actually managed to care about me."

"Yeah well, you got your temper under control and it was like dealing with a completely different person. After that, falling in love with you was actually pretty easy." I chuckled at her and leaned my forehead against hers.

"So was falling in love with you. Once I admitted that was what was happening and just, let it."

"So this..." She reached up and touched the scar, "doesn't bother you?"

"Only to the point that it reminds me of what happened to you because you're with me. As far as how I see you, how I feel about you? No, it doesn't bother me and it doesn't change a damn thing."

She smiled and wrapped her arms around my neck as she tilted her head and pressed her lips to mine. I pulled her closer and kissed her back, pouring everything I had into it. I couldn't believe I had been so blind to why the scars were bothering her. I reminded myself our bond was almost back to full strength and tapping into it wouldn't hurt either of us. I dropped the barrier I'd been holding in place and let what I was feeling drift through the link we shared. It worked exactly as intended and within seconds she had me pinned against the wall, working to remove the jeans I had just pulled on.

Chapter Twenty-Five

The Cold, Hard Truth

Once I had convinced Angel her scars weren't going to alter the way I felt or how I saw her, our relationship returned to its old pattern. The humorous banter picked up again, the sly looks and random touching returned and our sex life, thankfully, picked up right where it had left off. The nightmares had slowed, only interrupting our nights once or twice a month rather than every other night. She couldn't seem to shake her jitters though and remained jumpy at every little noise. Anything out of the ordinary made her nervous and I really couldn't blame her for it.

She had finally grasped exactly how close she'd come to dying and it had shaken her. Her attitude with me remained unchanged but her jarring confidence had been stripped away. She could fake it when I was right beside her but I had watched her from a distance when she hadn't known I was nearby and seen the truth. Without me to lean on, she was terrified and couldn't seem to relax. It ate at me, leaving a dull ache in my heart I didn't know how to ease. I spent weeks trying to come up with anything to help her regain her confidence, her pride but nothing was forthcoming.

I had started another round of digging through old texts in the library after enduring almost seven months of her newfound timid side. I didn't hope to find much but I couldn't bring myself to stop looking entirely. Somewhere in these old tomes I had read and reread a thousand times could be the answer. I flipped the pages of the leather-bound volume on the table in front of me, skimming each page quickly before turning to the next. I stopped suddenly, sitting up straight in my chair and reading over an entry I'd seen before.

It hadn't mattered to me in centuries but now it made all the difference in the world and a smile broke out across my features. The entry was old and the method it spoke of was drastic, not to mention forbidden and I remembered well why. At the moment, I didn't care. I dropped a sheet of blank paper from the stack in the middle of the table into the book, closed it and hurried out of the room. I took the stairs three at a time, skidding to a stop just inside the bedroom door. My rushed entrance and wide smile made Angel raise her eyebrows at me and sit up on the bed where she had been sprawled out reading.

"Everything okay?" She asked.

"Better than okay. Look at this."

I walked over and dropped the tome on the bed, flipping it open to the marker paper I'd dropped between the pages. She studied the page carefully, her brow furrowing down further the more she read. She finally took a long, deep breath, shut the book and slid off the bed, pacing silently to the other side of the room. Her hand came up, her fingers resting on her lips as she stared at the wall and I wondered what she was thinking. She finally turned around and looked at me, an unspoken question in her bright blue eyes.

"Silver, we can't."

"We can. I know it's extreme but it's the only way."

"The only way to what?"

"To make you feel safe again. Give you your confidence back."

"I figured you had noticed. Guess I should know by now that I can't hide things from you."

"Nope. This can fix that. It can give you the boost you need to know you can take care of yourself when I'm not around."

"At what cost?"

"What do you mean?"

"Silver, there's a whole set of laws devoted specifically to human consumption of Vampire blood and you know it. You helped write them!"

"I know I did, actually I should have thought of this solution earlier. This is what happens once you reach the two hundred year mark, the memory starts getting fuzzy." I chuckled but my mate didn't share my frivolity on the matter at hand. She fixed me with a glare and crossed her arms over her chest.

"We can't."

"We can."

"And when we get caught, because you know we will, how much trouble will you be in?"

"Probably more than you can fathom."

"Not worth it."

She turned to leave the room, apparently finished with the conversation but I wasn't ready to let it drop. I put a hand on her shoulder and stepped in front of her. My fingers brushed down over the scar my bite had left behind when I'd claimed her almost three years earlier. So much had happened in those years and I couldn't imagine what the future might hold if the beginning of our relationship had been so harrowing.

"Angel, when I claimed you almost three years ago I made a promise. This mark means that I'll be there for you, no matter what and that I will do whatever it takes to keep you safe, make you happy. *Whatever* it takes. Understand me?"

"But this is too far."

"Why? Look, I've got almost nine hundred years of mistakes under my belt. Stupid mistakes that I made for no reason other than being curious, bored or pissed off. They never made sense and none of them were worth the consequences. If this turns out to be another mistake that lands me in some crazy punishment, ignoring these rules to protect you, make you feel safe, it'll be the first time it's been worth it. *You* are worth it."

"Why not just turn me? I mean, you carry Vampire and Lycan genetics. Either one of those would have the same effect and is actually legal given consent from the leadership of one or the other."

"And the side effects would be drastic. I'm not willing to risk it."

"What possible side effects could turning me have that this wouldn't?"

"Either one will change you. Turned Vampires typically become..." I searched for the words to express what I was trying to tell her, finally deciding to just be open and honest. "They stray, they wander. The change is like a key to the locks on a human's hidden sexuality. Humans who were happily paired and married before the change frequently ditch their counterparts and go on a bit of a sexual rampage."

"Oh. Well we definitely don't want that to happen."

"No, I'd say not."

"And a more wolfey change?"

"I've never known a human to be changed after bonding with one of us. I don't honestly know what it would do to us and our bond. I do know that it's a lot harder to accomplish a change to Lycan than to Vampire. You'd have to come really close to dying and, well, I think I've had enough of how that feels for one lifetime, thanks."

"Okay so that's out too. I guess it really would leave this as the only option."

I nodded and then watched her turn it over in her mind, trying to find any other solution and knowing with the other two out, this one made sense. It was against the rules, yes but only because humans couldn't seem to regulate their own use and none of the Vampires wanted the hassle of paying attention. I could watch her, make sure she stayed within safe limits and keep her from a full blown addiction. She would be faster, stronger, more agile and a lot harder to hurt, or kill. The lasting side effect, she'd live longer. A *lot* longer. Her eyes snapped up to mine as the thought flickered through my mind and she stared at me hard.

"What else is there? I know there's more to it but you're blocking it from me."

"Damn it all. Sometimes this link is a pain in my ass."

"Yeah well, you're frequently a pain in mine but I still love you. Spill."

"Fairly major side effect. Extended life."

"How extended?"

"We don't honestly know. One of the pets we took custody of from the ringleader in China back then was well over two hundred. Looked like he had stopped aging at around forty."

"So then there's a chance it could let me live as long as you?"

"It's a possibility."

Her entire demeanor shifted in a matter of seconds as she spoke. "Then my answer is yes."

"Really?" I was a bit stunned she had changed her tune so suddenly and it caught me off guard.

"Yeah really. If I have an opportunity to save you from experiencing what you went through when you thought I'd died ever again, I'll do it."

"So you won't do it for yourself, but you'll do it for me?"

"Exactly."

"You really are something else."

I smiled as I gripped her shoulders, pulled her closer and pressed our lips together. Her arms snaked around my waist, her hands slipping into the back pockets of my jeans. Whatever the reason she had agreed I was happy she had said yes. It meant I could help her and maybe, in the long run, myself as well. I really wasn't thrilled about the prospect of losing her, even in a distant future. The pain and loss I had experienced in those few short moments I'd thought she was gone but really wasn't were excruciating. I would happily go several lifetimes without putting myself through it again.

I would need to find a willing donor to stock blood from. I would be tricky since I wouldn't be able to use my mind tricks on them. It had to be given willingly or I'd be in even more trouble when we eventually got caught. They also had to be discreet, I couldn't very well have them running their mouth about it or, worse, telling my mother. It would take a few weeks to pull together but after the months we had survived together, a few more weeks were nothing.

CHAPTER TWENTY-SIX

A NOT SO SIMPLE PLAN

ACTUALLY SETTING what we had decided on doing into action was a completely different monster than simply getting Angel to agree to it. The selection of a Vampire donor for our project had to be done so carefully it threatened to drive me insane. I finally tracked down the names of three Vampires who might be willing to help and would be less than willing to tell my mother about the arrangement. Each of them was fairly young, less than a hundred years since being turned. They were all pledged to a Vampire my mother had turned, not the woman directly and each was less than thrilled to be as they were. Not all Vampires were completely forthcoming when they picked humans to turn.

There were only specific things the Vampire doing the turning was legally bound to disclose by order of the council. They were what the old bloodsuckers had decided were the most important factors and, when it came right down to the safety of the community they were. However, they weren't high on the list of what humans would prefer to be told if they had the opportunity to know everything. I had discovered this completely by accident a few centuries earlier. I kept my ear to the ground for newer Vampires grumbling about being lied to in case I ever needed someone to help me out who I could pin things on later.

This time, I needed one of them for a different purpose and I had meetings with each of the three to try and figure out which would work best. I couldn't come out and tell them what I was planning, I had to circle the subject without letting on the truth. That in itself would be a dangerous game since I would have to judge if I could actually tell them everything. I had to hope I would make a good choice and we wouldn't end up in a world of trouble for our efforts. I strode into the first meeting head held high, feeling confident and ready to tackle the task at hand. Thirty minutes later, my self-assured attitude had deflated severely and I was ready to go home.

"So, you need me, but you won't say for what? You've skirted the subject a few times now. You really won't tell me the details of what you're up to?"

I sighed heavily and rubbed a hand down my face, exasperated at the woman sitting across the table from me. "As we've been over several times in the last half hour, I can't give you any details until I'm sure I can trust you."

A wicked smile pulled at her lips and my eyebrow arced up as she eased out of her chair and into the one directly to my right. I attempted to keep my eyes forward but the slight chill of her hand sliding up my thigh a few seconds later started a growl low in my chest. I grabbed her wrist, halting her progress only inches above my knee and turned my glare on her. She had the gall to smirk at me and wink which forced me to stifle another growl. A sudden tingle at the back of my mind told me Angel was feeling my irritation and attempting to soothe the heat rising in me.

I slammed the barrier shut on our link, I didn't want her calming this particular irritation. It would upset her, hurt her feelings but I would explain myself later and she would understand. I had every intention of remaining irritated until this woman got it through her head. She needed to keep her hands off me, she knew who I was and knew damn well I was mated, she should show some respect. I took a few breaths, not able to get one deep one in so settling for many average ones in a slow rhythm. I set my jaw as I exhaled the last one and then narrowed my eyes at her as I flicked her hand off of me in a quick, easy turn of my wrist.

"Awww, what? Not up to playing tonight? I figured that was why you refused to tell me the details and wanted discretion. Just assumed you were looking for a little something on the side and thought I'd be just your type, I hear you like blondes."

"You're wrong, I like one blonde and one only. You crossed the line and it's enough to prove you aren't the one I'm looking for. Excuse me." I had managed to rein in most of my temper, just the very edges of my words tinged with the growl I'd loosed earlier. I slipped out of the chair and turned for the door as she spoke again.

"Oh come on Silver, I was just playing. Come back and tell me what you need. You can't blame a girl for trying, right?"

I stopped and turned to face her, brow knit, eyes narrowed and a dangerous set to my jaw. She was treading on thin ice and it didn't appear she even knew it. I would happily tell her all about her brush with my temper before leaving.

"Heather, I can blame you for it. You aren't just a girl, you are part of my mother's bloodline and therefor you should know better. You know I'm mated and yet you still had the nerve to lay your hands on me. This conversation is over. Please know that whatever I came here to discuss with you is unimportant. As a matter of fact..." I didn't feel bad about what I was about to do considering what she had pulled. I leaned over, one hand on the table and the other on the back rail of the chair I'd been in as I got right in her face and locked eyes with her. "You won't remember any of this. We never met."

"Never met."

"You came in for a drink, tried to pick up an older vamp and got shot down so you went home. Alone. Right?"

"Right."

"Good girl. Now get out of here."

I turned and made my way to the door, trying to feel a little bad about rolling the younger Vampires mind but couldn't manage the sentiment. She'd had it coming after what she'd pulled and I wasn't about to let her run off and tell her master out of spite since I'd shot her down. I left the bar, Heather exiting two minutes later and heading in the opposite direction, paying me no attention. I shook my head as I slipped into my jeep then started back toward the manor. I knew I would have Angel to answer to when I got there.

I parked the jeep in front of the steps, hopped out and hauled myself up to the front door a step at a time, in no mood to bound up the stairs like usual. I opened the door to see Angel standing at the bottom of the staircase, leaning on the rail, arms crossed over her chest and one brow raised at me. I gave her a small smile and walked over, dropping my keys on the side table just inside the door on the way. I stopped just out of arms reach and held a hand out to her, she narrowed her eyes for a second but then smiled at me and took my hand.

"Why did you shut me out?"

"I'm sorry. Your presence was calming me and I needed to hang on to my anger right at that moment. So I had to shut you out."

"Uh oh. What did she do to piss you off?"

"Decided to not keep her hands to herself."

The slow growl creeping up through my mate as she stepped closer and wrapped her arms around me pulled a full smile across my lips. She pulled me close and leaned in, brushing her lips up my neck and leaving a shiver rushing through me.

"Mine."

I chuckled at the possessive tone in her voice, my growl caressing each syllable as it left her lips. Of all the things she had inherited from me after we had bonded, the growl was the one I enjoyed the most. It was sexy and dangerous all at once and when it came out like this it made me wonder if she liked my possessive side as much as I liked hers. She nodded against my neck and I raised an eyebrow, leaning back to look at her, the question written on my features.

"I do. I love it when you go all alpha wolf on someone and remind them that you claimed me. That I'm yours."

I realized I had dropped my barrier against our link and her mind the moment I had stepped into the house. She had heard my question without any need to voice it. The connection had been handy when she'd been missing all those months ago. It had kept me from going completely insane the weeks she'd been held captive since I could still talk to her. I pulled her back in and kissed her lips gently before I leaned back again and looked at her.

"Well, I'm glad you like it. Though this meeting did not go the way I expected. I'm hoping the next one is a bit more productive."

"I'm sure it will be. When is the next one?"

"In about three hours. His name is Diego. Hopefully he's less interested in testing the limits of my bond with you and more interested in what I'm offering."

"Here's hoping. Where are you meeting him?"

"He's a bartender at The Red Room. I'm meeting him out back after his shift."

"The Red Room is only about twenty minutes away."

I nodded and then raised a brow at her as she smirked at me. I almost opened my mouth to ask her what she was grinning at but the images that hit me from her mind told me everything I needed to know. The left corner of my mouth ticked up in a half grin and she winked at me before she turned and started up the stairs, my hand in hers. I didn't bother pretending I wasn't right behind her, she already knew I was up for the encounter, no reason to play games. I followed her up the stairs and into our bedroom, more than happy to kill off the next couple hours with our favorite activity.

CHAPTER TWENTY-SEVEN

A WILLING DONOR

I STEPPED into the lot behind The Red Room two minutes early with a smile plastered on my face. I doubted there was much that would be able to remove it for the next several hours. I leaned against the wall across from the back door of the club and put on boot against the brick behind me. A minute later the door swung open and a Vampire about an inch shorter than me with shaggy brown hair and sharp green eyes stepped into the space. He shot a smile at me, crossed the space as he fished around in his various pockets and then offered me a cigarette as he stopped a few feet from me.

"No thanks. Diego?"

"That's me, and you're Silver."

"Yep."

"Good to finally meet you, heard a lot about you the last couple years."

"I'll bet." I chuckled a little. He smirked as he lit a cigarette and stuffed the pack back into a random pocket.

"So, what can I do for you?"

My sensitive Lycan senses made me wrinkle my nose as he exhaled a cloud of toxic smoke and he looked confused for a moment. He finally raised a brow, looked down at the lit cigarette in his hand and seemed to click the pieces into place. He took one more drag, snuffed it out and tossed it out into the parking lot.

"Sorry about that. I forgot you have those heightened wolf senses. That had to be particularly nasty. My apologies, honestly." I liked him more than Heather already and hoped the trend would continue.

"Don't worry about it. Most actually assume I partake as well. Guess I never saw the appeal."

"Since I was turned there really isn't one. Addiction isn't an issue any longer. I think it's just habit more than anything. At least now I don't have to worry about it killing me, eh?" He laughed and I found myself laughing right along with him. He had a sense of humor, I liked that, overly serious always worried me.

"I suppose that's true enough. So, I'm sure you're wondering why I wanted to meet you tonight."

"I admit to being more than a bit curious. It's not every day your Princess wants a face to face in a darkened bar lot. So what can I do for you?"

"Well, I can't exactly out and tell you that. Not yet anyway."

"Don't trust me yet?"

"Something like that."

"I can understand that. So, what do I need to do to ease your mind?"

"What are your ties to my mother?"

"Virtually non-existent. I've never actually met her. My master is three sires removed from her so my blood bond to the Queen is virtually nil. As far as allegiance, I've sworn my loyalty to her so I can stay in this realm but that's the extent of it. Honestly, I haven't even seen my master in well over four decades. He's rather hands off."

"Okay, honest enough. How do you feel about humans?"

"Humans? Well, I'm a bartender at a blood bar. I regularly set up our human patrons with Vampires looking for a quick, live feed. We make sure they keep them from being in pain and that every one of them leaves as alive as they walked in. Other than that I don't have an opinion one way or another."

"Are you bonded?"

"I am actually. Parker works here as a bouncer three nights a week. We paired a little over fifteen years ago."

I smiled at the comment, unable to stop the happy little flutter in my chest at hearing it. Knowing he was bonded meant he would be stronger and we could take a little more blood if he worked out. It also meant he wouldn't get attached to either of us during the process, his heart already taken. I pursed my lips, considering my next step and let out a sharp sigh. I had to make a choice, quickly, it was late and I was ready to go home and crawl into bed with Angel.

I decided to go for it, if all else failed I could roll him and wipe the meeting out of his memory. It would be more difficult since he was bound to another Vampire but I could manage it.

"Okay, I'm taking a leap of faith here Diego. I'm sure you already know that my mate is human."

"Yep, well known in the realm."

"And I'm sure you heard what happened last year."

"Her kidnapping. Yeah, we heard about it down here. Parker and I wanted to join you in looking for her but we couldn't leave the bar. We had you in our thoughts every day though."

"Thanks for that. Well, here's the sticky part of the situation. She's been different since we found her, anyone would be after three months held captive and another two and a half in a coma."

"Damn. Definitely. I would be affected by that so I can only imagine how she came out of it all."

"She's holding together surprisingly well but there are some long term effects we're dealing with. Another issue is that I've come to realize how horrific it will be when I lose her. In the grand scheme of our lifetime, hers is so short as to cause me more than a little emotional distress."

"I can see how it would be. I never considered how it might feel to be bound to someone with such a short time on this earth. So, what do you need from me?"

"I know this is a lot to ask but, I want to start her on a regular dose of Vampire blood."

He raised an eyebrow at me, his expression telling me that I'd lost my mind but he was silent. I watched his face as he seemed to mull over the information, its consequences and the long term effects of it. He coughed, clearing his throat and then exhaled sharply through his nose and nodded several times before meeting my eyes.

"Okay, I get why you would want to go there. I just have to clear a few things before I even consider it."

"Of course. Please, ask me whatever you need to."

"First, how much are we talking about?"

"Well, I want to pull a little more from you than what she actually needs so we can build a store just in case. She'll need about a cup every week. I planned on splitting that into smaller daily doses though, less noticeable. So I figured if we can pull something like three pints a week, that's five cups more than what we need and easy for you to take an extra feed for without anyone noticing."

"Alright. So if I agreed to a single, three pint draw per week, you can collect for about nine months and have enough stock to last you close to four years."

"That's the plan. Then we can revisit the deal again to restock when we get down to less than six months of stock."

"And what exactly is the deal?"

"First, I take any and all blame if we're found out. You can't say I rolled you, that could be a death sentence for me but you can definitely claim I threatened you."

"Okay."

"And I'll pay, well."

I pulled an envelope out of my pocket and handed it to him then waited. He glanced around the lot to ensure it was empty then opened the packet. His eyes widened and then shot up to meet mine, disbelief evident in his gaze.

"That's only a down payment. I have control of my own accounts. We'll call that the first eight draws. Every two months you'll get another payment."

"This is enough to pay the rent on the bar for at least six months."

"I know. I figure if I'm risking getting you in this much trouble, it's the least I can do."

"Okay. And what else do you expect from me? From us?"

"Nothing. I just want to protect her, keep her in my life as long as I can and help her feel like she has some confidence again. I do expect some serious discretion of course. No one but you and your partner can know about this."

"Oh of course. The last thing I want to do is run off and tell someone! I can imagine you don't want your mother finding out about this. All right. Well, I'm inclined to say yes. Would you mind going with me and discussing this with Parker?"

"Of course not, I want to make sure he's open to it as well. I won't push the subject if he is set against it."

He nodded and then waved me toward our vehicles, telling me to follow him before we climbed in and left the lot. We drove through town for ten minutes before parking in front of an average looking brick house. I parked my jeep at the curb and followed Diego to the front door, keeping several paces behind him as he stepped inside. The house felt surprisingly comfortable despite being home to two of the undead and I smiled a little. I scanned the space as I was led through to the living room, my host calling out to his partner as we progressed.

Once we all settled in the subtly decorated, very homey-feeling space I started explaining to Parker what I had requested from his partner. He stayed silent through the entire speech and then Diego handed him the envelope I had given him at the bar. Parker flipped it open, studied the contents for a minute then closed it and handed it back to him. He leaned forward, elbows on his knees and his fingers linked together, his chin resting on his knuckles. He appeared to be deep in thought and as the minutes passed with nothing but the steady tick of the clock on the mantle to break the silence I worried he would say no.

"I don't see a problem with it. As long as we are discreet and don't get caught."

My heart almost leapt out of my chest at his calm words but I managed to control my excitement. I'd been hoping for this and I could finally begin to relax. Angel would be able to protect herself better, she would be safer. She would also be around a lot longer, even if it wasn't forever, every extra minute was a gift and I would cherish it. I inhaled in a long pull and then let it out slowly, pushing down the urge to jump around and hug them both.

"Thank you. Both of you. I can't express how much this means to me."

Apparently the excitement made it into my voice anyway as Parker chuckled a bit as he spoke. "I think we can imagine. It's the least we can do to help out."

"When do you want to do the first draw Diego?"

"As soon as you can get set up for it."

"How about I bring my supplies over tomorrow night after the bar closes?"

"Sounds good to me. Meet me here and we'll get the ball rolling."

I nodded, shaking each of their hands as I stood then making my way to the front door, my new donor and his partner following to show me out. I thanked them again before I stepped onto the porch, praying I'd made the right choice and they would be as discreet as they claimed they would. I waved to the pair as I started the jeep then pulled away from the curb. As I pointed the vehicle toward home, I knew Angel could feel the elation pulsing through me. I couldn't wait to tell her what my meeting had brought us.

CHAPTER TWENTY-EIGHT

STOCKPILES AND NEW HEIGHTS

AS THE next few months passed, Diego and Parker proved themselves to be the perfect choice for donors. Parker had stepped in after the second month and offered himself as a secondary source. They never demanded extra payment but I provided it anyway. I'd repaired the cooling unit on an old walk-in cooler in the basement we had frequently used when the entire family still lived in the manor. With Lycans wandering in and out of the place all the time, having loads of fresh meat on hand made sense. Once the boys had moved out and my parents had relocated to a home closer to the center of their settlement, there was no need for it.

Once it was working again I had set locks on it and bought new shelving, perfect for storing vials of blood. Each rack held premeasured doses, easy for me to walk in, grab and mix into whatever Angel was eating or drinking. At the eight month mark Angel had regained her former confidence, the cocky little sway back in her step. The mental scars seemed to have healed completely and the nightmares ceased. As her sleep returned to a normal pattern, her mood shifted drastically and she was once again the woman I remembered from before her ordeal.

The physical scars were taking a bit longer to vanish but since our talk about them several months earlier, she didn't seem to pay any attention to them. She had developed enough strength and agility to spar with me in our gym a couple times a week. I still went easy on her, she was definitely more than human but I was still twice as strong. She enjoyed the workouts and engaged me in them whenever I would agree. That was how I ended up in the gym, standing across a sparring mat from my mate, a cocky grin plastered across her face as she stared me down.

I had underestimated her skill level, helped by the fact she'd been going easy on me too the last couple months. She had landed one hell of a blow to my ribs, cracking one and bruising the muscles around it. I was bent slightly, cradling my side with one arm, waiting for the injury to heal and she was gloating. I narrowed my eyes at her but couldn't find any malice to put behind it. She looked damn cute standing there all smug and it made me want to call the match just so I could walk over there and kiss her.

I winced, closing one eye on a soft grunt as the crack in my fifth rib on the right side began to mend. Repairing bones hurt like hell and I was thankful she was allowing me the chance to heal at all before starting on me again. The thought was torn from my mind as she decided I'd had long enough and charged me again. At the last minute I dodged left and rolled across the mat, popping up behind her with a small cough. The movement hurt but had been worth it as I got the upper hand, sweeping her legs out from under her.

She fell to the mat face first, flipping onto her back before I could pin her and put a foot out. The bottom of her shoe met my stomach and she pushed hard, extending her leg and throwing me back a few steps. I stayed upright but staggered enough to give her time to get to her feet. I narrowed my eyes at her and grinned, she was giving me a good run but I was still taking it easy on her. I waited, not about to charge her the way she had come at me, she wasn't likely to do the same again either. After circling each other a few times her weight shifted subtly, barely a minor twitch of muscles but I caught it.

I was ready for the punch she threw at me, sidestepping her right jab and grabbing her wrist. I twisted, pulling her arm behind her and pinning her wrist between her shoulder blades. I kicked the toe of my right foot against the back of her knee and then used my own knee in the middle of her back to drop her to the mat. I pressed my body down into hers, a smirk on my face as she stopped struggling, no longer trying to get away. Her whimper reached my ears seconds later and in a flash I had released her and was on my knees beside her. I helped her roll over, brows furrowing as she pressed a hand gently to her right shoulder.

"I think you dislocated my shoulder. So much for going easy on me."

"Oh Gods Angel, I'm so sorry."

I reached over as she shook her head and flashed me a small smile tinged with the pain she was no doubt feeling. I laid a hand on the shoulder and closed my eyes, using our link to probe the injury and then sighing as I opened my eyes again.

"Was I right?"

"Yeah, it's dislocated. Come on. Let's get it taken care of and take it easy for the rest of the day."

She nodded and gave me her left hand so I could help her up, cradling her right arm against her and trying to keep from moving it. She didn't cry, made no noise to indicate she'd been hurt at all after the initial whimper and followed me from the space. I marveled at her pain tolerance and wondered how much of it was from the Vampire blood and how much was simply her. She had endured some terrible things at the hands of her captors after her kidnapping. Since our bond had repaired itself I had seen enough flashes and flickers of memory to piece most of it together.

We handled her shoulder then decided we should eat something and moved to the kitchen. By the time I was done cooking she could move her shoulder without pain and only minor stiffness. Her healing had increased remarkably and was almost as fast as mine these days. I grinned at her as she rotated her shoulder slowly, easing the ache from the joint as I set a plate in front of her. She smiled back, not saying a word as she grabbed the fork I handed over and started eating. Her appetite had increased thanks to her already amazing metabolism kicking into high gear. She was eating twice as much to maintain her weight the last few weeks.

"Sorry about your shoulder."

"Sorry about your ribs."

"Oh yeah, that. Guess we're even then, eh?"

She laughed a little and winked at me in agreement then turned her attention back to her food. I let her eat in silence, doing the same until we had both cleared our plates. Once I picked them up and deposited them in the sink I turned and leaned back against the counter. I braced the heels of my hands on the edge of the countertop and stood there studying my mate. I watched her until she looked up from the wine she had been studying and quirked one pale brow at me.

"What?"

"I was just thinking."

"About?"

"Over the entire time I've known you, that we've been together,

I've never asked your thoughts and opinions on human customs."

"What do you mean? Customs like what?"

"Well, like birthday parties and such."

"Okay. What brought this on?"

I shrugged and pushed away from the counter, crossing the room to where she was still seated and wrapping my arms around her waist. She tweaked a little half smile at me as her arms slipped around my neck and then her head cocked to one side slightly, urging me to continue. I thought about the things I'd been meaning to ask her for months now, not sure how to approach any of the subjects. I'd never given much thought to human practices but since I'd claimed her the ideas had been nagging at me more and more. Of course some had been helped along by the thoughts and images our bond allowed me to catch from her on occasion.

"I've just been thinking a lot lately."

"Well that can't be good. When you start thinking, someone gets in trouble."

"Not true! Okay, mostly true but you're still a brat for pointing it out!" She giggled at me and kissed the tip of my nose as she moved one hand to massage the back of my neck.

"Seriously though. Thinking about what? I mean, I don't really care about birthday parties. We never really had them before I came here anyway so it's not like I'm missing something."

"All right. Well, what about, like... I don't know... Marriage?" Her brows shot up as she leaned back a bit, looking at me as if I'd grown two extra heads and begun speaking Greek.

"Marriage? Isn't that a little redundant now that we're bound? I mean, a Lycan claiming is a lot stronger than any human marriage."

"That's true but it doesn't mean we couldn't have some kind of ceremony. I've been considering actually meeting your family. They probably think the rumors are bullshit and it couldn't possibly be you people are talking about."

"Oh I'd put money on that. My mother would never consider this scenario. I suppose I've thought about it."

"I figured you had, I've caught flickers of it through the link."

She grinned and my heart melted for at least the ten millionth time. It seemed ridiculous that it had taken almost four years for my brain to catch up with what she might want. I reached up to play with the ends of her hair. The golden locks slipped between my fingers, smooth and silky and my gaze lingered on the flow of the strands through my grip. She let me play with her hair for a full minute before she stilled my hand and used a finger to lift my chin so I would look at her.

"You okay?"

"Yeah. Just feeling nervous suddenly."

"You, nervous? Silver, that's really not like you." She let out a small laugh and I smirked at the sound, she was right after all, it wasn't like me.

"I know. It's just a weird thought, meeting your family. You met my parents before you ever met me. I've never done this before."

"Not even with Desdemona?" The little half smile and quirked eyebrow she shot at me told me she was playing with me, the twinkle in her eye confirmed it.

"Not even with her. It's not like we were playing house or anything. There were feelings there but nothing like this. Neither of us ever talked about claiming the other. I always knew it wouldn't last forever."

She nodded and brushed my hair out of my face, planting a light kiss on my forehead before pushing me back and sliding off the seat. She grabbed my hand and started for the door, thankfully giving me a reprieve from talking about my former flame any further. I was glad to drop the subject but as she turned and headed for the front door I wondered where she was going. I stopped and gave her hand a gentle tug, bringing her progress to a halt and pulling her back against me.

"Where on earth are you headed?"

"Taking you to meet my family of course."

"Now?"

"Sure. No better time than the present, right?"

I swallowed the lump in my throat and nodded, releasing my hold and letting her lead me out the door and into the jeep. I handed her the keys without a thought and climbed into the passenger seat. It would be a thousand times easier to let her drive considering the state my emotions had crawled into. I spent the first part of the drive considering how sad and confusing it felt to be terrified of meeting a bunch of humans. The idea made me chuckle and she shot me a look, clearly concerned I had lost my mind in the first hour of our trek. I waved her off, not wanting to discuss my rapidly decreasing sanity and started up a conversation about who I would be meeting.

CHAPTER TWENTY-NINE

MEETING THE IN-LAWS

BY THE time we pulled up in front of the home Angel grew up in I had a better idea of who I would be meeting. Her father had been killed in a fire when she was only seven but her mother was alive and well. She had two older siblings and three younger and I was surprised to learn that, like myself she was the only girl. I would have sworn to anyone asking I was prepared for the meeting about to occur as we slipped out of the jeep. Deep down however, my insides were a mess and I couldn't remember ever being this deep into our human settlement. It left me feeling surrounded and on edge, a paranoia I couldn't shake crawling up my spine as we walked to the front door.

She knocked on the door then smiled at me and reached over to take my hand in hers. She gave my fingers a squeeze and winked at me. I felt the nudge of her will against mine seconds before her calm soothed its way over the panic I'd been building for the last hour. I took a slow, deep breath and smiled a small thanks at her for the help then prepared myself for the terror of meeting my in-laws. The whole concept was strange and foreign to the Vampire half of me. The wolf understood, but that other side kept trying to make sense of something which had never been a normal part of Vampire life.

The undead didn't have families, at least not in the traditional sense after a few decades. Once turned, your maker and their other 'children' became the closest one had. Sure I had parents and siblings like normal people but the extended family and ideas like in-laws were awkward and new to me. I would need time to adjust but, thankfully I had all the time in the world. I exhaled the breath I'd held longer than intended on a barely audible sigh, the noise terminating just as the door in front of us opened. The woman standing framed in the soft lighting of the house looked exactly like Angel, almost six decades older.

"Angel? Oh dear Gods, is it really you?"

"Yeah mom, it's me."

My mate let out a laugh as her mother pulled her in a hugged her. The display caught me off guard until I remembered she had been gone for more almost four years. Almost half a decade with no contact, her family not knowing if she was even alive. The sudden knot in my gut and tightening of my heart told me I should have made sure she got out to the settlement to see them earlier. She shot me a quick look, telling me she had felt the guilt stabbing at me through our link and to let it go. She wasn't angry with me.

"Mom, you can let me go now. I can't breathe."

"Sorry, dear. It's just been so long. We were worried about you. Are you all right? They didn't hurt you did they?" She was already shaking her head in response before the older woman even finished the question.

"No. I'm perfectly fine. Look, are the boys around? I have some news but I want everyone here so I don't have to keep repeating it."

"All but Nathan. He should be here any time though. Come on in, I'll get them in the living room for you." She turned away from the door, casting a curious glance in my direction before leaving us to enter the house without her guidance. "Boys!" Her shout managed to echo through a space which shouldn't have allowed such a thing and I grinned. Apparently it was a mom trick, mine could do the same but I had always assumed it was a Vampire thing. Now I had to rethink that.

"Come on, we'll grab a drink and settle in."

I gave Angel a nod and followed her into the kitchen, waiting as she pulled two glasses from a cabinet and filled them with water. She nodded toward the opposite side of the room and we walked through the door into a moderately-sized and well-lived-in room. She handed me one of the glasses as she took a seat on a small sofa and glanced at the open space beside her. I lowered myself into it and set the untouched water on the side table near the arm. I was far too alert to drink anything, at least until everyone was in one room and settled down.

We didn't have to wait long, within five minutes her mother

and four of her five brothers were seated in the space with us. I looked around the group as they chatted excitedly and noticed they all shared the golden blonde hair and two of them shared their sisters sapphire eyes. The other two had irises as green as hers were blue and just as stunning. They had just begun to pester her about telling them her news without the eldest of the brood when the front door opened and slammed shut again. A man with my mate's angelic good looks stalked into the room but stopped when he saw everyone gathered.

His eyes swept to Angel and a massive smile took over his features, making him light up and I saw the heavy family resemblance. His eyes, blue but several shades lighter than his sister's, gleamed as they misted over at the sight of her. He took two large strides toward the loveseat we had occupied, scooped Angel up into a bear hug and held her silently for what felt like eternity. He finally chanced another look around and when his baby blue eyes landed on me the look turned icy and his arms dropped away from his sister.

"What are you doing here?"

The venom in his voice caused most of those present in the room to suck in a gasp and narrowed my eyes. My temper prickled defensively but I tamped it down, doing my best to lock it away and keep from losing my cool. It wouldn't do anyone any good if I went crazy on Angel's family, the last thing I wanted was for them to hate me. I was beginning to get the feeling at least one of them hated me already. Apparently none of the others had recognized me, this one, the oldest, he had.

"Someone better answer me, and fast. What the hell is that thing doing in our house?"

"Nathan, stop it."

The growl tinging her voice made my gaze flick over to Angel, finding she was meeting his angry expression with one of her own. Mine softened instantly as I realized she would handle anything her family threw our way. I didn't need to. I leaned back and crossed my arms over my chest, right leg lifting as I propped my ankle on my left knee. I was the picture of settling in and getting comfortable and it seemed to poke at Nathan's temper. Angel dropped herself back onto the seat beside me as she calmed herself some.

"Don't tell me to stop it. What did you bring into this house, little sister?"

"Nathan, calm down. What on earth are you talking about?"

His gaze found his mother for a split second before returning to Angel and me.

"So you didn't bother telling mom you invited a Vampire princess into our home then?"

Five pairs of eyes accompanied by shocked expressions shot to Angel and then fell on me. She let out a huff, rolled her eyes at her older brother and leaned into me. She needed comfort, support and I was more than willing to make sure she got it. I uncrossed my arms, wrapped one around her shoulders and leaned her head against me. Her muscles relaxed almost instantly and her eyes returned to her brother, still standing over us and trying to look intimidating.

"Angel, what's he talking about? Who is this?" From the tone I could hear her mother was as confused as she looked.

"Guess people don't know me as well as I thought they did." I let out a small chuckle as I said the words, deciding I should probably get out and meet more people.

"Apparently not. Mom, this is Silver." I watched the older woman's eyes narrow as she considered her daughters words and then widen as she seemed to process their meaning.

"Not just a Vampire then. About four years ago, Ayana knocks on our door and tells us you've been chosen to serve at the manor. We aren't given any choice in the matter, she just leaves with you. We get nothing, no letters, no visits, no signs you're alive for this long and then you just show up here with... That. What is it you hope to accomplish with this visit?"

"Well for one I figured I'd let you know I was alive." The bite had returned to Angel's voice as she pulled away from me and stood again. Nathan's words had prickled her anger and left her getting as close to being in his face as she could when he had well over ten inches of height on her. "And you need to back off and stop being a dick. There's no need to get all bent out of shape. She's here with me, so relax would you?"

Despite looking every bit of not being happy, Nathan backed down and took a seat near the door. He was tense and the set of his shoulders said he'd rather be attempting to beat the hell out of me. I shook my head and turned my attention to Angel as she glanced at me with a small smile. I returned the gesture, winking at her to widen hers to a smirk before she refocused on her mother. She was doing the best she could to decide what and how to tell them without causing a riot. I could feel the options running through her mind and see the tense set of her shoulders.

Relax love. Just be honest with them. I'm right here, no one will hurt you. I swear it.

"Look mom, I came back to tell you all that Silver and I, we're getting married."

Chaos erupted on the heels of her comment and Nathan bellowed his dissatisfaction with the announcement the loudest. The shouts became a jumble of negative energy and anger and I finally couldn't take any more. I slowly stood from my place on the loveseat, drew in a breath and calmed my rapidly fraying nerves. I needed to be forceful but losing my temper wasn't an option, force didn't need to include anger.

"Enough!" The force behind the single word vibrated the walls and the tone in my voice quieted the room almost instantly. "You all need to sit down and let Angel finish what she came here to say."

"You will not walk into our home and start giving orders. Mangy bloodsucker," Nathan said.

I kept my temper under control but only with a lot of help from Angel, biting back all the comments trying to spill out. Eventually, she turned toward her eldest brother and spoke, saving me from having to keep the growl out of my voice.

"You need to watch your tone, Nathan. Silver has been nothing but polite since we set foot in this house. You really need to remember who she is and what she could do to you if you keep pushing. Now if you'll kindly shut it, I'll finish what I was saying." She raised a questioning brow at him and he huffed but sat back in his chair, obviously consenting, so she continued. "From what I just heard being thrown around this room, none of you are happy about this announcement."

"Of course we aren't. Sis, its bad enough they walked in here and carted you off without so much as giving you a chance to object. I can't believe you would agree to marry one of them, much less this one. We all know her reputation and it isn't good."

"I know Caleb." I thought back on her chatter about her brothers on the drive, Caleb was second in line, right before her. "Believe me I heard all the same stories you did growing up. If you'd just give me a chance, give her a chance, you might find out how wrong we were." I knew she was trying to defend me, get them to like me but they deserved the truth, she shouldn't have to lie.

"Angel, wait." I stood up and put a hand on her shoulder until she took a step back beside me then I looked around at her family.

"Look, I appreciate what she's doing but the truth is this. All the stories you heard about me, they were true. I was terrible. Humans had always been less than nothing to me and I won't insult you by trying to deny that. Even right after she came to the manor I was horrid to Angel. She spent more time crying than anything those first couple months."

"Not helping your case, here," Nathan snarled.

"I know, Nathan. I'm not trying to help myself, I'm trying to be honest. The fact is, I've been known to be a real piece of work. Angel changed that though. It just took me some time to allow it to happen. I fought it and it made me a real bitch. Once I stopped fighting myself though, everything changed. Have I gone through a total transformation in four short years? No, definitely not. But I've been trying and I've made progress. I do everything in my power to make sure Angel is happy."

"You expect us to believe you suddenly care about something other than yourself?" The contempt was clear in Nathan's tone, he really hated me and I couldn't say I blamed him for it.

"I guess that is asking a lot of you but, yes. I am."

"And now you want to walk in here and tell us you expect to marry my daughter?" My gaze drifted to her mother and I nodded. "Well I'm sorry but I can't agree to that. The answer is no."

"The question and even the wedding itself are just formalities. Fact is, Angel is already mine. She's marked and none of you can change that." My focus was pulled to the woman in question as she pulled her hair back, a smile on her face as she revealed the scar my bite had left four years earlier.

Chapter Thirty

Anger and Invitations

I STOOD shoulder to shoulder with Angel and waited for the second wave of hysteria to pass. I didn't bother to curb this one. I simply let it play out, giving them the chance to get the shock and anger out of their systems. As long as they kept to shouting and hurling insults I could just let it slide off of me. Thankfully, they didn't attempt to get physical with either of us. Once the angry shouting had died down to only Nathan and her mother, I stepped in and got them both to shut up.

"You're pissed about this, I get it, but like I said, there's nothing you can do about it. This wedding will just be a formality, my way of honoring the fact that my mate is human and has human traditions."

"How dare you claim her without our permission!" Nathan was still fuming, and shouting but I simply sighed and turned a bored expression on him.

"I didn't need your permission."

"Like hell. She's just a kid, for crying out loud."

"Well, that I can sort of agree to. She is young. But the fact remains that when she was brought to the manor, and when she was claimed, she was eighteen. She knew what it meant, what she was agreeing to and she consented."

"Eighteen? Wait, so you claimed her right after she was taken from us? And we're just now finding out about it?" I raised an eyebrow at the young man as if he was some sort of alien lifeform since he didn't seem to understand that I didn't have to inform them at all.

"Nathan. Come on, I'm sure you heard the rumors flying around about Silver taking a human for a mate." The tone around the edges of my mate's words told me she didn't believe for a moment her brother was that stupid. He had to have known all along.

"Yeah, we heard them. They started a few months after you were taken."

"Exactly. Who did you think it was?"

"Not you apparently. We didn't even know she was..." He waved a hand at me as if trying to say the word without actually voicing it.

I couldn't help it, I laughed.

"What? Am I funny?"

"Right now, yes, you are. Come on, say it, I know you can. Lesbian, just say it." He rolled his eyes at me and even Angel laughed as a smirk took over my face.

He said, "Whatever, I don't care. All I care about is that you took her from us. How do we know you didn't pull some kind of creepy Vampire mind trick on her?" This guy had a serious issue with me and it seemed to have very little to do with my reputation and more to do with what I was.

"If I had, the claiming wouldn't have worked. A human can only enter the bond with a clear mind because they have to consent to it willingly. None of that matters. We're here because I wanted to meet you all and Angel wants a human marriage ceremony. If it will make her happy, then I want to do everything I can to make it happen."

"Whatever. Do what you want, it doesn't mean we have to like it." I rolled my eyes at the man, caught Angel doing the same and then turned when her mother spoke.

"I have to agree with Nathan. Angel, I don't know what happened to you these last few years but this isn't you. The girl I remember wasn't at all happy to be taken to that manor. The idea of having to share space with something like that made her physically sick."

She pointed directly at me and I caught Angel's eyes meeting her shoes out of the corner of my eye. Her mother was telling the truth and she was ashamed of it, hadn't wanted me to know. I stepped over and brushed her hair back behind her ear then raised her chin and smiled at her. None of it mattered. We both had things we weren't proud of in our past and mine left hers in their shadow, I was in no place to judge.

I'm sorry Silver. I never meant for you to find any of this out like this.

Or at all I imagine.

I guess you're right. I was terrified of sharing space with you.

And I don't blame you for it. Don't worry about it, I'm not upset. I understand.

"Be that as it may, things changed. She had every right to be worried about coming to the manor, definitely to serve me. I'm different now, with her at the very least. She knows that." I had addressed the older woman but my eyes were locked on the sapphire ones tearing up in front of me. "We won't take up any more of your time, we did what we came here to do. You've been informed of our plans, the ceremony will be held in a few months and you are all welcome to attend. We'll send a messenger with the exact date once we have it."

I took the familiar hand in my own and led Angel toward the door then out onto the porch. We were almost to the jeep when our path was blocked by a very human wall. I pulled up short and looked up at Nathan as he glared down at me. Even though he was close to eight inches taller than me and I should have felt like a dwarf next to him, I didn't. I met his eyes and he managed to prove dumb enough to hold my gaze. A low growl started in my chest and after ten seconds, the taller man flinched and took a step back. His eyes instinctively went to the dirt and I smirked as I walked around him, opening the passenger door of the jeep for Angel.

Once we were in and settled, I started it up and glanced out at Nathan with a shake of my head. He had recovered from his minor retreat into submission and was glaring at me again. Some people just didn't learn but I wasn't going to waste any more time or energy on him. He probably wouldn't show up at the ceremony and that was fine. Whoever in her family did decide to attend would be welcomed and even invited to visit the manor on occasion. Those who didn't would be forgotten and fairly swiftly I imagined. Thanks to the infusions of Vampire blood, Angel had a very, very long life ahead of her and worrying about her mortal family approving of us seemed pointless.

CHAPTER THIRTY-ONE

CAUGHT

OVER THE next week we settled on a date, sent a messenger to her family and my wayward older brothers and then began planning the elaborate thing. I had to admit I'd never much understood human traditions and ceremonies but the whole ordeal was proving to be fun. Thankfully we didn't have many guests to plan for, though Xander and several in his household as well as the Lycan elders wished to attend. I could only imagine throwing Angel's very human family into such a mix. If nothing else I would have some strange looks and uncomfortable shifting in seats to chuckle at. After all was said and done, the whole thing was about Angel and her happiness, everything and everyone else could vanish.

We were sitting in the kitchen nine days after the visit to her family when my mother stormed in, pure rage on her face. She swept the table we were seated at out of the way in one quick movement, leaving Angel scrambling toward the wall and me standing in front of an upended chair. I looked at her in confusion, wondering what on earth had caused my normally even tempered mother to react in such a physical manner. She hadn't thrown furniture in centuries and the last time she'd tossed a table had been when I was still in my teens.

"What the hell is this, Silver?"

It took me a minute to figure out what she was talking about but then my gaze focused on the object in her hand. My pulse shot up from one heartbeat to the next, my throat tightened and my blood ran cold. There in my mother's pale palm sat a vile of thick crimson fluid I recognized far too well. I tried to speak, failing and clearing my throat before trying again. It didn't work, words refused to leave my lips and I took a deep, shuddering breath. Finally, on the fourth try, sound worked its way from me and formed words.

"Mom, I can explain."

"You'd damn well better and do it fast."

"I was terrified after Angel almost died. I almost lost her and it damn near killed me. Then she came home and the pain she was in, the emotional scars the whole thing left behind, they were eating away at her. I had to do something to ease her pain, help piece her emotions back together and make sure we stood a better chance of avoiding such a close call in the future."

"But this? You know the use of Vampire blood by humans is outlawed. You helped me ban it!"

"I know I did. Do you think that didn't cross my mind when I decided to try it? It did and believe me it ate away at me. But we were careful mom, I kept it locked up and regulated her intake. We were safe about it." She took two steps toward Angel and I let out a warning growl. Mother or not I wasn't about to let her take her anger out on my mate without a fight.

"Relax, I don't intend to hurt her. I just want a closer look."

I huffed at the elder Vampire but backed down, keeping a close eye on her as she stepped over to Angel. Angel shivered, the cabinet she had cowered against rattling with the force of it. I moved close enough to crouch down and reach out to her and she carefully took my hand, her movements slow. I knew she was having a flashback, my mother's anger triggering her memories of her time held captive by Yvonne's henchmen. The moment her skin met mine I pushed my calm over her, easing the shaking and allowing her to take a solid, steady breath. My mother knelt beside her, the expression on her face softened a bit over the one she'd held me with.

"I'm not angry with you, Angel. Forgive me for frightening you. Look at me, child."

Angel glanced at me and I nodded, giving her the push she needed to turn her eyes to my mother. Ayana studied her in silence for a few long minutes. I knew she was easing her way into Angel's mind when I felt the familiar Vampire energy meet my own. I slipped back just enough to let her touch my human's mind, knowing she needed proof of my claims. She had to know Angel hadn't been overdosing on the blood I'd been feeding her. Finally her energy ebbed away and I replaced it with mine once again as she stood and turned away with a sigh.

"Mother."

"Don't, Silver. She's been dosed properly, I'll give you that much praise, at least."

"Thank you."

"Don't thank me yet." I narrowed my eyes at the older woman as I helped Angel off the floor, her shivering finally halted and her breathing stable once again. "It stops now."

"You can't seriously expect me to..."

"To what? Follow the laws I hold everyone else to?" I couldn't really argue with that but I would damn well try. I pulled in a breath, prepared to attempt reasoning with her, try to change her mind when she turned and met my eyes. "Silver, I understand why you did it and I do admit that you have been responsible with her dosing. That doesn't change the fact that the practice is illegal and very dangerous. If I allow this to continue and anyone finds out, we could be facing a serious firestorm. My hold on the council is already strained and any sign of weakness or favoritism could tip the scales."

"So the council is more important than me, than Angel?"

"That's not what I'm saying. Please try to understand."

"I do understand. You could easily take back every shred of power you originally gave that council and there's nothing they could do about. Instead you fold, bow out, cower and cater to them and their stupid rules."

"Watch your tongue. You'd do well to remember that this particular set of rules is of your own making."

"I know it is!" I growled the words out at her, knowing I was backed into a corner and was honestly lucky Angel and I were still alive and free. I reined in my temper and bit back the roar of rage that wanted set free as I looked up and met my mother's eyes again. "You can't ask me to let that darkness back into her life. She wasn't sleeping, she was falling apart and there wasn't a damn thing I could do about it. Except this."

"I'm not asking Silver. This is an order. You will cease the doses and destroy your stock, immediately." I opened my mouth to argue but she raised a hand to silence me. "You only have two choices. The one I just offered or a silver barred cage in the basement of the council hall. I don't think I need to remind you what the council wanted. Give them this and they *will* sever your bond and most likely execute Angel. It's your choice."

"Fine. Consider the doses stopped. I'll get dad to help me

destroy the stock tonight."

"Who was your donor?" I shook my head, unwilling to give up Diego no matter how bad things got. "You won't tell me?"

"No. It doesn't matter anyway, either way I'm the one at fault here."

"True. Fine, we'll consider this discussion closed but I expect that stock in the basement to be destroyed by sunrise. Don't test my resolve on this, Silver, I don't think you would appreciate the outcome."

I nodded since there was nothing else I could do and slipped my arm around Angel's waist. I led her from the kitchen and up the stairs to our bedroom. She deserved to know what was probably coming her way once the doses stopped. There was really no effect from stopping the blood cold-turkey, a few minor cravings which could be handled with coffee or tea. The major effect would be the probable sudden return of her flashbacks and nightmares. While they had slowed before she had started taking the blood, they hadn't been completely gone. Since she'd been dosing they'd both stopped totally, until the sudden one in the kitchen which I could admit had been provoked.

"Angel, I need you to understand something."

"It's all going to come back isn't it?" I expelled a heavy sigh and nodded as I dropped to sit on the edge of our bed. "I figured as much. It's fine Silver. They were almost gone anyway. It wasn't the draw of all that vanishing that made me agree to this anyway and you know it. Are you going to be okay?"

"I... Honestly don't know. I can't handle the thought of losing you. I was grasping at any chance I had to avoid that ever happening. I knew we would eventually get caught I guess I just figured it would be once my mother realized you weren't aging in fifteen or twenty years."

She giggled and I looked up at her with a smile and shook my head, patting the mattress beside me. She sat down and I pulled her over against my side and leaned my forehead against her cheek.

"Don't stress, we'll get through this." Her fingers brushed through my hair as she spoke.

"How do you manage to be so optimistic?"

"Comes with having a short lifespan. We tend to give up sweating the small stuff."

"This is small stuff?"

"Can we change it?"

"No."

"Then it's small stuff. Look, there's nothing we can do about it so why worry and stress over it?"

"You're right. We'll figure something out."

"Yes we will. Besides, we have plenty to focus on instead, we still have a wedding to finish planning."

Chapter Thirty-Two

The Wedding

After months of planning and frequent re-planning, we finally had everything set for our wedding. We had chosen to have the ceremony on the five year anniversary of the day I claimed her. She had insisted on a strange tradition of spending the night before the ceremony apart and after not seeing her for eighteen hours I was going a bit crazy. I smiled as I adjusted my tie, catching fleeting flashes of her emotions through the link and knowing it was eating at her as well. She hated being separated as much as I did and I knew we would never be repeating the process if we could help it.

You nervous?

Hey wolf, no contact means you stay out of my head as well.

Well that hardly seems fair. Besides, you didn't seem so eager to keep me out of your head last night.

Oh shut it.

I laughed into the empty room, I could practically feel her blushing through the link. I could have pushed and made it even worse but decided to be nice and leave her be for the last hour before our ceremony. I finished fussing with my tie and smoothed the imagined wrinkles out of my shirt. She had chosen to wear some elaborate dress I had yet to see, as I'd figured she would, while I was in a suit. Having decided my clothes were in order I sat on the nearby footstool and pulled on my shoes. After tying them and pulling on my suit jacket I pulled my hair back into a loose ponytail. I made sure to leave a few strands hanging free to frame my face, just how Angel liked it and then checked the mirror again.

"You're fidgeting." I shifted my gaze in the mirror and grinned at the tall, suit-clad figure of my father leaning in the doorway, hands in his pockets.

"Hey dad."

"Hey princess." He walked over as I shook my head and smoothed the shoulders of my jacket then turned me around and smiled down at me. "Weird tradition isn't it?"

"To say the least. I don't mind it though. The whole process has made Angel so happy."

"Yes it has. Do your best to keep her that way and you'll be a lot happier. My life is terrible when your mother is unhappy. When she gets all twisted up about something, I hide."

"Chicken."

"Mmhmm, just wait until it happens to you. See how fast you suddenly feel the call of the forest and need to get a run." We both laughed and I adjusted his tie for him then buttoned my own jacket and blew out a sharp breath. "Relax kiddo, everything looks great, including your mate."

"Thanks. Did her family show?"

"Most of them. Her oldest brother isn't here and her mother looks irritated but the rest of the boys look happy enough."

"Good. All right, I'm ready when she is."

"I'll go let her know." I nodded and he turned a left the room and after one last look in the mirror I followed. I made my way out, across the back lawn toward the woods across the property. We had chosen a place near the tree line we loved weeks earlier and now the space looked amazing. I approached and walked through the crowd, my mother's smile shining from the front helping to counteract the scowl on my mother-in-law's face.

"Agatha." I offered the older copy of Angel my hand but she simply glared at it then turned her eyes forward again. "All right, well, lovely to see you too. Enjoy the ceremony."

I rolled my eyes at the 'harrumph' the woman let out and moved to take my place at the front of the crowd. Less than two minutes later my father hurried out and took his seat just as the music began. Angel appeared at the other end of the aisle formed between the chairs on Xander's arm and the sight of her took my breath away. I knew nothing about the details of the gown she was wearing, dresses had never been my thing, but she was stunning.

The upper fit her perfectly, following her natural curves and accentuating every one. The neckline allowed a teasing view of cleavage and left her neck and arms bare. Just below the waistline it flared and my mind flickered to old images of fairy tale princesses which made me smile. I was the literal princess in this scenario but she definitely had the look down. I remembered to breathe as she reached the front of the gathering and Xander handed her off to me. I thought about voicing how amazing she looked but the light blush on her cheeks told me it was written all over my face.

Casper stepped up in front of us, a massive grin on his face and tears glistening in his eyes as he looked between us. He had asked months earlier if he could officiate the ceremony and it was decided he'd be perfect for the job. He drew a breath to begin but didn't manage to get any of the words out before a sudden shout pulled the attention of everyone present toward the woods. My eyes had to process what I was seeing for a few seconds before it registered as being real. A small group of humans, seven in total, had emerged from the trees, all carrying weapons.

My eyes narrowed dangerously as I found Nathan among the men who had interrupted what had started as a special day. I knew Angel had seen him when her hand tensed around mine three seconds later. I glanced at her and caught the glare she had leveled on him, the intense set of her jaw showing her anger. I pulled back my own anger and let my calm surge forward, flowing down my arm and meeting Angel where our hands were joined. The tension eased from her hand first then her arm and finally her shoulders and jaw relaxed and she shot me a small smile of thanks which I returned.

"Nathan, what's going on? What is this?"

"This, little sister, is an intervention. I can't stand by and do nothing while you join yourself to this freak. She's a monster, Angel, why can't you see that?"

"You show up at a wedding with weapons and I'm the monster?"

"Shut up, no one was speaking to you." My nostrils flared as my temper did the same and I took a deep breath to calm myself. It was Angel's turn to send me the easy, calm, and relaxing waves I needed to not rip into the whole group of them.

"Just leave, Nathan. We'll forget your insults and pretend you were never here."

"Afraid we can't do that, sis."

I didn't register the weapon his friend had trained on me before it was fired, the twang of the bolt leaving the body of the crossbow turning my head. Angel had apparently seen the threat before I had and thanks to our link had the movement speed to do something about it. At first I thought she intended to tackle the attacker but I realized her real intention too late. I caught her as she collapsed against me, and had a moment of confusion to wonder what had happened. I wrapped her tighter in my arms as her legs gave out and sank slowly to the ground, cradling her against my chest.

Chaos erupted around us and I finally looked down when I heard a whimper escape the woman in my arms. I registered the pain written across her face and then trailed my gaze down to her chest. My eyes widened at the crimson spreading across the front of her ivory gown and soaking my white shirt. A howl of rage from Nathan's direction barely reached me as the crowd swarmed the men. He was shouting, his fury obvious in his voice as he was restrained. I wasn't sure what he was angry at, being captured or what had happened to his sister. It didn't really matter to me so I shut him out, along with everything else around us.

Everything seemed to be moving in slow motion and my eyes refused to focus, didn't want to see what was right in front of me. I wiped at the tears streaming down my face with the back of my sleeve and forced myself to take it in. I couldn't hope to help if my mind wouldn't accept what I was seeing. The arrow had been fired at such close range that it had gone right through Angel's chest. It had missed her heart, but not by much and she was losing blood at an alarming rate.

I reached for her back and found the head of the bolt, cutting my hand on the razor sharp edge and wincing at the immediate sting of fire the cut sent through me. It was tipped in silver. I pulled my hand away, no longer sure what was her blood and what was mine and met her eyes. She was breathing but it was labored and raspy and the pain I could see in her eyes cut through to my core. I was vaguely aware of someone kneeling beside me, my father's voice telling my mate to hold on, they would get her help. I knew he meant well but I could feel her slipping away.

"I love you, Silver."

"I love you, too. Just hold on, you can pull through this. Please, don't leave me."

I was crying again and I couldn't have cared any less as I watched her struggle to breathe. The pain I'd felt rip through me when she'd been held in Ghent was nothing compared to what slammed into me moments later. Angel shuddered out her last breath and it was like my heart was being ripped from my chest. The sound I let loose stopped everything around me and forced everyone back a few steps, giving me a wide berth. Fire tore through my veins, ice close on its heels sending a shockwave of anger followed by pure, unhindered pain rocketing through me from head to toe.

I snapped off the end of the bolt shaft, pulling the broken thing from her body, not wanting to leave the offending object lodged in her chest. I surged to my feet, pain still coursing through me in waves, leaving me void of the ability to think straight. I lunged at the man who had fired the weapon, silver tipped bolt in hand, fully intending to kill him, and every one of his friends. It took my father and Xander each on an arm and Casper's arm around my waist to hold me back. With their grips all failing against my struggle, my father leaned over and put his face near my ear.

"Silver, calm down. Killing him won't bring her back. Stop it."

I wanted them all dead but the wolf in me couldn't ignore the commanding words of her alpha and the anger crawled away to a dark corner of my mind. My knees gave out and I collapsed to the ground, choking out sobs as Casper wrapped me into his arms. Once the rage faded, the pain took a firm hold and the reality of what had occurred settled in. As had happened in Paris when a piece of our bond had been severed, my entire system rebelled against the situation. My twin held my hair and rubbed my back as my stomach contents emptied onto the grass.

The elders carted off the offending humans, Nathan with them and still shouting at the man who had fired at us. It was good to know he hadn't intended for his sister to get hurt during his stupid display but it hardly made it better. By the time my grief had turned into dry sobs, no tears left to shed and the ground beneath me tinted red with blood from my hand and the final few minutes of crying crimson tears the sun had set. Darkness settled on the area and I looked up, finding the field deserted except for Casper, still sitting by my side, my hand grasped in his.

"We need to get you to the house, sis. Your hand needs cleaned."

I looked down at my left palm, the thin red line the sharp edge of the arrowhead had left behind angry, swollen and obviously infected. I flexed my hand, reopening the wound and making it bleed again. I watched the crimson seep from the cut, not feeling it despite knowing it should be like hellfire on my palm. Somewhere deep down I acknowledged I might be in shock but I didn't hold onto the idea or think on it too long. I let Casper pull me to my feet and followed him back to the house in a daze. We stepped into the house, making it all of seven feet before I caught my mother's scent and turned on her.

"This is all your fault!" My anger returned in spades as I stepped into her space, my eyes flaring as red ringed the irises. She stood her ground, not backing down in the face of my anger but that simply fueled my rage further. "You and the council and your damned rules! You forced me to stop dosing her. You made me destroy our stock. You let this happen. I could have saved her!"

"No Silver, you couldn't have. It wouldn't have made a difference. I know you're angry but even if she'd still been taking the blood, this would have killed her." She slowly reached up and wrapped her arms around me and I allowed myself to sink into her embrace.

"No. No I could have saved her. She could have pulled through."

"You're lying to yourself. That arrow was meant for you, nothing you could have done would have kept that wound from taking her life. Nothing." The anger welled back up and I directed it the only place that made any sense to me in the moment.

"Let go of me." I shoved out of my mother's arms and glared at her, the perpetually cool, calm, collected woman suddenly making me want to lash out.

"Silver."

"Fuck you. I'm done talking, leave me alone." I turned and tore up the stairs, exhausted but needing to be anywhere other than in her presence. Somewhere in the dark recesses of my mind I knew what had happened hadn't been her fault. I needed someone to blame and she was not only present but a rather easy target since my current state would keep her from returning my anger.

I slammed the door behind after entering the gym and locked it, wanting to keep everyone out. I didn't bother wrapping my hands, just stripped off my suit jacket, kicked off my shoes and started wailing on the punching bag in the middle of the room. I couldn't do anything about the pain searing its way through my system, I could only focus on the anger. Since the rage was easier to work with I let it surface freely. Eventually I would work through the anger and all I would be left with was pain, but for the moment, I clung to the rage flowing from deep within me.

CHAPTER THIRTY-THREE

LOST FAITH

TIME PASSED but I hardly noticed, spending my time locked away in my gym since I hadn't been able to face our bedroom alone. I worked myself until I dropped, only stopping to eat when Casper gave me no other choice. I was running on pain and denial, telling myself she wasn't really gone between flare ups of anger that left me pummeling my punching bags into oblivion. I'd stopped blaming my mother for her death but I hadn't managed to actually speak to the woman. Admitting out loud that the dosing wouldn't have saved her meant her death had been completely out of all of our hands. I didn't know if I could live with the idea, so I held onto the false anger, clinging to it for comfort.

I had taken out another punching bag, its contents spilling out on the floor and leaving a thin cloud of dust lingering around it. I backed up until my shoulders contacted the cold plaster of the wall and slid down to the floor. My knees pulled up toward my chest, arms propped on them and hands hanging limply as I fought the urge to cry. I'd cried more in the last few weeks than I had in the previous four hundred years. Just as I thought I had it under control, a choked sob broke free and the wall tumbled down, setting the flood loose. I let the pain surge forward and take over, getting used to just giving in to it when it was obvious the battle was already lost.

An arm fell across my shoulders and I knew instantly it wasn't Casper, the energy sweeping over me as the scent of lilacs and dirt surrounded me. I leaned against my mother, done raging at her for things she couldn't control any more than I could. She held me while I cried and eventually the tears dried up, the sobs broke and I could breathe again, though I didn't really want to. I took a deep, shuddering breath and leaned away to look up at her. She wiped the wetness from my cheeks and offered me a small, sad smile.

"I'm sorry, mom. I know it wasn't your fault I just..."

"Shhh. I know, you just needed someone to blame and I was an easy target. I don't hold it against you sweetheart. Believe me, I understand."

"She's really gone isn't she?"

"She is. Do you plan on using your room again? Your father and I considered just moving you but decided to leave it up to you."

"I don't know, the thought of sleeping in there alone is terrifying. But then, the thought of sleeping *anywhere* alone anymore is bad. I don't know if just having a different space will really help." She nodded and brushed my hair out of my face then kissed my forehead.

"Well whatever you decide, we're here to help. You do need to get some real sleep though. Not just pass out in here after working yourself into a fit and blacking out. You haven't had a decent night of sleep in eight weeks." My heart ached at the timeframe laid out bare before me, eight weeks. Two months I'd been without Angel and every day felt like the first. I couldn't imagine eternity left living like this, it was killing me.

"I'll try sleeping in the room tonight and let you know."

"Maybe you could have a talk with Hephaestus. He's visited a couple times to check on you."

"No." I shook my head as I said the word, not even wanting to consider the idea and not sure the response would ever change.

"Silver."

"No, mom. Look, I'm glad he and Hades were there when I needed backup on those other matters the last few years but where were they in this? Huh? They just sat back and let her die."

"You're projecting again. First me, now them."

"Maybe, but I'm not ready to let them off the hook just yet. She didn't deserve to die. Any one of them could have saved her if they really have the power they claim to have. I don't know that I believe it anymore."

She sighed but didn't bother to argue with me, seeming to understand I wasn't in a place to be understanding or forgiving. The faith in the Pantheon I'd grown up with had been shaken to its very foundation and I wasn't sure the cracks could ever be repaired. She stood and offered me a hand, which I took then let her pull me to my feet. We made our way to my room in silence. My room, it sounded so strange even in my head after five years sharing the space with Angel. My mother helped me out of my hand wraps and into a shower then left me to clean and dress on my own.

Free of workout sweat and in clean clothes I had dropped onto the empty bed and promptly broke down. After an hour spent crying and another spent staring at the ceiling a mild tingle in the back of my skull alerted me to another presence in my space. I drew in a lungful of air and closed my eyes as I took in the distinct tones of spring leaves, cool mountain air, steel and ink. I opened my eyes and turned to look at my rather unwanted company.

"Athena. Hermes. Come to try and talk me back into my faith?" Athena's laugh sent an unwanted shiver down my spine. She was stunning but dangerous and her laughter was like blade against shield, the sound of battle. Hermes simply quirked a cocky smile at me, often silent and always amused by something.

"Haven't the humans taught you anything? We exist whether you believe or not. Your faith is welcome but not necessary." She could be really annoying when she wanted to be, not that I was about to be the one to tell her so.

"Great. So why are you here? Hephaestus get tired of asking to see me and send you to breach my sad little bubble?"

"Oh not at all. Actually, he doesn't even know we're here." I arced a questioning brow at Hermes, wondering what the two had up their sleeves. Their expressions gave nothing away, they never did so I gave up searching and waited for them to actually tell me something.

"Silver, you must believe that what happened those weeks ago was not our will. However, it happened all the same. We will do all we can to ease your suffering but it will take effort, and faith, on your part. Confusing days lay ahead, don't fight the truth despite its improbability. Embrace it."

"Completely confusing and unhelpful as always, Athena. Care to be more specific?"

The request was made to emptiness, both deities having vanished as her last words were spoken. I gave an exasperated roll of my eyes, slid down the mattress and tried to settle in. I had promised my mother I'd do my best to get a solid night of sleep. As I laid there, watching the light fade behind the curtains I began to grasp the futility of relaxing in a room that coated my very being in the familiar scent of Angel. A rogue tear slid down my cheek and onto my pillow as I hugged hers closer. The dueling tones of her vanilla body wash and the sage and sandalwood that were her natural scent all at once soothed my battered soul and made me ache all over.

CHAPTER THIRTY-FOUR

ANGEL WINGS

I WOKE with a start, my eyes scanning the dark room in a panic until I remembered where I was and relaxed a fraction. The minimal easing of my frayed nerves went out the window when an unfamiliar scent hit me. The odd mixture of rain and feathers was undercut with something I had smelled before but my sleepy brain was having trouble placing. As the rest of my senses returned and sleep pulled away completely, I managed to place the scent. My breath caught at the unique whiff of sandalwood I'd only ever found naturally on one person.

I sat bolt upright in the bed and stared at the closet door, the old full length mirror long since smashed in one of my fits of pain. I refused to look at the door, knowing something, or someone, was playing with my senses and not trusting what I might see there. I fought to swallow around the lump forming in my throat and forced the muscles in my jaw to relax so I could speak.

"Who are you and what do you want?"

"Silver." My eyes closed tight at the familiar sound of that single word, not believing my ears any more than I thought I would be able to believe my eyes. "Look at me, please."

"I can't."

"Why?"

"Because you aren't real. You can't be and if I look and let myself believe you are, it might finally break me."

"What if I am real?"

"You can't be. You died." The mattress beside me shifted with the weight of another body moving onto it and I pressed my eyelids tighter, refusing to give in to my curiosity.

"Baby. Look at me."

I knew the tone of the voice, the brush of warm breath against my cheek and the sensation of familiar fingertips across the back of my wrist. Despite my repeated internal chant that I wouldn't look, I gave in, peeled my eyes open and turned my head. The sight that met me made my heart stutter and my stomach clench tightly as a handful of tears slipped free. I reached up and touched her cheek, the skin cool under my palm but then shook my head, dropped my hand and slid off the opposite side of the bed.

"No. This can't be happening. I watched you take your last breath, I felt you die, felt our bond shatter. You aren't real."

"Silver, please."

"Get out. Whoever, whatever you are, leave me alone. Stop playing with me like this. It isn't funny."

I was approaching angry now, a force behind my words that made the specter of my former mate flinch and etched a hurt look across her features. For a moment I wanted to apologize, wrap my arms around her and beg her to forgive me for snapping at her. Then I reminded myself she couldn't possibly be real, she'd been human, fragile and I had watched her die. Something in the back of my mind tingled, trying to get my attention but I ignored it.

"Give me a chance."

"No! Get the hell out! Stop messing with my head!"

The hurt scrawled across her face turned to a deep pain, her brows furrowed and tears shining in her sapphire eyes. Those eyes I remembered staring into, like perfectly faceted jewels cut by the Gods themselves. The tingle in my skull started again and this time I thought better of ignoring it. I reached toward it with my mind, drawing it forward and embracing it. It began as a whisper, barely a breath of what might have been words but grew louder. After repeating several times, Athena's words came back to me, hitting me and knocking the air from my lungs. *Don't fight the truth despite its improbability. Embrace it.*

I dropped to my knees, struggling to breathe and just as I forced a full draw of oxygen into my lungs familiar arms wrapped around me. I choked out a ragged sob and leaned into the embrace I had missed so much, willing it, her, to be real. She felt real, she smelled real though admittedly not like herself and I allowed a moment of belief that she had somehow come back to me. The absurdity of the thought overwhelmed me, pushing Athena's words from my mind. I withdrew from her embrace and put her at arms-length, shaking my head again.

"How? This isn't possible."

"I know but here I am anyway. I don't remember much, just a weird conversation with Athena and Hermes."

"Yeah well, weird conversations are their thing."

"I gathered as much. All I remember is they said we were needed, together. That neither one of us was any good to anyone without the other. Then something about an act of love and a sacrifice of life."

"Sounds cryptic enough to be Athena."

"I do remember her telling me the humans would need me. That there are others like me, special with a purpose but they might find themselves in danger in the future. She said she'd give us another chance but she might call on me at any time and I would have to answer. Silver I... I think she brought me back."

"Right you are, love."

I rolled my eyes and groaned as I turned my attention toward Hades.

"There have been far too many Gods in my personal space this week for my liking. What do you want?"

"Oh, do you really think I would just give up a gift like a soul purified by willing sacrifice without some kind of deals or strings in place? I don't think so ducky." I looked between he and Angel then focused a glare on him.

"What kind of strings?"

"As well as Athena's little deal for your darling here, I added my own. She gets to come back, but she has a job to do. Every so often there are human souls which are less than enthusiastic about joining me in the underworld. They like to cling to this awful place for some unknown reason."

"Ghosts? Are you seriously talking to me about ghosts right now?" I sat staring at the woman I'd spent the last couple months thinking was dead and suddenly wondered how she could find ghosts so unbelievable.

"Why yes, blondie, I do mean ghosts. If they refuse to comply with my timeline, you'll be sent to help ease their way into my realm. Shouldn't be more than a handful every few weeks. Quick and easy."

"And how am I supposed to accomplish this?"

"Oh didn't Athena tell you?"

"Tell me what?"

"Angel isn't just your name anymore love. It's what you *are*. Keep your ear to the ground for my calls." With that he gave us a two fingered salute and disappeared, leaving me sitting there stunned, the look on Angel's face telling me she shared the sentiment.

"Athena!"

My shout reverberated off the walls and startled Angel out of her shocked silence, earning me a confused look. Despite my worry the Goddess wouldn't bother responding, she appeared leaning in the doorway a breath later.

"What's with the shouting?"

"Tell us what the hell is going on, and try to give it to us straight, and in English please."

"Earthbound lifeforms, so touchy, sheesh! Fine, so the deal is this. Your girl here gets to come back but we had to rebuild her a bit. After a couple months dead there's not much left to work with. Form is a lovely copy though, don't you think? Pretty accurate if I say so myself. Whatever. Her soul was obviously altered a bit because what self-respecting angel is mortal? Ewww, no. She probably smells different, yes? Of course she does. So now she owes big ones to me, and Hades of course as I'm sure he told you. There it is, enjoy."

She vanished before I could even take a breath to respond and I rolled my eyes but then looked at Angel and ventured a smile. She smiled back and I realized the scar that had bisected the left side of her face was gone. The thin patch of missing eyebrow where it had once been remained but the skin on her forehead and cheek was smooth, flawless. I reached over and brushed her hair behind her ear then pulled her close. She fell into my arms and held on tight, like I might disappear any moment. I couldn't say I felt any different as I held her close and pressed a kiss to her temple.

"I missed you."

My soul missed you.

I jumped at the sound of her voice in my head after so long without it and spent a moment confused before I leaned back away from her. I reach up and brushed her hair away from her shoulder then tugged down the neck of her shirt and smiled. There, in the soft spot on her lower neck was the only scar she still appeared to have, the mark I'd left when I'd claimed her. A new and very different set of tears welled up in my eyes and trailed down my cheeks. She had a set to match and neither of us attempted to wipe them away.

"So, you're literally my angel now, huh?"

She grinned and shrugged then pulled me in for a kiss, obviously done talking. I wasn't one to argue, definitely not when I had spent so many weeks missing her so I kissed her back. I lifted her from the floor and carried her over to our bed, glad I didn't have to sleep in it alone anymore.

The pink tinted light of sunrise filtered through the crack in the curtains as I watched Angel sleep. My mind was still reeling over everything that had happened over the last four months. Our wedding had been interrupted by an assassination attempt. Angel had died, I'd fallen apart and then in a strange twist she'd been brought back to me. Sure there were strings attached but they'd been easy to deal with. She'd only had to disappear on me five times in the two months she'd been back and only once had it taken longer than an hour.

We'd finally had our wedding and two weeks later I was still getting used to the feel of the titanium band on my left ring finger. I pulled the blanket down off her shoulders and let my fingertips drift lightly over the addition Hermes had inked onto her skin. The pale outline of wings was just visible against her skin but we both knew they were very real under the barely there tattoos. The revival and second chance she had been given came with a side effect we were both looking forward to. She was immortal, maybe even longer lived than me but we would deal with that if the time ever came.

She stirred under my touch and I smiled as she grumbled and turned over, squinting one eye open to look up at me. She returned the smile and stretched as she let out a yawn and I reached over to tickle her halfway through the motion. She broke into a giggle and slapped my hand away, and then glared at me.

"Bitch."

"Foul language from such a pure, angelic creature." She flipped me off and we both burst out laughing as she pulled me down beside her and cuddled into my side.

"I may be an angel now but I was human first, then your mate. Neither of those things is angelic."

"Or pure." I smirked and waggled my eyebrows at her, she rolled her eyes in response but then kissed me hard.

"Suppose that's true enough."

"Feel like starting your daily quest toward further impurity early this morning?" She didn't bother with words, just agreed to my less than subtle request with a wicked smile and a kiss that promised even more wicked actions to come.

ABOUT THE AUTHOR

Kaden Shay is a 30-something crazy-cat-lady in-the-making who currently resides in Arizona with her partner and miniature zoo, which does currently include 4 cats. When she isn't writing or playing mom to several fur-kids she's singing, playing guitar, or playing online video games.

Kaden grew up in a very musical household and was singing with her family early on in life. Having an English teacher for a dad gave her a love of the written word and encouraged her to begin her own path toward writing. She spent middle school and early high school penning poems, songs, and short stories before beginning her first book at age 16 (a project she still hasn't completed)!

Her furry family, currently consisting of two dogs, four cats, and several rodents, is always available to help her procrastinate in finishing projects.

www.ingramcontent.com/pod-product-compliance
Lightning Source LLC
Chambersburg PA
CBHW070952190726
48292CB00004B/1432